the Dove.

BOOK ONE OF THE LEGEND

CASEY VOIGHT & BARBARA WENDLETON

To Victoria,
For unknown
adventures ahead!
Dream Big and with no excuses.
Casey Voight

COLUMBIA, MISSOURI 65202
hauntpublishing@gmail.com

The Dove:
Book One of the Legend
Casey Voight and Barbara Wendleton

Copyright 2011 by Casey Voight

Cover and Book Design by: Casey Voight
Edited by: Bill Ramey, Courtney Shove, Gail Hagans

Library of Congress Control Number: 2012953856

ISBN 978-0-9886104-9-1

Printed in the United States of America
Haunt Publishing
Columbia, Missouri 65202

Available in ebook format.

For you, our beloved reader
and to the beautiful Native American ancestors who stimulate
the imagination through their histories. They have enriched us
all through their art, music, language and lifestyle.

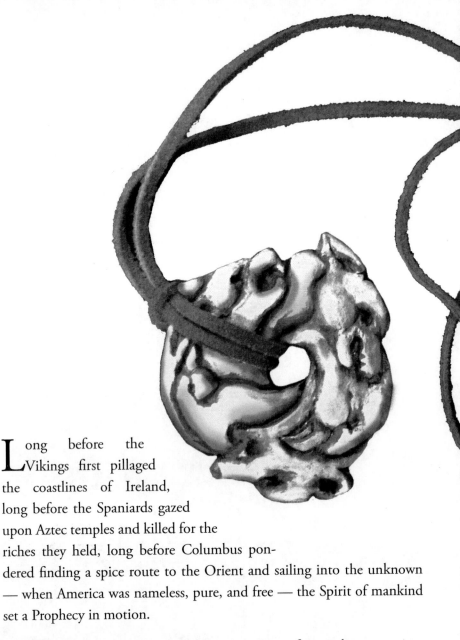

Long before the Vikings first pillaged the coastlines of Ireland, long before the Spaniards gazed upon Aztec temples and killed for the riches they held, long before Columbus pondered finding a spice route to the Orient and sailing into the unknown — when America was nameless, pure, and free — the Spirit of mankind set a Prophecy in motion.

The Great Spirit knew there would come a time of great disaster, a time when we would dangle from the chords of technology, held by fingers of corporations that would let us fall just to make us need them more. Our rivers would flow with the vile backwash of our society, and our food would leech into our bodies the pesticides we used to produce them. The Spirit knew there would come a time when we would ride steel ponies that exult poison into our once pure air and dragons that would dump jet fuel onto our heads but that we would nonetheless smile in oblivious bliss because we would call it "advancement," "achievement," "evolution."

The Great Spirit had foreseen this future and set out to change it. He created two gyre-shaped pendants, each alike except for the material they were made of; one was made of black onyx and the other of bone-bleached pearl. Each had carved in it five heads: the head of a bear, an eagle, a sibahé, a cougar, and a dove, each representing a piece of the Prophecy, each a chosen one from the calling. The Prophecy was to lie idle within the gyres until the time came for the first wave of the great unbalance to sweep over the land. The Spirit of mankind held the gyres, one in each hand until they ignited into a sphere of fire and flame at which point they were swept into the sky as a great blue comet. Good and Evil formed in that moment. To balance Evil, the Great Spirit prepared the people with a silent weapon, one to defend against the death of purity.

The gyres fell, forming a massive crater in what is now the northern Arizona desert. A Chief tribesman found the gyres many years later and held on to them until his twin sons were of age. To help others tell the boys apart as they grew up, one wore raw, light-colored buckskin, the other a dark-stained skin. So it was only fitting that the dark son receive the onyx pendant and the light son receive the pearl pendant. This is the story of what the gyres bore and the small crusade to stop the death of purity.

Table of Contents

PROLOGUE

Have you ever traced a pivotal moment to the exact second when one path in your life suddenly transitions into another? I was tracing such a moment now, back through the well-beaten grooves of my previous life, and searching feverishly for the moment it all went wrong. The fear in my head was winning control of my thoughts. I had never been faced with this type of unknowing, this type of fear, this much confusion. My life was perfect; my life was an uncomplicated path. I was, after all, the daughter of the Chief. I had just turned seventeen, common marrying age, a time in my life where things were supposed to change for the *better*. Every girl in my tribe looked forward to this time of life, but suddenly I found this was no longer my path.

CHAPTER ONE

It was a typical start to a typical day here in Chikitan Canyon, the place I had spent everyday of my life thus far. Usually these kinds of days were boring at best, but today there was much to look forward to. I woke up in a good mood and was daydreaming of the life I had hoped to be living in a few short days. The noisy hoot owl had gone silent shortly before dawn, the cook fires lit shortly after that, and the smell of my mother's tea brewing was right on schedule. All seemed routine except this wasn't a normal day — it was three days before the Summer Maiden March.

I didn't really have my eye on anyone in particular ... well, no one I would reveal to my father anyway. There was one Brave whom I secretly admired when no one was watching. It was hard to miss him. He was a "mischief maker," as my father put it, and "not of my standing," and my mother described him as having "a wild soul." Regardless, Tallenhill was my secret crush. Despite what my father thought of him, I was planning on letting him know I liked him, just in case he liked me back. I'm usually hesitant of disclosing this kind of information, but I have liked him for a long time now; and if I didn't at least try, then I could get stuck marrying Squatting-hoof, the odd, pit-faced toad that to this day still throws frogs in my hair.

Squattinghoof had one advantage as a husband; his father had a substantial dowry to offer and would need it to marry off his insanely irritating son, who is infatuated with me even though I duck out of view every time I see him. The Maiden March was only three days away and if the stars were lined up in my favor I would be starting a great new chapter in my life; if they weren't, then I could be marrying Squattinghoof, and nothing would be worse than that.

I sat alone in deeper thought than I am able to achieve with Ottowa and Tecka around. My two best friends are nothing like me, yet extensions of me all the same. Ottowa is very petite. To look at her, you would think her tiny frame would crumble under her large head. Her long, dark hair hides her thin frame like a cloak. Of the three of us, she is the shyest and most insecure. Tecka and I always assumed this was because her father died when she was little and her mother sort of "turned into herself" — or so that's what we hear others whisper. Ottowa never talks about it much, but she has always seemed eager to grasp any stability she can find for her life and hold on as if any moment it would be ripped from her; because of that, she is a very loyal friend.

Tecka, on the other hand, is one of the more outgoing girls in our tribe. She is the kind of girl who talks before thinking and routinely gets caught with her foot in her mouth. I think that is why she latched onto me. Others are more lenient with you when you associate with the Chief's daughter. Still, my polar-opposite friends complement my wild Spirit and strong personality well.

I'm not sure why or how I ended up with the personality that I have. I'm not like my mother or father, and I've always felt a degree of isolation from my tribe, as if I were an outsider looking in. As far back as I can remember, I have never felt content with the life my parents or the tribe expect of me. I feel there is something else out there calling to me. It's almost eerie. Whatever it is, it pulls at my soul like the Northern Star, beckoning me to follow. Unfortunately, the unknown is also something that terrifies me, so I've worked hard to suppress those feelings.

I gazed at my reflection in the creek, as though I was looking at someone else. I studied my features and tried to get an outsider's opinion of myself in hopes it might help me make improvements before the Maiden March. Each summer, the single women of the tribe dress up and celebrate with a feast and a march as the available men watch and decide who, if any, is ready to marry and if they are prepared to present our fathers with a worthy enough gift. It's the way marriage has been done in our tribe for hundreds of years, but often a father's acceptance of a less-than-worthy offer will upset the tribal lines and create tension for years to come. Not accepting an offer is risky. I knew three maidens whose fathers rejected offers twice, and their daughters are now the oldest in the group and will most likely never be picked as a wife. I know my father, for that very reason, is equally nervous about any offers for me. I certainly hope I am worth more than a couple of buffalo hides.

I wondered what type of woman I was becoming and if it showed on the outside. Was I skilled enough, pretty enough, friendly enough? A frog leaped into the creek, and the ripples washed my face away and scattered it into unrecognizable fragments of liquid silk. I took it to mean that I need-ed to stop questioning myself and start this day out fresh and productive, but that was nearly impossible because I was meeting up with Tecka and Ottowa, two of the most unproductive girls in the tribe, especially lately.

Our new daily habit is to flaunt around conspicuously, always smiling and making sure that our hair is nice in case we catch an eye. I never let on that I care, but I do love the way we turn the Braves' heads when we walk by. I try to come across as the mysterious, hard-to-get type, but I'm not convinced that I actually come across that way.

The Braves were the men of the tribe who had passed the test of manhood but had not married yet. It was customary for them to marry within three season cycles of becoming a Brave. Many of our Braves were in their third cycle, so there were quite a few looking for mates. My mother and father would talk about the new Braves unencouragingly. I would hear my father say things like "in his dreams," and "over my dead Spirit." My mother would humor him with, "Yes, dear, the Braves just aren't the men they use to be when you were young." My father promised that I would get a say in the final decision, which eased my anxiety a little bit, but I knew it would be a very small say.

Some Braves ran by, chasing each other as I came up from the creek. Their sweaty hair whipping in the wind and slapping their deeply tanned shoulders.

"Hi, Tallenhill," I called out, leaning from a screen of cattails and trying not to appear too eager.

"Oh, Natani, I didn't see you standing there. You're looking nice today; you better watch out — someone will snatch you up at the Maiden March looking like that." His bronze face was smooth and youthful — even smoother than mine — as his eyes passed over me.

"Thanks." My heart sank — he must not have considered me to be an option. "Are you going?" I asked, hoping that he could see that I was interested in him.

"Of course." He looked back and saw that his friends had all left him. "Well, I better catch up. I'll see you later, Natani." He turned and ran off, leaving me irritated, confused and sighing with discontent. I stood watching as he sprinted off, the sound of the buck hide flapping on his legs with each turn. I knew I shouldn't overanalyze our encounter, but I had gotten contradicting vibes. I should have been more direct, *but guys hate it when girls are too direct*, my mind shouted back to me. What's the use — my father would never approve anyway.

My father is a warm man though he is forced to put on a stern face as Chief. He is always in thought and always focused on something else, which made it easy for my brother and I to get away with things as children. One minute he would be disciplining us, and the next he would be off meeting with the Elders about issues much more important than our childish mischief. My mother, on the other hand, is a silent mountain. She is as stable and traditional as any woman in the tribe and is relied upon by most for advice on everything from medicines and food to crop plotting and so on. Those things just come naturally to her, and many of the older women have always envied her. I wouldn't say that my brother, Natan, and I were necessarily neglected as children, just that the straps weren't pulled as tight around us as some of our peers. There just wasn't time.

As a child I spent a lot of my time daydreaming. Even now, if allowed, I could sit out in the field all day staring at the clouds and dreaming. Usually two things fill my mind: thoughts of the Brave I'd marry and the tepee

I'd have one day and the other, a more menacing thought, of the eerie calling I had in the pit of my stomach. This week, though, all thoughts were on the Braves.

I wasn't a picky girl, but I did have standards. I didn't want to marry a Brave just because his father was willing to pay mine more; I wanted someone with substance, someone I felt lucky to have. To be honest, none of them really made my heart sing, even Tallenhill, but I knew the older I got the less likely I'd get picked by someone I could tolerate. I wasn't the prettiest girl in the tribe, but I could turn heads. I always dreamed of catching the eye of someone great. Tallenhill would do.

My only sibling, my annoying little brother, was both my chagrin and my delight. He was an irritation to say the least — similar to having uneven ears — something you have to live with but are always conscious of and something you worried would make itself obvious at the worst moments. I love my brother, like any sister would, but even at the tender age of fourteen, he finds great pleasure in following me around asking inappropriate questions and making passes at my friends. I know he does it just to irritate me. He also knows I wouldn't lose my cool this close to the Maiden March for fear that the Braves might see. He uses this to his advantage and knows that on a normal day I'd be able to chase and tackle him. Now I just have to endure his remarks and his flirting with my friends. One advantage in having Natan as a brother is that I always have an excuse to hang out around the Braves because he is always with them.

My brother looks like me, only boxier in the face and with a bigger nose. Thank the Spirits I didn't get that nose. We looked even more similar when we were younger, and people would always get us confused with one other. Natani and Natan — even our names are irritatingly similar. I was glad that as we grew up our similarities grew apart.

I met Tecka at our usual meeting place by the shade tree north of the village. She was sporting a new turquoise necklace. "Isn't it gorgeous?" She ran up to me twirling it around in her hands.

"Wow, that is … where did you get it — or did you steal it?" I asked sarcastically. We always gave each other a hard time.

"My mother gave it to me as sort of a good luck charm to wear to the Maiden March. She wants to see me get picked by someone good just as much as I do. See the turquoise sun symbol? That's my favorite part. I just love it; it was my grandmother's." She jumped around speaking in fragmented thoughts, giddy over her new possession.

"Wow, your grandmother's? I'm surprised she trusted you with that," I said laughingly.

"Of course, she did. What are you saying, Natani? I'm responsible — besides I would die before I let this out of my sight." Her voice sobered up as she tied the necklace around her neck. I understood the importance of treasured heirlooms. I had a necklace that had been handed down many generations to me that I felt the same about. Becoming an extension of me, it had hung on my neck for two years now.

"I have my eye on you Tecka — the Maiden March is only three days away!" Natan was on the other side of the bank shouting like a buffoon. The thought of someone actually accepting my brother's proposal made me laugh out loud. Ottowa and Tecka put up with his boldness always telling me how cute he is, but it still gets old, and I think they do it just to be nice.

"You have to become a Brave first, Natan, and I'll probably be taken by then," Tecka shouted back in a flirtatious tone. Natan just grunted and smiled and then chucked a flat stone across the water. It plunged into the muddy bank at our feet and sent Tecka jumping and shrieking from its path. Natan laughed and disappeared into the field grass.

We three girls have a good relationship, and we spend most of our free time together, walking through our village and watching the Braves practice their skills. There is a popular hangout near the river where they congregate to practice hatchet throwing, riding, and shooting. It's nice because it's out of the Elders' sight, and we are free just to have fun without watchful eyes. The Braves are always competing, and we enjoy the show, especially Ottowa. She is giddy by nature, but her silent awkwardness comes across as odd, which is fun to watch because it doesn't take much to get her going.

I was crossing camp with Tecka to gather baskets when Ottowa intercepted us.

"Want to take the long route past the river and see if the Braves are swimming?" Ottowa was always one to put off work when there was flirting to do, which is surprising because she is not good at it.

I think out of the three of us, I had the most focused approach to life. But it was only three days until the Maiden March, so the more exposure we got, the better our odds would be. Plus, I needed to find Tallenhill. The wind was still, and I could feel the heat radiating from the dirt path as we walked. The morning was heating up fast.

The cicadas buzzed in the distance as sweat beaded up on our noses. It was the dead of summer, and I could tell by the sound of the cicadas that their cycle was about over. That meant that tonight would be close to a new moon, usually those nights brought a much- anticipated cooler breeze.

"Hey, Natani, wait up!" Squattinghoof appeared out of nowhere. He was kicking up dust on our heels as he barreled through us and gasped for air with whistling wheezes.

"Well, don't pass out, Squattinghoof." That was all I could think of to say. I was surprised I hadn't heard him coming from across the village.

"Wooowheee, it's hot!" He stood one stride from my face sucking in so much air that I could distinctly smell the venison jerky on his breath. He finally calmed down and seemed to change personalities. "So how are you?" he asked, trying his best to sound suave.

"Good," I answered politely.

"Good, good, that's really good to hear. I'm doing good, too ... you know, in case you were wondering how I was." I didn't know how to respond, so I didn't. "So are you going to be in the Maiden March?" My stomach clenched as the words came out of his mouth.

"Yes," I said hesitantly.

"Good, good, that's really good to hear. I will be there, too, in case, you know, in case you were wondering." He wiped the sweat off his forehead and slapped it against his belly. This left a dark print on the buckskin to match the sweat rings already formed around both arms and neck. I stood silently and felt slightly sick to my stomach. Ottowa saw that I was in distress, so she piped up.

"Nice talking to you, Squattinghoof, but we have to go now." She put an arm around mine and lead me past.

"Oh good, that's good. Well, I will see you all later then. I will be around." He was still talking as we headed through a blind of river birches.

"Oh, no" was all that I could say.

"He's not *that* bad," Tecka said with smile. "And his family is really well-off. Just think about the tepee you could have."

"Oh no, I have to find Tallenhill. I have to just come out and say it — does 'pick me' sound too desperate?"

"Yeah, kind of," Tecka responded while scrunching up her nose.

"At this point, I don't think I have any other choice." I headed off with more determination in my step. We walked silently, the importance of the next few days weighing on each of our minds.

"Ottowa, I don't think you could have picked a hotter part of the day to be looking for Braves," Tecka said as she tried to keep the sweat off the band of her new necklace.

"Tecka, this is like a battle, the battle of our futures. We might not get picked again this year, or even worse, Natani could get picked by that buffoon Squattinghoof. Think about how she will feel then."

She was right. I had to find Tallenhill and seal the deal. I needed to have something in the works, at least another option or two. We finally reached the river, but oddly no one was there.

"Great, it's too hot even for the Braves to be out." Tecka kicked the dirt in disgust.

It was strange that no one was around. Usually the river was full of people on hot days.

Something seemed different, almost uneasy to me. Tecka was still twirling around showing off her necklace to Ottowa, but their voices slowed, almost as if time was slowing in that very moment. "Hmmm, that's odd," I thought. That feeling of puzzlement barely had time to flash across my mind when it happened.

I suddenly felt the flight instinct shoot through me like a bolt of lightning. *GO, GO, GO!* my mind roared. A stick broke under someone's foot, and like a flame turning to smoke, suddenly everything was frozen chaos. A form appeared. It was unlike anything I had ever seen, and it took me a minute to register what was happening — a minute too long. Before I knew what was going on, leather bands whipped around my hands, and the three of us were bound. A rope wove violently around our waists and cinched us together with one hard jerk. I could feel the friction of the leather burning into my side. It all happened so fast. Before I could even react or do anything to stop it, it was over, and we could no longer move.

My mind raced until it was suddenly brought back to the current scene. There was such a blur of dust and fur and whipping hair and ropes, I couldn't grasp what was happening. *What is going on, what is going on, what is going on?* My mind was trying to process the events, but it could only perceive a frantic fragment of threat.

I looked up through the cloud of dust and saw at the other side, the face of a man, a monstrous man. He jerked the rope lurching us forward, and trying to make us walk faster. I tripped several times before gaining my footing. No one said a word. I could hear the sounds of our breath struggling to keep up with our pounding hearts. I felt like I was consuming handfuls of dirt, the taste of the dust cloud was settling on my tongue. Behind us, several men poked anyone who did not take our captivity seriously. I glanced at Ottowa and then at Tecka. Their faces were as white as flour and their eyes were full of terror, each was searching mine for some sort of answer. Even in my wildest nightmares, I would have never been able to have made up anything like these creatures.

This couldn't be happening, right? *Was this really happening?* It took all the strength in my body to keep moving. My legs were tingling, and I felt like I could collapse at any moment. But I knew this was not a time to be weak.

What was going on for the rest of the tribe? Did anyone know what was happening to us? Was my family safe? Questions replaced fear, and I searched desperately, looking back for clues. Tears were streaming down Ottowa's face as the color of her copper skin highlighted on her cheeks – but she didn't speak a word. Her blank face reminded me of the Spiritless face of the rabies-stricken coyote that had wondered into the village just before my father killed it. Its eyes were glazed, and its mind absent. I could hear the forced, panic-stricken breath of Tecka and Ottowa behind me. It sounded hard like mine, and I hoped no one would hyperventilate.

Still in disbelief, we followed the monsterous men. Down the river just a few paces, two other girls from the tribe joined us. One of them, Tanna, began struggling and screaming as she realized this was not a prank. One of the men whaled a whip through the air and cracked it against her feet. She gasped in pain but remained silent after that. I watched the welt form and rise with each limp, and I could feel her pain. We were all bound together in a tight huddle, our knees knocking together with each step as we were led further away from our home. The sound of frantic breathing and suppressed whimpers surrounded me, and I could no longer hear the cicada.

As we walked I searched my mind for some sort of plan. Surely the Braves would come for us; surely this was not the end. Maybe Tallenhill would be just over the ridge planning an attack with his friends.

I remembered my father once saying, "Know your enemy, and you can outthink him." But at this moment, that notion seemed ridiculous. I had heard stories of other tribes, bad tribes, coming and taking the women and children for their slaves. Could this be the Denriks or the Cutinaws? My childhood was full of scary stories of those tribes, and I suddenly felt like I was living one. The thought entered my mind that we might not return to our families.

From the corner of my eye, I studied the men. They wore hides of bears. Tanned, black -matted fur ran down their backs and onto their huge arms giving them the appearance of being half-bear, and half-human. The bears snout hung out over their brow concealing their eyes under rows of white teeth. Strapped to their backs they carried long knives, as long as my arm. The sight was terrifying. Their arms alone were like tree trunks, and their muscles bulged from their massive bodies.

This had to be some kind of dream. My life was perfect. I was the Chief's daughter, and things like this don't happen to the Chief's daughter.

But here we were.

To be honest, I had never been truly afraid in my whole life, so the feeling was foreign. Once, my father got mad that I let my brother wander into the forest when I was supposed to be watching him. I finally found him, but my father was furious. That kind of fright did not compare at all. No, these creatures were too powerful to be stopped by even a mad father. I searched my mind trying to make sense of what was happening, but nothing was clear. I felt disoriented and in shock, and everything had happened so fast that I still couldn't piece it together.

What did these men want with us? Where were we going? I looked at Ottowa and Tecka, and they had the same dazed look on their faces that I'm sure I had on mine. Our heads were shoved into sacks, and for a moment I wondered if this was some sort of evil prank by the Braves—maybe it was a new Maiden March ritual that we hadn't been told of? Even through the sack I could smell an awful odor. I was about to tell one of them they needed to take a bath when the bag was lifted, and I saw one of the monsters eye to eye. It was now clear to me that these were not the Braves and that this was not a prank. I could hear the whimpering cries of my companions, but as the Chief's daughter, I needed to show more strength than that; it was expected of me. For their sake, I needed to be strong even though I didn't feel that way.

I collected my thoughts. I told myself it was all going to be OK. My father would come for us; he was probably getting men together right now, a war party to rescue us. It would be just a matter of time, and we would be back to our normal lives, back to flirting with the Braves, back to making baskets, and back to the chores I so wished I were doing right now. I closed my dust-coated eyes, and they watered with irritation.

I turned to Ottowa. She was in so much shock that I feared that she might pass out.

"Don't worry, they will come for us … you'll see … they will save us … it's just a matter of time," I whispered, barely making a sound, hoping that I could calm her down. She looked at me like I wasn't even there. That's when I noticed behind her the dark gray smoke rising toward the sky in the direction of our village. Tears of rage filled my eyes, and I forgot how afraid I was.

"You evil monsters!" My voice shrilled to the point that my throat hurt. I screamed, thinking of the rugs I had spent weeks on and the baskets my mother was making to trade. I just knew all would be gone. A back-breaking lurch of the rope made everyone gasp, but I kept quiet. Why would anyone be that cruel? And what about my family? Were they alright? A feeling of helplessness came over me, and the dizziness returned. A fresh round of sobs broke out from the captives. I knew that they too were thinking of their families, but I knew my father and the Braves would be coming. Even as I asked myself the question, doubt entered my head. In the back of my mind, I felt the need to prepare myself for the worst. I wanted to break down, but I held it together. Part of me held out for hope, and I focused on that. Our captors just laughed and hurried us along. I could feel their eyes on our every move.

Soon we had gone past the outer rim of the village, and the smoke was just a distant speck on the horizon. Everything I had known was probably in that cloud of smoke looming over the familiar grounds of our burning home. It would never look the same. I just knew my poor family was running around trying to save as many tepees as they could. With every step I built up more fury.

CHAPTER TWO

Screaming Mountain

We traveled through the grassy plains until evening, stopping only to drink and rest for a short time. Then we started on our way again. The brush was tall, and it was difficult for us to walk because we were all still tied together. Sticks and thorns were ripping at our legs, but there was nothing we could do to prevent it. When we finally came to a clearing and stopped for the night, exhaustion overtook our fear. The girls huddled together and picked the dried blood from their scraped legs and wiped the crusted dust from their tear-swollen cheeks.

"We will get through this if we stick together."

My words of encouragement seemed useless, and I wondered if anything I said could possibly lift their spirits.

"You always think you know it all, Natani."

I looked into the face of Pinotteh, one of the other girls from my village. We had never gotten along. Her father was on the Council and didn't approve of all the things my father did. I didn't know if that was why she disliked me so much, or if I had done something to her in the past that she just could not get over.

"No, I don't know everything. It just stands to reason that our fathers would want to get us back. But in your case, I might be wrong." I couldn't resist the jab.

She raised her arm out to strike me, but Tecka grabbed it.

"Please, you two, don't make things worse than they already are; she is still the Chief's daughter." Tecka said as she flashed Pinotteh one of her famous don't-you-dare-looks. Tecka was a big girl, easily six inches taller and twenty pounds heavier than Pinotteh, so it was smart for her to back down.

"Not here she's not — it's everyone for herself." Pinotteh seemed to be releasing some stored anger, and it only made the other girls more anxious. I didn't know how long I was going to allow her to stir up emotions.

"She is not the big shot she thinks she is just because her dad is Chief. That doesn't make you any better than the rest of us, so don't think we are all going to listen to you just because you're giving us a pep talk." Pinotteh glared at me, but I could tell that she was just as scared as I was.

"I never said I was," I replied smiling half-cocked.

Pinotteh looked away irritated. I could tell out of the corner of my eye that Tecka was giving me the look now though I know in any other circumstance she would have been egging it on. We both stopped when we heard two men laughing at us. Their deep bellows settled in our ears with an unwelcome tone. One man in particular was staring with an odd smile on his face; I looked away quickly and then back again through my hair, a convenient blind. They sat at a fire. The gold hues illuminated their already exaggerated features, and the flames whipped between us and them. I whispered as low as I could and turned away from Pinotteh in hopes of getting support from the other girls.

"We need to make a trail so that the Braves will be able to find us," I whispered out into the darkness not sure who heard me or if anyone would answer.

"What do you mean?" A voice whispered back. It sounded like Ottowa's.

"You know, drag your feet; break branches — anything you can think of to show we passed through this way."

"That's a good idea."

Ottowa was on board. I was glad someone was on my side.

One of the bear-men appeared, handed out dried meat and bread, and then stood over us while we ate. The meat was horrific. I wanted to reach out and bite our captor's grizzly leg with all the fury I had been suppressing but I knew it would not be an equal fight. I knew we needed to keep our strength up so I ate the rancid meat without a grimace and sat quietly until he left. I noticed Ottowa could not bring herself to eat and I was worried that she wouldn't be able to keep up.

"You must eat and stay strong; our Braves will come for us, and we need to be able to run back home with them when the time comes. Please eat it," I begged her. She gave me a faint smile of hope and stuck a small piece in her mouth.

"When will our Braves get here?" came a voice, but in the dim light, I couldn't tell whose it was.

"I don't know; I just don't think we should give up. We are going to live through this; that's all I know."

"That's easy for you to say. You are stronger than we are." The voice was weak, but I could tell it was Tecka's. I could tell she was referring to Ottowa.

"We just need to stick together. That's all." No one responded, and the sounds of the night screeched around us. I sat there cloaked in the darkness and wished I felt as confident as I sounded. That night I allowed myself to think the worst. — "Maybe they would not be coming" — but that possibility sank me into such despair that I would not allow myself to think it again, at least not anytime soon.

In my dreams that night, I was dancing freely around the campfire while many friendly eyes watched. My soul knew them, but I did not recognize their faces. I felt so happy, but when I looked closer, the eyes changed to hungry animal eyes. I woke startled, thinking I would be inside my tepee safe with my family, but that was not the case.

The sun was not even up by the time we were on the move again. We had survived one night, so I was confident that we could survive many more. One of the men walked close to me and grabbed my arm when I tripped. I caught his eye, and his stare made me uncomfortable. His eyes weren't like mine; they were wild and hard to read, I broke away and watched my steps more closely.

Trees started popping up in places among the prairie grasses. Unlike the pines I was used to, these had thick, twisted trunks with huge branches resembling arms that could reach out and grab you. We were no longer in Chikitan Canyon. They grew closer and closer together until they blocked out the sun. An abundance of birds flew from branch to branch and chattered at us as we passed. The twisted forest felt cooler, and the earth was damp, which was a relief to our tired bodies and swollen feet. That night, strange sounds filled the air around us. They were deeper, scarier sounds than the night before. It truly felt like a different land. I no longer recognized anything. Dried leaves under our feet made every step sound ominous. This new land was so strange that it reinforced my disorientation.

Once the men had gone to sleep, I worked at freeing my hands from the ropes. I had always been flexible, a seemingly worthless trait until now. I worked for several minutes and was able to twist my hand enough to get at the other one. The twine cut into my wrists, but I was able to wiggle them free and loosen the slack. Soon we were all free of the ropes.

"What should we do? Are we going to run? I'm scared — maybe we should stay." Ottowa's voice was so soft and weak that I actually considered telling her to just stay behind, but I didn't.

"OK, let's go slowly and quietly. If they spot us, then run and don't look back. Just run as hard and as fast as you can — until you can run no farther." I knew some of the girls were faster than others, and if possible the fast ones might make it and be able to get help.

I whispered these instructions in hopes that we'd be able to escape without being detected. I stood up first, and we started to sneak into the forest. We advanced about twenty feet — the plan seemed to be working. My heart pounded, and I could feel it pulsing down into my hands. Although the darkness was comforting, it also hindered our ability to see the best paths through the trees. Then suddenly a loud cracking sound rang up from the forest floor. It was nothing more than someone stepping on a stick, but the sound cracked and echoed like thunder. The quiet suddenly turned to a rushing fury of insanity. My heart sank like a deadweight. I could hear movement. I was sure the men were jumping to their feet, but I was already running. I felt like I had been running for several minutes already.

"Run!" I shouted behind me.

It was impossible to see in the dark. I was clawing through branches and over rocks. I could have been headed for a cliff. I couldn't tell, and I didn't care; I just had to keep going forward. In the back of my mind, I wanted to turn around and see if Ottowa or Tecka were behind me — should I go back for them? My hands stretched out in front of me, defending my face from branches but getting ripped and cut as I went. I wanted to gasp for air, but I was afraid it would be too loud. I hadn't been caught yet — would I make it?

The next thing I knew, I was on the ground with a heavy weight smashing me into the dirt; someone was on top of me. The smell of the damp, pungent dirt burned my nose, and the rocks ground into my ribs. I had been caught.

"You're not going to get away from me; I have waited too long for you." The voice was deep, so deep that it resonated with an echoing chill. I felt comforted by it and yet terrified by the huge forceful body that it came from. He ran his hand down my arm and along my leg. It sent chills down my spine. I had expected the capture to be more violent and for him to be angry that I had tried to run, but he wasn't. Instead it seemed like he enjoyed catching me; in a way, that disgusted me even more. Who was this man? How dare he touch me? I was the Chief's daughter after all.

"A perfect fit," he whispered through the darkness, his slimy voice pooling in my ear.

"The only perfect fit would be a dagger in your side." My voice was stronger than I thought it would be.

I could hear the other girls screaming and crying all around me, but my mind could only focus on his words. A perfect fit for what? What did he mean by that? My imagination was of little help. He then scooped me up with little effort and carried me back to the others. I didn't fight. I just let him take me back because I wanted him to think I was weak. There would be a better time to fight, a better time to unleash the fury that had been brewing inside me. His fur was coarse and rough like spines. I could feel the massive weight of his body with each step; it seemed the earth shook with each colossal stride.

"What do you want with us? Where are you taking us?" I asked into the night, hoping my voice wasn't too muffled by his fur. He didn't reply.

Soon I was back and disappointed to see that all of the other girls were too. This meant no one had escaped and now there would be no one to find us help. Everyone's disappointment weighed on my shoulders, as no one spoke a word.

We continued traveling. The terrain was rough, and the sharp rocks gave way to even sharper thorns as the thicket rose to waist high. By the second day, the vegetation had subsided to random twisted sage bushes. I could see a forest in the distance, but we were headed in the opposite direction and climbing close to rocky cliffs. By now everyone's panic had subsided a little, and we agreed that if they had wanted to kill us, they would have done so already. The confusion, though, was still apparent, and I had no comfort to offer. I could tell that the upward climb was wearing on everyone. Signs of exhaustion where obvious on Ottowa's face as we continued to climb.

Finally, at the end of the third day, we were untied from each other. It was nice to have my wrists free of the ropes; they were raw with blisters, and bruises were setting in.

Maybe this is my chance, I thought to myself. I could slip away and head for the thick forest where these men could not find me. I would bury myself in the dirt if I needed to. My eyes brightened with hope, but before I could put my plan into action, the same man who had caught me before flung me over his shoulder. I was really starting to get irritated by this beastly man.

"I am going to enjoy this a lot more than you are," he said with a snide smile. His words made the hair on my neck stand up. We were all being carried in this uncomfortable manner for a very long time. The blood had all rushed to my head, and I felt like passing out. I assumed this was why they were carrying us. My face was in the small of his back, and his fur smelled raw, like old pine needles. My hips hurt as his shoulder blades dug into my empty stomach. If only I could have mustered up enough courage to reach for one of the knives on his back, but I kept telling myself there would be a better time for a revolt when I wasn't dangling four feet off the ground. I had time to think, and I wondered: if given the chance, would I be able to slice his neck in the silence of the night? Did I have what it took to kill a man, even a man as evil as this? What would my body do in that situation? Could I even rely on my hands to do what my head told them to? I didn't know, but I also didn't care. I was going to escape no matter how I had to do it, and if I was going to die, I might as well try and take one of them with me.

By the dim light of a hazy moon, we made our way along a stone path next to a sheer mountain side. Even in the fading light, I could see the outline of what looked like a looming face above us. It was as if the mountain was calling out in a frozen silent scream. The rock face was dark, and the moonlight bounced off the facade's enormous brow, adding a foreboding cast to the blue shadows that hung in the sockets and mouth. It was apparent this was the congregating place for these evil men. The mouth appeared to be a cave which I feared we would eventually be entering – and I knew there was nothing I could do to stop it.

I felt shrouded in doom and bound by fear, but I swore to myself that eventually I'd come back out.

CHAPTER THREE

The Wives

Hundreds of tiny-winged bats flew precariously across the sunken cheeks of the mountain's face. To my horror we weren't the only ones entering that black cavern. Their tiny bodies whipped past my head as we entered, and I knew there was a high possibility that one of these winged beasts would get stuck in my hair.

Whether from sheer terror or the position in which I was being carried, my stomach churned as I fought back the need to vomit. Once inside, we were put back on our feet. I nearly fell but was held in place by my captor, whose touch repulsed me. Ottowa collapsed on the floor. I took a step towards her but was knocked back.

"Stay in place," his rough, deep voice commanded.

We all froze, and I was relieved when she started to come around. Ottowa made it to her feet, and we were pushed along the cave floor toward a dim light that grew brighter as we approached it. The air smelled as if it had not moved in a thousand years. I could feel the damp droplets of stagnant water oozing from the roof of the cave like blood, the minerals staining it a dirty crimson.

"OK, so where are all the Braves that were going to rescue us? No one is ever going to find us in here!" Only Pinotteh could think to be snotty at a time like this.

"Does that really make you feel better?" I asked, whispering without looking at her.

"Yeah, you know, in a small way, it does" she replied. I could feel her hateful eyes burning into the side of my cheek.

"Well at least that's something. Glad I could help," I replied, still looking ahead.

This was not the time to be arguing with Pinotteh. Our lives had just taken another turn for the worse, and we could be walking to our deaths this very moment. Pinotteh did not respond, and I was glad because I needed to focus. Yet nothing could have prepared me for the scene that was coming. As the image came into focus, I felt my throat tighten, and with one last gulp, I had stopped breathing. My knees wanted to give way. I couldn't walk; instead I began to stumble.

I saw a figure sitting in the center of the cavernous room we were entering. He sat on a stone-carved throne that looked like skeletons joined together to support him. He wore the same bear hide, only massive horns came out of his headdress making his appearance even more menacing. From the looks of him, I assumed he was their demon Chief. His wild eyes flickered in the torchlight as they zipped feverishly back and forth, scanning us from the other side of the room. Finally, they slowed and fixed upon us in a greedy gaze that sent chills down my spine and extinguished the last bit of hope that I was holding inside.

"Welcome home, my sons," he said in a low, raspy voice. "Looks like you had luck on your hunting trip." His moves were very slow and fluid like that of smoke. The veins in his hands and arms protruded like snakes from under his pitted skin. He was not as big as the other men. In fact he was probably no taller than I was, but he had an aura about him that set him apart from the other men and hinted at a more keen intellect.

I quivered in my skin and tried not to make it too obvious how repulsed I was. I didn't believe anything so disgusting could be a natural, living thing. One of the men stepped forward from the rest and bowed down on one knee; it looked like my irritating captor, but I couldn't tell because the headdresses made them all seem so similar.

"We did have luck, my Chief — these will make fine wives. You said the winner of the contest gets first pick?"

"Did I?" The Chief bellowed out as his voice echoed with dying vibrations through the cavern.

At that moment the words snapped into place within my head. WIVES! We were going to be wives to these monsters? I thought I was going to be sick, and when I looked at my companions, they all shared the same look of horror. Instantly my father's face flashed into my head. This was not part of the plan. My father was going to be angry when he found out I was forced to marry some hairy brute.

"Yes, but that one is mine," the Chief replied. I looked to see whom he was pointing to, only to discover that everyone's eyes were on me. "Lucky you," Pinotteh whispered with an evil little grin. I had been chosen as wife by the demon Chief himself. Pinotteh smiled at me again, and in that moment, my knees could hold no more. They gave out and hit the stone floor with a thud that shot a pain straight up my back. It hurt so bad that the pain snapped me back into focus as I gasped from the cave floor to the sound of laughter buzzing all around me. Everyone was laughing except my companions.

"Please get up," Tecka pleaded with me.

"See, she already knows to bow to her husband — how wonderful!" roared the horned Chief in laughter.

I stumbled to my feet.

"Don't be so excited my dear, just because it is your wedding night." The room echoed with laughter again. I could feel the blood rush to my face. He then turned to address us all, and I was glad that his eyes were no longer on me. It gave me time to focus my fury.

"You will be treated well if you do as you are told. After several moons you may be returned to your homes. If you do not obey, you will be punished.

I am sure you remember being carried here? That is in case you try to leave — there will be no old tracks to throw the wolves off — it will be a quick hunt," he paused with a suspenseful glance and then finished. "The unfortunate part is that they usually find you before we do, and there is not much left once we do." He leaned forward and made a slow, warning gesture.

"So let me make this perfectly clear: You leave this cave, you die." With that, he smiled and then addressed us as if talking to children: "What could be simpler than that? Do as you are told and perhaps you will go home." But I feared whether there was anything left of home.

This didn't reassure me. His promise was forced, his smile disingenuous. The Chief's silky words seemed edged with poison.

Three of the prettiest women I had ever seen stepped forward, gently took my arm and guided me down a long, torch-lit tunnel. I looked back to see my friends staring after me terrified. But the women's touch was soft and gentle, and a small sense of relief flowed over me. As we walked, many questions arose in my head. Did these women start off like me? Had they been through the same trauma of leaving their families behind? Would they be able to help me? No one spoke until we reached a cherry-colored room lined with beautiful rugs and a flowing pool of water. The warm wooden accents seemed out of place for the cave's interior. Illuminated by candlelight, the room glowed with a welcoming feel that I had not expected to find in this place.

"What is your name?" one asked as the group undressed me.

"Natani," I answered, still in a daze. The air was cold, and I could feel goose bumps forming in protest to the bare air.

"This is very pretty; is there a story behind it?" She held up the carved bone pendant that hung around my neck.

"My mother gave it to me," I replied, as I reached up to take it back.

"It is very unusual, and it looks very old," she said smiling.

"It is," I replied. I didn't feel like conversing; I didn't feel like making a friend. I looked into her face and searched for some relief from this nightmare. I was ready to pounce if she tried to take my pendant.

"She is in shock," one of the women whispered.

"Yes, but it's just as well; she will remember very little tomorrow," she replied.

I heard their words but did not react. I was just anticipating the worst night, and possibly the end, of my life. I was cleaned and dressed as if it were the most natural thing for them to do. I wondered how many other girls had been put through this before me. The water was refreshing even though it stung the scrapes and welts on my legs. It was warm and safe, and I wanted to just stay there. When they finished, food was put down, and we ate. It was a wonderful change from the dried meat and bread that we had lived off of for the past three days. The oldest woman gave me a gourd cup filled with warm tea. It smelled sweet and bitter at the same time, but I took it anyway.

"Drink this, little one. It will relax you, and things won't seem quite so bad. Don't worry — it's not poison," she assured me with a voice that reminded me of my mother.

I took the tea. At that point I probably would have done anything they told me. I sipped the tea to the last drop wishing that I'd had another helping. Maybe I would pass out and not have to remember anything, I thought. They led me to another room filled with beautiful rugs. At one side was a large stone bench covered with soft woven blankets and furs.

"Just remember it won't last long and when . . . well, when you are allowed to come back here, we will help you. You may not feel lucky, but you are; Chief Duran picks the best of the brides for himself. He is the Chief so that makes you important here." She took my hand and led me to a door.

Important? The word stuck in my mind.

They were all being so nice that I could only imagine the horror and dread that followed such a kind welcome. The tea drink had done its work. After three days of fear and anxiety, I felt a wonderful sense of well-being and relaxation. Deep in thought and in somewhat of a drunken stupor, I laid on the furs. Tonight would have been the Maiden March. I would have been celebrating, eating and dancing with my friends and possibly getting married to Tallenhill. All hopes and dreams I had a few days ago were now over. Now I was marrying a demon, the Chief of these horrid cave dwellers. It made marrying Squattinghoof seem like the best thing that could ever happen to me. I felt dead inside, emotionless, and I was grateful for that — the tea was sending me into another state of mind, a safer one. To my surprise, that feeling did not leave me even when I saw the imposing figure of the Chief standing in the doorway. He did not speak; he only eyed me approvingly. With one long, claw-like fingernail he raised the pendent from my throat. His face showed no reaction, even when he slowly raised his eyes to mine. I noticed then that his were a strange shade of green, one I couldn't quite place. Staring into his old eyes, I was no longer afraid of him. It was as if a trance had taken over me as I boldly stared back. His frightful headdress and skins were gone, and this made him look a little more human. It was impossible to tell his age, but as I gazed into his face, I got the feeling that at one time he might have been almost handsome. For whatever reason, many rough years had passed and taken their toll. Part of his nose was missing, and deep scars adorned his face and body. I could only imagine the many battles he had been in to receive them. This was not how I had thought my wedding night would be. I had dreamed of an actual ceremony, a feast, a dance, at the very least, happiness. This was simply a nightmare, one I hoped to live through, to wake from — to eventually forget.

I would not be the same after tonight. I knew tomorrow I would wake a woman, my purity ripped from me in the worst possible way. Part of me wanted to fight, but the tea rendered me calm and helpless. When he touched me with his rough, cold hands, I closed my eyes and mentally drifted off to another place far from where I was, a euphoric place filled with warm sun and gentle breezes that blew the tall grass like dry, sweet waves. I lay motionless, passing slowly and permanently into a darker side of existence. It didn't matter what he did to me; he would not reach my mind. The iron-clad doors to my soul had shut, and I waited safely behind them, void of all feeling.

CHAPTER FOUR

The women were true to their word; thanks to the tea, I did not remember much. I got up, still in a hypnotic state, and stumbled back into the pool chamber. I was glad to leave, the Chief's deep, ghastly snores faded behind me. The three women hovered around me and washed and changed my clothes again. I didn't speak, and I don't think I could've if I'd tried. I just sat drifting in and out of focus wondering if the same fate had followed the other girls. I sipped a different tea this time and was led to a darker, less-decorated chamber with a smaller bench covered with blankets.

"Sleep well, little one; you have earned it," a soft whisper floated through the dark air. I lay down, but before drifting off to sleep, I pictured my mother's, father's, and brother's happy faces. I couldn't hold back the tears as they welled up and rolled down my already-chapped cheeks, which wet my hair with cold droplets. Then I drifted off to a much-needed dreamless sleep.

When I woke there were cheerful sounds coming from the other room. It was hard to tell if it was day or night. I guessed it didn't matter much. This was a cave, and it may be a long time before I get to see the light of day again. When I tried to move, every muscle in my body screamed — the journey and events had caught up with me. My memory, like an evil friend, greeted me with images of the previous day. I felt dirty and disgusted. I wanted to sink into the dark corner of my little room and disappear, but I told myself to concentrate on an escape — today might be the day I do it. Sore and disoriented, I slowly rose from my bed and entered the other room. Three beautiful, excited faces greeted me; the oldest woman rose and put her arms around me.

"Here, dear, sit and eat. You must be starving. We were afraid you would sleep through the games."

"Games?" I asked confused. Games seemed like the last thing I would have expected in this place. Panic in my voice was leftover from the previous day and made me sound pathetic and whiny. I figured it was okay to allow myself to appear weak to them. I was getting out of here one way or another, and I might feign weakness to my advantage.

"Don't worry; you don't have to do anything," I heard one chuckle.

"The men spar with each other to see who is the best, and the winner gets first pick of brides," her voice faded out.

"But it's fun to watch them fight one another, so grab something to eat, and it will be time for the fighting to start. I'm sorry there isn't much time for introductions. My name is Tetoway. That is Eba, and over there is Abanea. When we have more time, we will tell you all about ourselves, but right now we need to get going." Tetoway's voice was full of energy. Just listening to her excitement seemed to exhaust me.

I had many questions for them, but before I could ask, the women rose, took my hand and lead me out the door. We entered another huge chamber with a large scooped-out circle that was twice deeper than any man is tall. Two wooden ladders on either end provided the only entrance and exit from the pit. Many torches surrounded it making it well lit, and the light refracting off the damp stone made it dance like a pool of liquid light. There was a second rock-shelf level that we walked up to, and from there it was easy to see the entire room. On the other side, I could see Tecka, Pinotteh, and the others; all around them were other women and men. They did not notice me, or if they did they didn't appear to. I wanted to be with Tecka and Ottowa. I hated being separated on my own.

I sat waiting for the games to start and filling my time trying to make opinions of my three new companions. Tetoway seemed the oldest and most regal looking of the three. She was the tallest and most striking. Her dark hair had a reddish tone that when caught in the light, almost shimmered like flames. Her movements were always slow and seemed well-thought-out, and she seemed to be respected the most by Abanea and Eba. Abanea was a stark contrast in personality to Tetoway; she was bubbly and spastic. Her hair was in a tight braid and from what I could tell so far, she reminded me the most of Tecka. I glanced to my right, where Eba was sitting. I wondered if she was the bride the Chief had chosen before me. She seemed to have the most sadness in her eyes, a look she seemed to wear clearly despite her obvious attempts to hide it. None of the women seemed to be unpleasant or dangerous, and that put me at ease.

I glanced out across the room. Eight huge men stood anxiously by the ladders. I noticed that one was the man who had carried me here. His stare caught me off guard and caused shivers to run down my spine. I tried to read the expression on his face, but from that distance it was hard to tell. I forced myself to look away, but when I looked back, he was still staring. I tried to shake the obvious discomfort from my face by turning to Eba.

"What is this place?" I asked desperately. Her eyes turned from happy to sympathetic.

"The pit," she responded shortly.

"No, I mean this whole place, the cave? What is this all about?" I asked again, but it was like speaking to a rock. She obviously didn't want to talk to me.

"In time, for now, we watch," she pointed to the pit and went back to smiling.

"So what did you say we would be watching?" This time I turned to Abanea.

She was eager to answer, and her bubbly excitement seemed odd and inappropriate in a place like this.

"There are eight men who need wives, and only five, well, four girls to choose from, so the winner gets first pick and so on and so on." I turned away without returning the enthusiasm.

Fragments of sentences pieced together in my mind. *First pick? Perfect fit?* I wondered if the one who had eyed me so much and had prevented me from escaping in the woods had planned on picking me as his wife? Why else would he have said "perfect fit?" The blood rushed to my face. I looked back at him; his eyes narrowed to bitterness, and he looked away. Was he mad because the Chief got to me first? That must have been what he meant by "a perfect fit." *You're just being ridiculous, Natani — they are not fighting over you. Focus on what is important, getting out of here.* My mind was dismissing these various scenarios, and on second thought, they did sound foolish. I was deep in thought when the beating of drums startled me. They echoed loudly off the stone walls and made the bats dip down in an irritated frenzy. When the resonance stopped, the Chief walked in. The sight of him repulsed me still and made my palms sweat as I sunk as far back into my seat as I could. He was holding his arms in the air as his voice rang out.

"Begin the games." The room roared with cheering people, and the girls from my tribe sat quietly huddled together. I could tell by the looks on their faces that they had no idea what was happening.

"Where do all these men come from?" I asked without trying to sound too suspicious.

"Just like all of us, they are chosen. We call ourselves the Chosen Ones. The tribe is made up of so many different tribes that it didn't make much sense to really have an official tribal name. We are kind of a secret in here, " she answered.

"But they don't look like the Braves from my village; they are a lot bigger." I had noticed from the first day that these men had huge, muscular arms and legs with bodies that made other men look delicate. "How do they get that way?"

"Well, they didn't always look like that. It's the Mushrooms that do that to them," she answered. "Shh, they are going to begin." Abanea raised her hand to silence me as the roar of cheering increased around me.

From each side of the pit, a man climbed down a ladder into the circle, each carrying a long pole as his only weapon. They stood across from each other, swinging their poles back and forth as they flexed their muscles for the audience. The Chief raised his hand again, and the battle began. The men heaved and ducked, each swinging violently to hit the other without letting himself be struck. The staffs collided with a loud snap that echoed through the chamber. The violent dance was somewhat poetic as the men pushed each other and tried to achieve dominance over the other. From what I could tell, it seemed like bones were being broken with each crack. Once in a while the pole would hit flesh, and you would hear a moan rise up from the crowd. I noticed all eyes were on the competition taking place, all but one. I looked over and caught his eyes on me again. I felt very exposed, sitting trapped between Abanea and Tetoway. I was on display, and the feeling made me self-conscious. I pretended to ignore the strange man, but even when I looked away, I could still feel his eyes on me. If I ever get the chance, I thought to myself, I'm going to tell him how rude it is to stare and that I'm glad I didn't have to be his wife. Who did he think he was anyway, stealing me away from my family just to try and fight over me? He could have just come to the Maiden March and asked my father. It would have been easier.

Cheers erupted and snapped me back to my surroundings. One man was on the ground, and the other had the pole to his throat. They left and two more men took their place. Besides a few bloody knuckles and some dark bruises, no one was seriously injured. Even though I hated these people, I was glad the battle was not to the death. I didn't think I could stomach that right now. When it came time for the strange man to fight, he jumped into the ring and attacked his opponent without even giving him a chance. His aggression was serious and brutal; the other man all but gave up willingly. Abanea leaned to me and spoke.

"That Colbryn is amazing, and he is so good looking. I wish he were fighting over me," she said while giving a wink.

So my creepy stalker's name was Colbryn? I quietly kept my opinion of him to myself. I sat watching until his icy gaze met mine. Our eyes locked. I could not fathom what thoughts were going through his mind. He was like a savage beast. It intimidated me, and I felt the urge to glare back with equal intimidation. But I knew it wouldn't work, so I finally broke eye contact. My thoughts were crazy, and I was letting my imagination run away with me again.

As the next match started, I tried to concentrate on the moving figures in front of me, but my eyes kept drifting back to him. *What's wrong with me?* I kept asking myself.

His face, as attractive as it was, represented all my pent-up anger towards this place and these people. I resented the fact that he thought he could take me as a wife after the horrible events that had taken place over the past few days. I wanted him to suffer as I had suffered. I wanted him to die so I'd never have to see him again. And yet, I couldn't stop looking at him.

Somewhere inside me something strange was brewing. I couldn't shake it, I couldn't dismiss it. Was part of me feeling...? No, I would never allow it. The most absurd thoughts forced themselves into my mind.

Was I feeling an attraction to him?

Without the bear-skin headdress, I could see that he was attractive. In fact he was beautiful. His dark tawny skin lay against his perfectly sculpted body, but it was more of a body I wanted to stab. I decided I would focus on the anger; it would be more beneficial in fulfilling my self-promise of escape.

The eight fighters were quickly reduced to one, but the contest was not much of a challenge. Colbryn had defeated the other men in a matter of seconds and was declared the winner. My palms started to sweat. Who would he pick? I didn't want him, I told myself, but I didn't want any of the other girls to get him either. When he was told to pick his bride, my eyes wouldn't look away. I was already the Chief's wife, which meant it would either be Tecka, Pinotteh, Ottowa, or Yanna. Colbryn walked slowly toward the seats where they were sitting. To my surprise, he held out his hand to Pinotteh, who reached for it hesitantly and smiled her evil little grin.

Pinotteh? Out of all of them, why did he have to pick the most unpleasant and unfriendly one? It serves him right, I thought. I wanted nothing but pain for this man, so he deserved to have snake-like Pinotteh for his wife. I was staring at the ground when the second picked Tecka; eventually, all were chosen. I was still lost in thought when I heard Tetoway speak.

"Come, Natani; our job is to get the ceremonial wedding dinner started." Tetoway motioned for me to leave. I wasn't sure how I was feeling at this moment — irritated, robbed, disappointed, angry — it was a strange mix. We traveled through a series of halls and tunnels that finally led to what I can only describe as the most beautiful place I had ever seen. It smelled of distant freedom and instantly lightened my mood.

"This is the Hall of the Sun. It's our favorite place," Eba said with a smile as she twirled past me.

"I can see why. It's like nothing I have ever seen." It truly was beautiful. The stone walls of the enclosure were a golden shade that reflected pink in the sun. Vines and bushes climbed effortlessly from the ground, and a reservoir bubbled up from the center where it met a waterfall pouring over from the top of the high stone walls. The floor was smooth, almost soft to walk on, but the best part was that you could look up and see sky, the same sky that lingered over my village, the same sky that I had stared into my whole life. Like the face of an old friend, it warmed my soul and whispered to me of secret escape.

"You see, this place isn't so bad after all," Eba said with an attempt to sound convincing. I just smirked without saying a word. I tried not to make it obvious I was sizing up every foothold and strong vine.

"We only let the men here on special occasions," she giggled back.

"We come up here and sit in the sun every chance we get. Over there is where we grow the mushrooms — that will take some time to explain, so I will show you that later."

"So this place is just for us?" I asked, surprised we would even be allowed this type of luxury.

"Well, all the women can come here. We are the only ones who take care of it, so we sort of feel we get first claim." Eba smiled, and I could tell she enjoyed the simple luxuries of being a Chief's wife, though I knew there had to be a secret sadness within each of the women.

"It's beautiful!" I couldn't think of any other words. Compared to the dark depths of the inner cave, it was simply breathtaking. The air was warmer and dryer, and the breeze across my face was softer than it had ever felt.

"We thought you would like it." They all sounded so happy. I could see through it, though, and I knew behind the smiles that they would not have chosen this life.

"So what is this place, and why are we here?" I tried not to sound too demanding even though this was the second time I had asked.

"You mean the Dwells? These caverns are now home, Natani. We know you are sad now and that you miss your village, but in time it will get easier. It helps to think of this as your new village. Just do as you are asked, and never break the rules. We have all been through what you are feeling, Natani," Eba said in a voice that was teetering between happiness and sadness.

"But I ..."

She cut me off.

"Come on, we have to get busy; everyone will be here soon!" Tetoway broke in. "I want you to hand out the rugs. They are over by the entrance.

Each couple gets one. Later, when it gets dark, you can light the torches." Tetoway pointed to the rugs and showed me where the torches were. I was somewhat glad to have a job. It made me feel less like a prisoner — *for the moment*, I reminded myself.

Cooking fires were lit, and food was brought up. Some was already prepared. Eba and Abanea simmered stews in various pots and laid out loaves of bread and berries upon rows of stone tables. The tribe began to arrive, and everything seemed to come together in unison. I wondered how often these feasts happened. My three companions seemed so prepared and at ease as though this happened all the time. For a moment I got caught up in all the happiness and cheer, and this did not seem like the barbaric place that I had first thought it to be. I should make the best of this situation, right? But I also should never let my guard down, in case an opportunity to escape arose — and I knew that it would. I couldn't get caught up in this place. I had to get back to my family and my tribe.

Colbryn and Pinotteh were the first to arrive. I became more anxious the closer they came. I didn't know if it was appropriate to speak, as no one had prepared me for this. What do I say? *Here, have a rug? Glad you could make it? Good job bashing in all those other guys today, Colbryn?* They walked up to me and stopped expecting something, so I spoke.

"Congratulations," I said, but my words were raw as I focused on the rug I held out.

"Thank you," came the familiar deep voice in reply. It seemed less threatening this time.

I glanced up and caught his eyes. I could read nothing of what he was feeling. I shoved the rug into his hands, and the new couple found a place to sit. I never had a reason to be jealous before, especially not of Pinotteh, so the feeling was strange to me. I fought conflicting battles in my mind. Part of me naturally wanted to warm up and embrace this situation, and the other was angry to be here in the first place.

It would have been better if Colbryn had picked anyone other than Pinotteh. As I watched her with him, she acted as though she hadn't been kidnapped, as though she loved being here, as though nothing had happened. All of the girls seemed to be acting this way. Were they being brainwashed? Had they already forgotten home? Was I the only one who wanted to leave? Well, I was the only one with an old, repulsive husband. At least everyone else had strong young men with attractive faces even though they wore bear heads and raided villages. I sat beside Eba and thought: That could have been me sitting next to Colbryn. It made my stomach churn. No, what was I thinking? Was I actually having these thoughts again? It was like someone else was controlling my mind. How and why were these feelings even being considered? An overwhelming sense of irritation came over me. The Chief picked me, so I should be happy given the situation, right? If this were where we were going to be stuck, I would have much preferred the handsome young warrior over the scarred-up demon Chief. I allowed myself a little pity.

I searched for Tecka and Ottowa, but they had not arrived yet. I hated being away from my friends. I knew that staying busy was the best thing for me now. I moved all about the room and plotted out each inch of the space. Before the night was over, I would memorize everything I could about it.

The food was served, torches lit — whatever needed doing, I did.

"Natani." I recognized Tecka's voice as she greeted me with a tight embrace.

"How are you?" I asked, trying to be sympathetic and brave at the same time.

"I'm doing OK, I guess — not really how I envisioned my wedding day," She said with a shrug.

"Tell me about it," I responded smirkingly.

"I'm so sorry you got chosen by the Chief; he scares me. Did he ... did you

...?" I could tell she didn't feel comfortable asking what was on her mind, and I didn't feel comfortable talking about it.

"Hey, it's OK. Don't be sorry for me; we are alive and together. That's all that matters, right? All things considered, you ended up with a good catch," I said with a smile turning the focus on her.

"Yeah, I'm surprised; we haven't really talked much." She glanced in his direction, and a watchful eye was glaring back. "Humpf, I really don't understand this place. I wonder how long before we can go home?"

"I'm afraid it will be a while. I better get back to work. Stay strong." I hugged her and then returned to my duties.

Couples began leaving early, and I didn't want to think about why. Just as I had not been saved, there would be no saving Tecka and Ottowa from this night either. Before I knew it, the celebration was over, and dread loomed over me like a claw.

"Natani, you must be exhausted," Tetoway said smiling up at me as I rolled up the last of the rugs.

"Just trying to stay busy," I replied politely.

"I know this is hard, but it does get better. Before long you will forget the life you left behind, and so accepting this one will be easier. The sooner you can do that, the better off you will be. Trust me." Much like Eba's, Tetoway's words had a hint of sadness still clinging to them.

"I didn't leave any life behind, Tetoway; I was ripped from it, and as long as I am here, I will never be better off." I felt a lump squeeze up into my throat, and I was afraid I might have hurt her feelings.

"Natani, listen to me, and listen to me very closely. What you are holding onto is sure death, so do not even consider trying to escape. I know, I was there just like you. I held on to those very same thoughts for months, even years, but I've seen too many friends leave here and only their heads return. You know, we are here for each other. It's not easy being in this situation. Talking it out always helps. I'm here if you need me." Tetoway sounded sincere, her tawny skin reflecting an old beauty. It was a shame that she had to be locked up inside this dark mountain.

"Thank you, but I'm not sure if it's anything I can talk about. It's nice to know there is someone I can come to if I need to, though." She just smiled and put her arm around my shoulder. I wasn't comfortable enough yet to trust any of my three new companions with my feelings about Colbryn. Tetoway seemed to be digging for something, and it made me nervous. For now it was best that I keep all thoughts and feelings to myself.

"Come on, let's make a cup of tea and get some sleep. You have another busy day tomorrow." She pulled me along, her arm still around me as though we were friends. I played along.

"Tea, yes, the magic tea." I smiled, remembering how wonderfully numbing the tea had been. "I am glad you are with me. I don't think I could ever find my way back to where I need to be; this place is twisted and confusing." I amused her with my small talk, and we smiled.

"I know, this place is like a maze, but you'll find your way soon enough," she said confidently. I didn't want it to become comfortable for me here; I wanted to leave and get back to my family. The thoughts erased any happy feelings I had after the feast, and I went to sleep alone and safe. The Chief did not come to my room this night, and I thanked the Spirits for the solitude. But I wondered how the other girls were faring tonight.

****

CHAPTER FIVE
The Lost Babies

Working with the mushrooms one morning, I asked Tetoway a question that had been on my mind since I got there. "Why aren't there any children? No babies, no toddlers — there is no one under sixteen even?"

"Oh," she paused. I could tell she was thinking. "I thought I told you; it's this." She held up a cream-colored mushroom dome. "While the mushrooms make them strong, they don't allow them to sire children. The only one who can father children is the Chief." She paused again and dropped her head in deep thought. "But you must not get pregnant." Her eyes changed to sadness and expressed a sudden concern. "If they haven't already warned you, then I will: Don't get pregnant if you can prevent it." I could see the pain in her face, and tears started to swell in her eyes.

"Oh, I am sorry, Tetoway. Did I say something to upset you? What is it; why are you so sad?" I sat with my arm around her for several minutes before she spoke again and revealed a hidden grief.

"I had a child, a little boy" was all she could mumble before breaking down again.

"Oh, how long ago has it been?" I wasn't sure how to console her. I was never very good with this type of interaction.

"A little over a year now, Natani. I didn't even get to hold him." She cried some more.

"Why? Why didn't you get to hold him? Was the Chief the father?" I asked.

"Yes, they take the children. Right after birth they take them before you can even touch them. Then they are gone, and no one knows where they go — just that they never come back." She sobbed, and I tried to comfort her but felt awkward.

"I...I don't know what to say...that's horrible. I appreciate you telling me. I know it must be hard. Have you been the only one?" I wondered if this happened often.

"I don't know how many for sure. If I had to guess, I'd say there have been many, but no one talks about it. Women become pregnant, and then eventually they aren't, and the baby will be gone. The men know it's not theirs, so they never have a problem with it being taken. It is just silently accepted. Abanea has been pregnant six times. She says it's a blessed curse, the wonderous feeling of motherhood yet knowing what will come – she refers to it as "the Ruins" because it does — it *ruins* you."

Tetoway's words were on my mind the rest of the day. We kept the conversation light from then on. I wondered why the Chief didn't take the mushrooms to be strong? Why did he sire children if he didn't want them? What happened to all the babies? Where any of the women "in ruins" now? I pushed my ever-growing list of questions to the back of my mind and settled into a comfortable routine. I was to take a basket of squash to the other wives' chambers, where I hoped to find Ottowa and Tecka.

The rest of the tribes' chambers were different from ours, and I wondered why we were kept secluded from the rest of the tribe. I entered the huge cavern. It was speckled with tepees. It reminded me of home, but the unmistakable darkness that surrounded us was a sure reminder that the sun and stars had been replaced by this cavernous prison. I wandered past the dwellings. No one stopped me, so I kept going through the maze of tunnels with my torch in one hand and basket in the other. I found myself in an area I didn't know existed. Curiosity had never been my friend, and it always seemed to get me in trouble, but I figured I could always say I had just gotten lost. Despite the risk of being caught, I might have found another escape route, so I continued going. Overhead I heard the growing sound of bat wings echoing off the stone walls. Their screeching vibrations warned me that I wasn't where I should be. I remembered the sound distinctly from when we first arrived here, near the entrance hall, and knew I must be close to the opening. My fear told me to stop, but my curiosity told me to go further — so I did. The dim light of the cavern was fading with each step as I entered the forbidden darkness. Suddenly the sound of bat wings grew more intense. I was under attack! Bats darted out of the darkness and rammed me with their claw-tipped wings. I turned and ran, not knowing where I was heading, or even if I was going back the same way I had come. It wasn't but a few feet, and the next thing I knew I was falling.

I reached out for something to grab, but there was nothing but air all around me. I barely had time to think or react when I suddenly plunged into freezing water, the shock like blades to my skin. My torch went out, snuffed by the icy water. I was surprised it had even remained with me through the fall. I gasped for air, but the water was squeezing the breath right back out of me. I found myself bobbing like my basket in the icy darkness.

What was this place? My mind was scrabbling to put it together as I gasped for air. I swam, struggling to reach an edge, but the sides were too steep and slick. All I could do was cling to the slimy stones with my fingertips.

"Help, help, can anyone hear me?" My echoes just came back to me and made me all the more angry for being so careless.

It wasn't long before I began to shiver. I struggled through the water desperately searching for a better place to climb out. I had no idea how long I had been here or how long it would take before my body would start shutting down. Shaking uncontrollably with each passing moment, I quickly became tired — maybe this wouldn't be that bad of a way to go, I thought to myself. I could just fall asleep and sink into this hidden grave. The water felt like it was full of vibrations, a comforting sensation that drew me to it despite the cold. Perhaps it was just my own shivering that I felt, but I had a feeling something else was there. Soft distant sounds could be heard, but I couldn't make them out. This mountain, this place of rock, seemed to speak.

Don't be such a coward, Natani; you're stronger than that. You're not going to take the easy way out, are you? Now it was my conscience speaking to me from deep within my soul, and despite the inspiring words, I just didn't see how I'd ever get out of this. I could no longer move my legs. Thoughts of my family went through my mind, and I could almost hear my father calling for me like he would do at dusk. "Natani, Natani, where are you?" His voice was so strong, yet so sweet; I missed him so much, all of them.

"Natani." I could feel my name slowly quiver down the shaft and ripple across the top of the icy water. Was it my father? Was someone or something calling to me?

"H … H … H … Here!" I mustered up as much energy as I could to spit the word out. A dim light provided a view of the vast pool I had fallen into. Next I heard a splash, and he was next to me.

"Can you hold on to me while I climb out?" It was Colbryn. His hard, warm arms around my torso contrasted the soft, icy water. How could anyone have heard me fall? My arms and legs were unusable, and I couldn't move.

"D … D … D … s … s … s …" I couldn't utter another word. The cold felt as if it had frozen my face and taken over the rest my body. All I could do was hold onto him to keep from sinking. He towed me over to a thin rock shelf and pushed me onto it. My muscles were so cold that with every movement my joints felt like they were ripping apart. Once out of the water, Colbryn pulled off my knee-high moccasins. I was shocked. Surely there was some rule about undressing the Chief's wife? It didn't matter. I was probably already a corpse.

"Lift up." He tugged at my dress. I was still too cold to move, but my eyes were questioning him in silence. It took one moment, and he had slipped my body from my dress in one effortless move. There I was — blue, speechless and naked, but I was too cold to care. He gasped for breath when his warm body made contact with mine. Laying over me in the eons that seemed to fill that one moment, his body seemed to slowly smother out the cold. I closed my eyes. Was I dying? Probably, but this was a pretty good way to go. I could feel my warm breath bounce off his wet skin, warming my face within the misty fog. After a minute of silence, he gently laid me on my dress and wrapped me in his arms. His skin felt burning next to mine, and my teeth were chattering so hard I worried they would break.

"I have dreamed of this ever since I first saw you, but in the dream you were a lot warmer than this." Was he making a joke ... at a time like this? He seemed to laugh, as if here were making light of the situation. I smiled and wanted to close my eyes and fall asleep inside the warmth.

"Natani, you can't go to sleep; please stay with me. Talk to me so I know you're awake"

"Wh ... Wh ... Wh ..." my teeth chattered together. His arms rubbed up and down my back.

"Well that's something," he said, his breath warming my ears.

I concentrated hard on making my mouth work again. I had questions. "Wh ... Why did you bring me here to die just to save me?" It didn't seem quite like the right time to be confronting him because he did just save my life, but I figured I wouldn't be this alone with him again. He owed me answers.

"Die, what makes you think that? That was never my intention." His voice sounded confused and surprised, but I wasn't satisfied.

"Why then, why did you bring me h ... h ... here? I was happy, I had a family, that was m ... m ... my tribe, and you just took us from our home for no reason." I could tell I was warming up because the numbness was fading, and the feeling was returning to my thigh making the pain of his weight bearing down on me grow. I could feel the emotions start to thaw and run from my heart. My pulse was now racing as I both appreciated and yet hated this man for the things he had done.

"I'm a fool," he spoke. I could tell he had looked away, and it seemed like he was hesitating to say anything more. "I'm a fool because I've been watching you, watching you for many moons. I knew that I would finally be granted first pick for wife from the Chief, and I knew I wanted it to be you. That is why we raided your tribe." He paused again. "I didn't mean you any heartache; I was just thinking of myself and what I wanted, and that was you. You were never in any harm, I assure you. It all went wrong. The Chief wanted you, and at that point there was nothing else I could do but settle for someone else and watch him take you. It angered me, and if I had known it would have turned out this way, I would have left you and your tribe alone. I would have taken someone else that day. My actions are unforgivable, Natani." His words came from such a sincere place that I couldn't help but feel pity for him. I didn't know what to say but I couldn't stand the silence, finally I just tried to console him.

"It's alright, Colbryn." It was the first time that I had said his name out loud.

"It doesn't even matter now. We are probably both going to die, you of the cold and me because I am lying with the Chief's naked wife."

This was the most awkward, emotional conversation I had ever had with a man. I didn't know how to feel. Part of me was still holding a deep grudge towards him for thinking he could take me in the first place, and another part of me was warming up to him … literally and physically.

"Well, are you enjoying you time with Pinnoteh at least?" I broke the silence, not quite ready to forgive and forget. I still had anger in my voice. I figured it was fair to ask because he had asked me.

"You got that out very well. Maybe you're going to live after all?" he said with a smile. "Now I am the only one who is going to die." The pitch of his voice rose as if he was smiling, but then it got serious again when I didn't respond.

"Pinnoteh was supposed to be a substitute for you, but there is no feeling there." He stopped. "I feel like I've already said too much. I've accepted the fact that there is no changing what I've done. There's no going back to try again. I just have to accept that you're the Chief's wife and forget about it." He pushed himself off of me and left the cold air to swirl in place of him.

"I need to get you out of here. This isn't a place the Chief's wife should be. I could hear his footsteps shuffling across the rock. I stood shivering in the darkness. I wanted to reach out for him and just have him hold me in his warmth. I also wanted to just break down and cry for my family that I missed so much, and lastly, I wanted to dive back into the water and just go to sleep.

He wrung out my icy dress and slipped it back over my head. I gasped for air, and then I felt him turn away. I heard him dive into the water. A faint light was reflecting off the center of the well. I watched him as he shimmied up the slick wall and searched for every finger and toe hold until he finally made it to the top.

"I'll be right back," his voice echoed down. The dark swallowed me up again. I sat clinching my legs and thinking of his warm body against mine. I knew that thought would need to last me for a long, long time, or as long as I was with the Chief. I wasn't sure if I was starting to have feelings for Colbryn or if it was the fact that I didn't have anything else to hold onto in this place. The separation from my family and friends was wearing on me — was I just needing to reach for something or someone? I had never loved a man before, so I wasn't sure what it felt like or if there was a difference between love and selfish desire.

I didn't have long to ponder my thought before he was back with two other men. Great, now half the tribe will know all about my clumsy escapade. Did he really think it would take three giant, strong men to pull me out of this pool? My vanity took over, and I felt a little humiliated. A rope was lowered, and I tied it around my hips. The slack tightened in the rope from above until I slipped away from the rock ledge and sailed across the water, swinging and twirling in the frigid air. The rise to the top didn't take any time at all. I knew they couldn't see me in the void of the hole, but their faces were lit enough so that I could see them staring down into the darkness. I watched Colbryn the most. His eyes looked endearing and defeated at the same time. I wondered if his apology would be enough to keep me from trying to escape or if he would grow to want Pinnoteh the way he wanted me? Once on top he scooped me up into his arms like he had done once before, and this time I liked it.

Putting me down in the wife's chamber, he turned and left. It was an abrupt end to our time together, but sadly that seemed to be the theme that surrounded Colbryn and me.

Undressing and redressing me, the wives hovered again like that first night. A cup of hot tea was waiting by my bed. They did not ask me questions. They didn't even speak at all. I didn't care. I didn't need to speak; I had other thoughts occupying my mind. When I closed my eyes, I did not feel alone. Something had warmed in my heart. I just wasn't sure if I was going to allow it to stay or if the morning would bring the same resentment I had felt before.

That night, in my dreams, my father and mother were fighting. I could hear angry words. A smack echoed and was followed by crying. I wanted to go to them and tell them not to fight, that everything was alright, but I could not get up, could not move. I had lost all control. Then my father came to me and stroked my hair. This was not my father; it was Colbryn. I sighed, and that woke me up, but this was not a dream. This was not Colbryn — it was Duran. I closed my eyes trying desperately to return to the dream. I drifted away from here, and turning inwards, I shut the door to my mind.

The next morning Tetoway and the other wives entered early. "How are you feeling?" she asked concerned. "Sore, but I am fine." I wasn't sure how much they knew about my escapade, so I didn't offer anything.

"I am, or I mean, we are so sorry we let this happen to you. The Chief was very upset." Tetoway looked down to the floor as though she was guilty of something. Her voice masked an obvious resentment.

"This was not your fault. Please do not be concerned about me. It was an accident. I just got lost delivering the basket of squash." As I spoke I noticed the bruise across her left cheek; all of them looked like they had been crying. I was suddenly alarmed.

"But you are our responsibility. We should have taken better care of you." She gave me an apologetic smile.

"You all take great care of me. This was not your fault. You realize it was an accident, right? I got turned around, there were bats, and ... did he hit you?" I couldn't take it anymore. Why had they been treated this way because of something I did? There was silence and more hesitation. I knew my directness didn't come across as sympathetic as I had hoped. "What happened to your cheek, Tetoway?" I looked into her eyes. "Did he hit you?" I demanded again.

"No, no, I fell in the dark. See, you aren't the only one who gets lost around here." I looked at the other wives, and I could tell she was lying. I had never imagined that they would be held responsible for my actions. I was angry. I was enraged because they had no way to protect themselves and I was horrified that he would treat them this way. I wanted to shake them and convince them that this was not the way to live and that they should try to escape and come with me. However, I knew that sharing my thoughts and including them in my plan could backfire on me, so I sat staring in silent disapproval.

I didn't push the topic any further. I was just glad it was all over.

"So what are we doing today?" I smiled, trying to change the outlook on our day. They all looked relieved that I changed the subject, and I was glad I didn't have to answer questions. We got busy, but the night's events never left my mind.

In the Sun Hall the next morning, I ran into Tecka and was very happy to see her. I was afraid she would be taking our captivity really hard. I had imagined her becoming depressed, so I tried to keep my voice upbeat for her.

"Tecka, I'm so happy to see you. It seems like it's been such a long time."

"Oh, Natani, I am so happy. Things are wonderful. I would never have gotten a husband this good from our tribe. And can you believe it? He likes me, too. I can't wait for you to meet him."

Did I hear her correctly? She was having a wonderful time? Was I the only one in agony here? I could feel the bewildered expression flash across my face, so I smiled to conceal it.

"I am so happy for you. I have been worrying about how you and Ottowa would be handling it. How is Ottowa?" Surely her life wasn't wonderful as well, I thought.

"She is good, too — just doesn't talk about it though. She is so shy about that kind of thing. You know what I'm talking about," she said with a wink. "But I can tell that she is really happy." I gave Tecka a strong embrace. It was just like old times yet nonetheless, drastically different.

"We have a get-together almost every night. We talk and tell stories while the other girls gossip. Hey, do you think you can come? It just isn't the same without you around. Then you can see for yourself." Get-togethers, gossip, stories — I was missing a lot by being one of the Chief's wives.

"Sounds like fun. Where do you meet? Do I need to bring anything?"

"No, tonight we'll watch the men compete in the main cavern. I have an extra rug for you to sit on. I'll be looking for you. See you later." She smiled, squeezed my hand, and darted off.

That evening when everything was done, I walked down to the huge chamber of tepees as I had a few nights back. Shouts and yells drifted up from a space that was set up for the men. Women sat to one side talking and laughing freely as they lounged on beautifully woven rugs. It reminded me again of my village, and I was suddenly aware of how homesick I really was. Ottowa waved eagerly to me, and I walked over and sat down. She leaned over and hugged me. I could tell that she, too, was happy.

"This is great, just like old times," she added. Pinnoteh came over and sat down by us. I wondered if our time here had softened her heart any.

"I see you have lowered yourself to come visit the common folk," she said as she glared at me.

"I see you haven't changed," I rebutted.

"Natani had never been invited before, Tecka said, turning towards her.

Ottowa quickly changed the subject. "So tell us about being the Chief's wife. You seem so busy all the time." I wanted to tell her how I was feeling: that I wanted to be with them, that I wanted to be with Colbryn, and about all that had happened with the Chief, but I didn't want to complain, especially in front of Pinnoteh.

"It's good," I lied. "I have Tetoway, Eba, and Abanea to help me, and they're like sisters. Abanea is going to teach me to make pots and baskets when we find time. There's just a lot to do." I left it at that, but I could tell that Tecka wasn't buying my response. She knew me the best and could see through my vague replies.

"We heard about you falling into a hole and almost drowning. Is that true?" Pinnoteh's ears perked up, and I could feel her eyes dart to see my expression.

"Yeah, tell us about that." Pinnoteh's voice was a bit snide. She must have found out that Colbryn was the one who rescued me.

"Didn't your husband tell you?" I smirked.

"Only that he had to fish you out. All the men were looking for you. They even got out the wolves thinking that you had run away." I could hear the old venom in her voice. Nothing had changed between us.

"So where is your husband tonight?" Tecka asked, cocking her head towards Pinnoteh and trying to change the conversation.

"Hunting," she scoffed.

"Wow, he hunts a lot," she added.

"Someone has to feed all these people," Pinnoteh shot back. The room got quiet; I looked up to see why. The Chief was standing at the opening.

"Looks like my escort has arrived." My voice sounded more light hearted than I felt. In fact I was terrified. Had I done something to break the rules? I walked over to him and stood behind him to one side.

"Tetoway said you would be here." His voice was slow and cold.

"I thought it would be nice to see my friends, to show them I am still interested in their lives," I said timidly.

"You really shouldn't be down here, Natani," he glanced past me.

"Look at their faces; they are so glad to see you," I pointed out. He gazed around. The contests had started again, and the men were trying hard to make an impression.

"Would you rather be feared than liked?" I asked, instantly wishing that I could retract my comment. I knew I had overstepped my place.

"Like I said," he finally looked at me, "you really shoudn't be down here." He turned, and we walked out. I wanted to stay, but fearing that I would look disrespectful, I followed behind him. I could feel the blood burning my cheeks as we walked in silence. The good feelings I had, quickly drained from me. We walked to my chamber.

"I will see you tonight," was all he said as he paused at my door before walking on in silence. I entered the room reluctantly. Part of me wanted to go back and be with Tecka and Ottowa. The other women looked up at me in surprise. I tried to seem cheerful.

"Looks like I will be needing that tea tonight, Eba." They looked down. Tetoway spoke.

"Natani, you need to tell me before you do these impulsive things. I can't warn you if I don't know what you are doing." Disappointment and anger were in her voice.

"So I can't go see the others? Am I confined to this space unless I am working?" No one had ever told me the rules, and I was finding my isolation irritating at best.

"We try not to interfere in the rest of the tribes' lives unless they need us. It just works out better that way. Besides, don't you get to see your friends in the Hall?" I didn't want to debate with Tetoway. I knew I had freedoms that the other girls didn't have and that I should focus on those, but I still felt the need to defend myself.

"I am always so busy taking care of things. I don't get to talk to them much. It was nice to see how they live and meet their husbands. They have fun — it's like a real village down there. I just miss it, that's all."

I got myself ready for the night, and as usual I thought of Colbryn. I closed my eyes, wishing I could see where he was and what he was doing and wondering, most of all, if he was thinking of me.

You do realize that you are the one making yourself miserable. My mind expressed what my heart was too blind to see. It had taken some time for me to realize it, but in that instant I agreed that I was the one making myself miserable. I had no one to blame but myself. I was holding on to a futile desire. Things were the way they were, and I was going to have to accept them even if I didn't want to. The sooner I understood this, the better off I would be, however brief or long my stay. When Duran entered my chamber, I felt a bold strength come over me.

"You are right, Master. I only want to please you." The words coming from my mouth disgusted me, but I felt that it would go better for me in the end. He glared at me with a strange look, but it seemed that I had pleased him.

****

The next morning I woke with my new resolve firmly in place. I was happy and determined to stay that way. I was sitting eating breakfast when Tetoway entered the chamber. She sat down and put her hands to her face but didn't say a word.

"What is it, Tetoway?" Abanea asked with concern in her voice. Tetoway seemed to think briefly and then turned to me.

"I am so sorry, Natani. I have bad news. It's hard for me to say, so I'm just going to blurt it out before I have time to think about it. The Chief wants to teach you a lesson; he thinks you do not know your place. He is sending you to the pit." I sat confused — didn't I just come from a pit? What had I done, what lesson was I supposed to learn?

"The pit!" Abanea shouted, overhearing Tetoway's news. "For how long?" Tetoway gave her a look that silenced her, and then she turned back to me.

"I had to spend three days there when I first got here. It helps to think up stories and songs and things like that, just keep your mind busy. You will have to stay positive." She stopped, and I could tell she was trying to think up something else to make it sound better than it was. "We will bring you food once a day; that is always something to look forward to. Take as many blankets and rugs as you can carry." There was urgency in her voice, but I was still trying to make sense of it. What was the pit? Why was I having to go? I had told the Chief that I wanted to please him. What more could I have done?

"What about my weaving? Can I take that to pass the time?" I was now irritated. Tears started to come to Tetoway's eyes. I did not know if it was for me or if she was remembering her time there. Eba walked into the room to find our solemn faces.

"What's wrong? You three look like someone died?" she seemed to joke, but her face quickly went blank.

"Natani is being sent to the pit for four days," Abanea answered.

"Oh no — just because she went to see her friends?" Abanea expressed the same question I had. Eba's look of horror and surprise caught me off guard.

"I will be alright. Surely it's not that bad. You all have done it, right? It will give me a chance to rest up." No one would look at me.

"What are you not telling me?" Before anyone could answer me, we looked up to see two men standing on either side of the doorway. Jumping up, the women started grabbing blankets and rugs and throwing them into my arms. Tetoway hugged me and whispered: "Do not lose hope. We will see you tonight."

Wondering what she meant, I dragged my feet as we made our way through the maze-like tunnels. I followed the torches going deeper into the bowels of the mountain and finally came to the huge pit chamber where the games had been played before. It looked different from this angle, like some huge crater dug out of stone. None of the torches were lit like before, and what little light the men's torches put out, the darkness seemed to swallow right up. I stood there frozen in place and remembered what it looked like the last time I was here. This was the same place that the men had fought for wives. As I was standing there, the ladder was put in place, and the men stood waiting for me to descend. Tossing my things over the side, I climbed down into the pit. At the bottom I hollered up: "Where is the firewood? Do I get a torch?"

"You will get one in four days," they yelled back as they left.

CHAPTER SIX
The Pit

The blackness was suffocating. The darkness was not like a moonless night or even the blackness you see when closing your eyes. You could feel this on your skin; you breathed it. It was the color of despair. I needed some comfort — where were the blankets? Standing alone in the darkness, I realize I had no idea where I had thrown them. Stretching out my arms, I took a step and then another hoping to reach the wall or feel them softly underfoot.

Strange sounds bounced off the walls and made it impossible to tell where they were coming from. Every muscle in my body was tense. Surely my eyes would adjust to this horrible darkness, and then I could see what was making the noise. Taking another step, I made contact with the cold and slimy wall. It was the most uninviting thing I had ever put my fingers on. Slowly I made my way in the direction of where I thought my blankets were, kicking a leg out, feeling for them as I went. I could feel cold, slimy, clumps on the floor — probably blood from the games. It repulsed me. If I had just paid more attention to where I had dropped my blankets. Surely I had gone far enough. Tears of frustration ran down my face. This place was just awful, and I was beyond being ready to go home. What had I done that was terrible enough to deserve this? I sank down to my knees and let despair take over.

"Natani, get a grip. You have four days of this, and you can't seem to cope with four minutes!" I couldn't just sit here. The cold was already getting to me. Why did I always have to be in these cold places? I knew now why they said to take lots of blankets. I retraced my steps and began a new search, this time circling farther out. Finally, my foot made contact with one of the blankets, and I gathered them to me. I couldn't help but laugh at the darkness. I lay there for what seemed an eternity, just curled up in the warmth of the blankets and trying to keep out the damp cold. The sounds of the mountain moaned up from below me. It felt like I was in the bowels of a living creature. With thoughts like these turning over in my mind, how was I ever going to last for four days and keep my sanity? I opened my eyes and noticed I could see color on the wall across from me. Was it possible that my eyes were getting use to the dark? The color kept getting lighter — someone was coming.

"Natani?"

"Yes, yes! I am here! I crawled out to see three heads peaking over the side at me. Their single torch made me squint.

"Are you OK? We brought you some food and a water skin.

"Sure, I am fine." I lied.

"We had to see that you were OK." Abanea's voice was so sweet.

From a rope they lowered a large basket full of bread, dried meat, and berries. I took a drink of water and looked up, afraid they would disappear.

"Do I keep the basket?"

"Yes, we will bring you another one tomorrow, so eat everything. We cannot stay long. He is waiting for us." I quickly fixed my bed and put the basket where I could find it in the dark.

Tetoway spoke up. "It's hard, but this might help: Each day make up a story or song, and we will do the same. When you get out, we will celebrate by telling our stories. We've done this in the past when one of us was in the pit. Now don't forget; do it each day to have something to think about." Eba and Abanea whispered, "Stay strong."

Then the light went out, and the darkness swallowed me up again. Did they have any idea how hard it was to have happy thoughts down there? If I did think of anything, the songs would be sad, and the stories would be depressing. I got as far as FAR, FAR AWAY IN THE LAND OF THE SCREAMING MOUNTAIN and then stopped. Far, far away ... in this consuming darkness, time just did not exist; nothing existed. No forms, colors, happiness, hope — just blackness. I tried to think of stories, but the darkness would take the words from me before I could even put them together.

The days and nights passed by this way. I don't remember them bringing the new baskets, but they did. That was the only way I knew a day had passed. I could feel myself slipping away bit by bit and not caring that I was. I thought about everything that had ever happened to me. I swear I traced back over every event of my entire life. I thought about my family, my tribe, my crush, and how I never got the chance to tell Tallenhill that I liked him. I held on to the images burned into my mind of Colbryn; they gave me much comfort. I played over every single encounter. I started with the trip there, the games, his look and touch. The thrill of his body so close to mine, the point in which my feelings for him had started to change, his hand running up and down my back to warm me. It still surprised me that I felt this way about him after everything that had happened. When the happy thoughts were gone, so was my will to survive. It all seemed like ages had passed since my previous life. I now yearned for its simplicity, its familiar comfort.

The strange sounds of the mountain became another language, another foreign being in this foreign land. At times, the sounds seemed to get louder, like voices conversing, or were they just voices in my head? No, it had to be the mountain. It was telling me it would not stop until every bit of sanity was sucked from my mind.

You're here because you allow yourself to be.

I have no choice!

You always have a choice, but you deserve this. You love the person that did this to you. It's your own fault.

That's not fair. What else do I have?

Come on, Natani, come on.

Do I really love him?

Silence. Perhaps it was my own inner voice, my own mind discouraged that I was in this situation. I knew I had crossed some line — sitting here just proved it. I couldn't stand listening to my own head any longer. Placing both hands to my ears, I resorted to the one thing I hate doing: feeling weak and whimpering. Rocking back and forth, I tried desperately to cling to anything stable. It seemed that the Chief was trying to break me of my will, and if that was the case, he had succeeded, for the time being anyway.

As I rocked and cried, I went back to the only safe haven I had left: Colbryn and the warmth of his smile. I dreamed that his touch was so real that I could feel him, that he was shaking me ...

"Natani, Natani, please come back!"

"I have truly lost my mind," I whispered.

"No, I am here — you have been in some kind of trance. I was getting worried. You're freezing — lie down, I will wrap you up." Once again I felt him close to me, his warmth, his skin pressed hard against mine. I had to be dreaming. His arms seemed inhuman as they wrapped around me both soft and strong.

"Are you sure you're not something my mind made up to keep me from going insane?" I questioned the darkness.

"I am quite real." He took my hand and placed it on his face. I felt his cheeks and hair. My fingers drifted down his thick neck and onto his hard chest. His beating heart was like music to me. I smiled for the first time in what seemed like days. It didn't matter; the darkness seemed to erase any accountability. His chest radiated such wonderful heat. My hand slid down farther to his stomach, and it rumbled in response.

"Are you hungry?" I couldn't do much, but I knew I had food. He just ignored my offer.

"I came here the minute I heard where you were. I should have grabbed something."

"I have food." I tried to move, but he only held me tighter.

"In a minute — I want to warm you first." I felt like a snake warming in the sun. My pulse beat faster and run with a wild desire. My hand was on his side, and I let it slide slowly down his hip. Slowly he retrieved it and brought it back to his chest.

"Careful," he whispered.

"Why?" I whispered back.

I knew the darkness had made me slightly crazy, but it also seemed to make me unconcerned with the possible consequences of my actions. In this darkness, no one could see, no one could know. I could offer myself up, and it would be like it never happened, like a dream. I egged my thoughts on with encouragement.

"You have no idea what your touch does to me." He restrained both wrists above my head. "So have you decided if I am real yet?"

"No, I've had lots of fantasies like this while I have been down here; the only difference is that you have never stopped me before." I could feel the warmth flush over my face, and the darkness continued to make me bold.

"I would like to hear all about them, another time." His voice was deep and curious, and his breath flowed and exulted a warm restraint. I chuckled and felt my dazed state of mind dictate my actions.

"This does bring back old memories. At least this time, you are dry. Why do I always have to be saving you from the cold?" His breath on my face was thrilling. I smiled but realized again that it didn't matter in the dark.

"Maybe because, thanks to you, I am trapped in the wettest, coldest place I've ever been. But, thank you, I do enjoy your rescues. You said you just got back?" I couldn't let the silence consume our time together.

"Yes; I have been on a hunting trip. It's spring, and the bears are out."

"You hunt bears?" I guess I had always assumed this given their head-dresses, but I asked anyway.

"Yes, but I do not want to talk about that right now. Tell me why you are in the pit? Did you kill someone?" His voice sounded truly concerned.

"Kill someone? Well, I've thought about it a few times but no. Tecka invited me to visit the village and watch the competitions, so I went. That didn't go over so well; apparently, it's a pretty serious crime." Despite my sarcasm, my voice was still weak and sporadic.

"I see, but I wasn't aware you were not allowed. This punishment still seems a bit harsh, especially for someone like you." His voice was smooth and relaxing.

"Well, that's not all. I think it's because I could not keep my big mouth shut. When the Chief came down to get me, I told him that it would be good for him to be a part of everyone's life; and I asked him if he would rather be liked than feared. So here I am."

"That would explain it." I think he smiled.

"I was just thinking of my village and how everyone there helped each other. This place, there are so many rules, so much that isn't talked about, so many secrets. It's just not our people's way to be concealed from nature and to have our freedoms taken away."

"Natani, this is not like any other village, and he can't be compared to other Chiefs. You should be able to tell that by now." His stomach gave another grumble.

"Please let me feed you something. The basket is right here, and Eba said she would make me stay another day if I didn't eat it all."

"Rather severe punishment for not eating isn't it? Why haven't you been eating?" he asked.

"This place doesn't make me very hungry. Besides, just lying around doesn't stimulate my appetite." We were silent for a minute. I could hear him eating. It was strange thinking back to all of our different encounters; from the kidnapping, tto the icy pool, to sharing a basket of dried fruits and meat in a dark pit. It still didn't make sense to me that I was already on the verge of forgiving him. I usually hold grudges for years. There must be something messing with my mind, I thought. This place had to be full of bad magic. I was probably under a spell, I amused myself.

"Colbryn, why is this place so different?"

"What do you mean?

"Well, the fact that you are stronger than other men, that everyone lives holed up in this cave, and that there are no children. How do you explain all of that?"

"I was wondering if and when you might pick up on that." He was silent.

"I understand about the mushrooms and the addiction to them, and I am told that this is why there are no children. What I don't understand is why everyone goes along with it?"

"We are stronger than most men, but next to the Chief, we are like children. I have seen him fight; he has no equal. He can slay several men at once. If I had not seen so myself, I would not have believed it possible. It's like some power that none of us have." His voice seemed content with his answer, but I was not.

"Well maybe one or two against him might be a hard fight, but if all the men stood up against him, I'm sure there would be no challenge." I tried to make my voice sound strong.

"Natani, there is much you don't understand. The only way to get ahead in this tribe is to obey and impress the Chief. Trust me, you will get nowhere by breaking away with your own thoughts and ideals. There is only one Chief; it's been that way for hundreds of years, and you can't just go changing things." The way he spoke made me regret asking, but I've never been one to just accept something because I was supposed to.

"Hundreds of years? Who was the Chief before Duran?" Surely the tribe hadn't always been ruled by such evil.

"It's always been Duran, Natani. Even the elders remember him being Chief when they were young."

"That doesn't make sense. That would mean he doesn't age. He would have to be several hundred years old."

"That is what it means." His voice seemed reluctant to be speaking about this, as if it were against the rules. I sat intrigued in silence.

"Is it the mushrooms?"

"No, he doesn't take the mushrooms. Only the tribe's other men are under their influence. No one knows the reason he is still living. It's one of the many things not discussed, just accepted and never challenged." He emphasized the word "never" as though to tell me to back off.

"What about the babies? Tetoway said that he will not let anyone have children. Wouldn't he want to be surrounded by his own evil offspring?" I asked.

"Oh, they can have as many as they want. They just do not get to keep them." He did not try to hide his disgusted tone of voice.

"Where do the babies go?" I was almost afraid of the answer.

"I don't know. Some say they are killed; some say they are sold as slaves to other tribes. There are many stories. Don't think about it, Natani. It's been going on for many, many years. They are just lost souls. If you think about it, it will consume you." His words sent chills up my neck.

"I've heard bits and pieces of stories whispered around the fire at night. Why does he hide in this cave? This is unusual to me that people would live this way. What is the real reason for all of this?"

"Ahh, you've been listening to too many stories, Natani. Don't let your imagination piece together things that aren't so." He quickly changed the subject, and I could tell he was hiding something. "Thank you for sharing your food with me. It was very good. If you haven't gotten up in several days, we need to get you up and see if you can walk." He helped me up, and we started around the pit. My legs burned, and my back ached but with him by my side, I would have walked anywhere.

"Colbryn? When we first got here, the Chief said eventually we would be going back to our villages if we wanted to. When does that happen?"

His voice dropped. Even in the darkness, sadness and betrayal were unmistakable. "It doesn't. It's all just a part of his act to make the new ones feel better — you know, give them hope. I'm sorry, Natani, but you're not going home."

The words were like a spear to my heart. Anger radiated from me again. I clinched my teeth so hard that I couldn't speak for several moments.

"So what happens if someone asks to go home?" I wasn't going to just accept the fact I'd be stuck here forever. There had to be options. He hesitated for several minutes. I was about to ask him again, when he slowly answered.

"He makes an example of them." He stopped me from taking another step and turned me to face him abruptly. I could tell by the power in his grip that he was serious.

"What do you mean, exactly?" I had already survived the pit and the well.

If another week or two of that was all it would take to go home, I could and would happily manage that.

"Natani, I really don't even want to discuss this with you. The thought is unbearable, and I know how stubborn you are." His voice was now strict.

"Tetoway or Eba will tell me," I answered with determination in my voice. By now he had his arm around my waist, and I had my arm over his neck and took steps again so I couldn't fall or easily turn towards him.

"They are brought here to this pit." His voice was hollow sounding.

I interrupted. "They stay in the dark? After three days you become part of the darkness. It becomes easier, really. It's not too bad." My voice sounded promising, but I knew freedom couldn't be as easy as spending a little time in the pit.

"No, the pit has five wolves waiting in it. They are given a choice; to make a run for it before the wolves are unleashed, or stay and live in the cave with utter obedience. If they choose the wolves, then they are given the chance to run and fight for their freedom, but no one ever makes it out of the cave."

The thought that others had died here in the very shadows that I was standing made me gasp for breath as my knees weakened. He scooped me up into his arms and spoke softly.

"I am so sorry to be the one to tell you, but you need to know whom you are dealing with. Do not cross him ever, please," he pleaded. I didn't respond. I just let the security of the darkness consume his words and fade off. He guided me silently back to the blanket.

"As much as I enjoy being here, they must not find me with you." He reached to my face and ran his hand across my check. I was emotionless. I stood in the realization that the only way I was getting home was to escape, to take my chances, as grim as they were going to be.

"Natani, I must go. They will be coming soon." He took a step back. Raising his hands, he held my face. His warm lips touched my forehead, nose, and then lingered on my lips. It was like throwing a rock in a still pond. The ripples radiated from that spot all the way down to my toes, taking my breath with it.

"How much longer do you have down here?"

"I don't know. I have no concept of time down here. Months, days, years, who can tell? What does it matter anymore?" My words were full of despair, but I didn't care.

"It's just this pit. It's wearing on you."

"No, it's not just this pit, it is this place," I whispered back.

"Be strong, Natani. You are in my heart always. I will see you soon." The warmth of his lips and hands lingered on my face. I could hear movement against the wall, and then all was silent. I dropped to my knees. Had this all just been a dream? My imagination was working overtime to save my sanity. Had he really been here? With the overwhelming blackness all around me, I wasn't sure. I didn't care. My mind was full of thought and whether it was real didn't matter. It was something to fill my mind. So much to think about, but the only thing I wanted to concentrate on was the feeling of his lips against mine. A steady light grew on the opposite wall. Someone else was coming.

"Natani," I heard three voices call out.

"Let's get you out of this awful place!" The ladder lowered, and I could see two men standing beside them. To my surprise, Colbryn slowly came down the ladder with a torch. He walked over to me and smiled in a way that once again took my breath away. "We would have been here sooner, but we were looking for Colbryn to help lower the ladder," Eba shouted.

He didn't say a word to me, but his smile through the torch flame said everything. Putting me over his shoulder, he carried me up the ladder and then gently placed me back on my feet next to Eba, Tetoway, and Abanea. They put their arms around me.

"Come on, the men can get your things." Tetoway put her arm around me, and the four of us headed off. I had survived the pit.

It took a while to feel comfortable with the light. Even the candles flickering across the wives' chamber gave me a blinding headache. With Eba's tea, the pain soon lessened to a tolerable sting.

"So did you think up stories like we suggested?" Eba inquired.

"I got as far as FAR FAR AWAY IN THE LAND OF ... I already forgot. That place sucks everything out of you."

"Yeah, we know. None of us came up with stories when we were there either. It just helps to try and think about something other than the dark." Eba shook her head agreeing. Luckily, I had Colbryn to fill my head, so fairy tales weren't needed.

Tetoway came in the door. "Bad news. After you clean up, he wants to see you," she said with her head looking down. "Don't try and act brave, Natani; just be submissive, and don't say anything to make him angry. I fear you are on thin ice with the Chief."

"What now, do I get thrown to the wolves?" At this point I was considering that to be my final fate anyway, so why not get it over with?

"That's not funny, and don't joke like that. You better go now. I wouldn't leave him waiting." She seemed persistent, so I didn't argue.

Rising slowly I made my way out the chamber door and into the darkness again. I was feeling brave. I wondered where the bravery was coming from. I quickly concluded that it was the part of me that was giving up. I didn't care anymore. He could throw me in the pit or feed me to the wolves. This wasn't the life I wanted anyway. The few secret moments I had with Colbryn weren't enough to make up for the desolate isolation I lived in the rest of the time. I no longer had anything to lose because Colbryn wasn't mine to begin with. When I reached his chamber, the Chief was watching the door before I even came through it. His eyes were motionless, seeping straight into my soul from across the room. He slowly raised his eyes to appraise the damage the last four days had inflected on me. Until he told me to come closer, I just lingered in the doorway.

"Come here, Natani," he spoke, settling into each word completely. His voice seemed to come with a silent force that drowned out all other sounds around me. "Well, I hope you have spent the last few days wisely, thinking just where your place is here." His voice was still unmistakably slow and fluid.

"Yes, I have had plenty of time to think." I responded. His eyebrows came together.

"I am glad to see you have retained your usual spark that I enjoy so much." The words did not match the expression on his face. I looked away in a submissive manner and remembered Tetoway's words.

"You have been given a great opportunity here. I expect you to live up to it." I bowed, not knowing what else to do or how else to respond, and he waved me away. As I walked down the tunnels, I thought: What opportunity have I been given? To do as I was told? To not have a say in my life or those around me? What opportunity? Perhaps the opportunity to forestall my death a few more days?

I had always thought that at this stage of my life, I would start to make my own decisions, my own choices, and no longer have to obey someone else's orders. I had earned that right. But instead I was in a new kind of prison, a mental and physical one. I wasn't even allowed to be who I was. Everything had a rule, everything had a consequence, and everything here had control over me in some way. It was changing me. I could feel it altering my soul with every day. I was no longer the same girl who had entered this place, not at all. I was different. I just couldn't decide if that was a good or a bad thing.

CHAPTER SEVEN
Preparations

Eba came into the chamber smiling. "It's time to plan the Spring Celebration," she said as she took my hand.

"That sounds like fun, but what is there to celebrate?" Her enthusiasm was appreciated and necessary because mine was lacking severely. It sounded like something new to concentrate on.

"Oh, Natani, the sooner you accept this place and this life, the sooner you will be happy." Her words were not new to me. I had heard this a hundred times, and a hundred times I've told myself, *never*.

"Well, what can I do?" I tried to muster up as much positivity as possible when I replied. I even flashed her a smile to show I was trying.

"The Hall needs to be cleaned of the dried leaves and brush. Would you like to do that?" I could tell by her tone this was a job that she didn't want to do and was making it sound more pleasant than it was. I smiled. I actually do enjoy the jobs where I can be alone to think, and this would be one of them.

"Abanea was going to show me bowl-making today, but I can do it afterward." I wasn't going to give up my pot-making time for anything, especially not for cleaning. Tetoway smiled.

"I knew we could depend on you." I was eager for my pot lesson to begin, so I hurried through the morning chores and finished them as fast as I could. I had always enjoyed making baskets with my mother, so getting to learn something new would give me the sense of being at home.

"Abanea, you're a pro!" I was surprised how talented she was. She already had a bowl spinning when I arrived. A spool rotated on a sharpened pole. It was crude but worked well and made even my first attempt look pretty nice. I was amazed at how much fun it was to be creating, possibly the most fun I'd had since coming here — other than the time I had spent with Colbryn.

"I was thinking, if you want me to, I could carve your pendant design in your bowl for you, sort of like your signature symbol. What do you think?" Abanea held up a sharpened rock point.

"Yeah, sure, I'd like that." I handed the pendant to her and was eager to see how she was going to do it.

"This is really interesting: The animal heads were carved really well. I wish I could be this precise." Carefully she etched the design into the soft, grey clay. Her brows pinched together as she worked. "I have seen this design somewhere before. I've been trying to place it ever since I saw it."

"Where? Do you remember?" I asked. I knew the pendant stood for something, but my mother never told me much about it other than it was old and must always remain in our family.

"Not sure, but I will let you know if it comes to me." We put it on the shelf with her others to dry. "When they are no longer cold to the touch, we can bake them, probably around the time of Spring Celebration."

"Great, it's nice having something to look forward to," I said excitedly.

"Which one: the Spring Celebration or the bowl?" she asked with a smile.

"More so the bowl," I laughed with her.

That night, as we sat around the fire, I wanted to know more about the Spring Celebration. I wondered if it was like the Maiden March, which I had been denied and would eternally be angry about.

"So what happens at the Spring Celebration?" I knew Tetoway would be happy that I was showing interest.

"Well for a week prior to the event, all the men leave and hunt. Some hunt animals; some fish for days. When the week is up, they all come back with mounds of food. Then, we get to prepare a giant feast, and the men have competitions — friendly ones, nothing like the pit fights. It really is a fun time. Everyone looks forward to it, so you should too," she added, smiling.

"It sounds fun, but why do the men get all the fun and leave us to all the cooking and cleaning?" I felt a little cheated.

"What? Do you want to hunt and compete with the men?" They all laughed but me.

"No, compete with other girls ... it would make it a little bit more exciting?" Their faces went from giggles to deep thought to twisted frowns.

"Hmm ... that could actually be fun; I know a few girls I wouldn't mind competing against." Tetoway seemed intrigued by the thought.

"Yeah, the men enjoy competing. What about having the women join them?" I tried to urge the conversation, but they still looked at me a bit confused. "Well, we could play pull the rope, hide the rock, relays, things like that. You know, things men and women can do together." The idea wasn't a new one; it was something the young people did in my own tribe, but I tried to keep it new sounding.

"That sounds like fun," Eba cut in.

"Yes, we could have prizes, too" I added.

"Prizes? What kind of prizes?" Tetoway asked.

"Natani and I could make bowls," Abanea shouted out.

Tetoway looked pleased: "I can go to Duran tomorrow and see what he thinks."

"Do you actually think Duran would go for something like that? I'm actually surprised he allows any kind of celebration in here." My voice was harsh and bitter.

"Well he tries to keep the tribe happy despite all the rules, so I think there's a good chance he will say yes. I think it is a good idea, something to get us out of the winter blues that everyone seems to be in. It's worth a try." Tetoway shrugged, aiming her comment at me.

"Abanea, how long will it take you to make the bowls?"

"I am about out of clay, so I need to get some more, then I think it would take about a moon."

"We have the full moon in fifteen; can you be ready by then?"

"I can make that work with Natani's help," she smiled back. I was elated. Thoughts of the Spring Celebration were on my mind until the following day. As I was working in the mushroom garden the next morning, Abanea entered, looking like she was going to bust.

"How would you like to go get some clay with me?" She laughed at my look of confusion and disbelief. "I just saw Tetoway. She got the OK for the party — games, prizes, everything. I really hadn't expected the Chief to agree to all of it, but somehow he did. So when I found that out, I asked if we could go get clay, and he said yes!" She jumped a few times and clapped her hands with excitement.

"Wait, so you get to leave this place? Now?" Was I hearing her right?

"Yes, not often, but sometimes, with permission," she added. "Eba gets to go out and collect plants and seeds — stuff like that. Tetoway goes with her. I get reeds for baskets, so we are allowed to get out occasionally. It's a lot of fun. As you can guess, we really look forward to it. It's one of the benefits to being the Chief's wife. You will see tomorrow. I am going to get things set up — see you later!" She ran off, though I wanted to pick her mind some more. My own mind was suddenly full of wild ideas and scenarios. I was going to be leaving this place — this could be my chance for escape.

That night I could not help but feel excitement for the first ... well, maybe the third time since I got here. I had something to look forward to, something that I wasn't going to get in trouble for — *unless you get caught,* the voice in the back of my mind reminded me.

****

Morning came soon enough. Abanea was standing by my bed and holding a leather strap with a crooked smile and goofy twinkle in her eye.

"You will need these," she said smiling. I could tell she had been up early, just waiting for me to wake up. We ate quickly with excitement in our eyes. Tetoway and Eba told us to have a good time and that they would take over our chores for the day.

"So are we really going to leave this place?" I asked again, unsure if I had dreamed it all up.

"You'll see — aren't you glad now that you are one of the Chief's wives?" Her comment hung in my mind. Nothing about being one of the Chief's wives made up for what I had lost. I followed her to the mouth of the cave. It seemed like so long ago that I had been carried here by Colbryn, so long ago I was ripped from my old life. I thought about how scared and worn out I had been. The memory reminded me that despite the special treatment I got for being the Chief's wife, this was still not my home. My thoughts quickly disappeared when I turned the corner to see Colbryn standing against the face of the cliff and holding a large leather strap. Three other men stood with him. Another also had a strap. When I got close enough, he smiled, turning the edge of his mouth up ever so slightly.

"Lucky you, huh?" He held out the strap.

I looked for Abanea for clarification. She had already put the sling around her rear and was dangling from his back.

"It's just a harness. Hurry up, we don't have all day, and the Chief is strict about when we get back." She responded to my confused stare.

I wedged myself awkwardly into the sling the same way she had done, and Colbryn easily picked me up and wrapped his massive warm arms under my legs. I was in heaven; this must be the best day ever, I thought. Lost in bliss, I just sat staring at Colbryn's face. My expression must have reflected my thoughts because Abanea felt the need to explain more.

"Don't worry, the straps are just a precaution; it keeps us in place. It keeps us from escaping." She glanced at me raising her eyebrows. "Even though we are out, we still can't be untied to walk freely," she smiled.

I knew there would have to be a catch and that was it. Escaping was going to be harder than I thought. Before I knew it, I was saddled up, and we were headed down the trail. I leaned forward and whispered in Colbryn's ear.

"I am going to enjoy this a lot more than you are." I could see goose bumps rise up on the skin of his arms, and I loved the fact I had that kind of effect on him. He smiled.

"I remember saying that to someone not too long ago. I did enjoy it, too; it was the part that followed that I didn't like." I could tell he was trying to appear a certain way around everyone else than he did when he was alone with me. There seemed to always be two sides to Colbryn: the side of him that was calm and loving around me and the side of him that was guarded and withdrawn around everyone else.

Eventually, we were far enough ahead on the trail so the others could not hear us. He looked behind us to make sure, and then added:

"Speaking of that day, if I had only known things were going to turn out the way they did for your family, believe me … I wouldn't have … I hope that you believe me."

"You saw me with my family?" My stomach clinched.

"Yes, we watched your tribe for two days. We picked out who we wanted and plotted the best time to make our move. I wanted you so badly, but even so, I would have gladly let you escape in the forest had I know this is how everything would turn out. I would never have taken you away, and I am sorry." We were silent for a long time.

"If that is how you felt, then why did you seem so mad at the competition?" I recalled the angry stares he had given me from the pit.

"For three days, as I walked by your side, I was thinking of ways to make you fall in love with me. I knew it wouldn't be easy considering how things started out. I knew you would hate me, but there wasn't any other way for me to be able to have you. I had so many plans to win your heart so you would see that taking you from your family was not a mistake. I knew that we belonged together. I waited for four years for you and never took a wife because I knew you were and are perfect for me. I am drawn to you. It's impossible to describe; it's like you're made of magnetic loadstone. But I knew you wouldn't feel the same, at least not at first. That's why I had to take you." He looked away and focused on the path.

"You could have just come to the Maiden March and asked my father." I was half smart with my reply.

"It doesn't work like that for us, Natani. There are methods, rights, rituals, traditions that must be followed. This was the only way."

"What about my traditions, my rituals? I could have married Tallenhill and had my own tepee. I could have been free to pick herbs and have friends. What about all of that?"

"Tallenhill? You were selected to be married?" His face lost a little color, and it surprised me.

"Well I was going to be. I was on my way to let him know when I was kidnapped." I wondered if I could make him mad enough that he would stop and put me down. I could feel the heat in my face radiating through my hair.

"You have a bit of the buffalo in you, Natani." He chuckled, and his face smoothed over again.

"Buffalo? What are you talking about?" His accusation offended me, and I didn't even know what it meant.

"I can see where you're going before you get there, You put up a face that is tougher than your real one, and you are clumsy with your attacks — you're predictable." He spoke as though he knew me.

"You don't know me. You might think you do because you stalked me, but there are hidden things in me that I don't even know about," I shot back, wondering if my defense was any stronger than the last.

"See, that's exactly what I mean." He chuckled again. "The escape in the woods that day was your idea wasn't it?" He asked with a smile.

"Yes, obviously, it didn't work, but that doesn't mean I'm predictable. If I were, you would have caught me sooner. As I remember, I got pretty far before you tackled me."

"I was just playing with you and giving you a head start, but your escape was never a real threat. We are very good trackers, and I never let you out of my site."

"Just playing, huh? Well I'm glad this has been one big, fun game for you, but for me it's been Hell." I wasn't going to honeycoat my words right now. I was speaking without restraint. "Cruel — that's the only word I have for you right now. You let me think that I was going to make it to freedom by giving me a head start, only to rip it from me?"

"I was just ... that's not what I meant to say. I was just trying to ... it came out wrong ... really wrong."

"No, it came out true." I could feel a little piece inside of me sever in that moment. I released my grip from around his arm and held onto the leather strap. It was silent between us. I knew he was thinking of some way to smooth things over, but I was hurting inside.

"If I had only known, known how it would end, I would have grabbed you, kept going, and never looked back. When the Chief picked you, I thought about not competing and waiting for someone else. But if I was going to settle, it wouldn't matter who it was because I knew I would never feel the same for anyone else. I didn't mean for it to sound like a game. That was wrong of me. I apologize." It took me a few moments to let his words settle and calm the anger that had percolated up my spine. Whether Colbryn had meant for this to happen, I was still here, still dangling above the soft grass I use to lie in but was now forbidden to touch.

"So if it didn't matter who you ended up with, then why did you fight so hard to win?"

"Rage. I could not help myself. The person I really wanted to fight wasn't even in the ring. I felt like the Chief stole you from me. He took what I felt was my destiny with no effort at all." There was a strange similarity between us. Colbryn and I both wanted something other than what we had; angry that we didn't have control over our own destiny.

"You could keep going now." My words were short, but I knew the weight they carried. If Colbryn could have taken me away then, he could take me away now, right? He was silent. I could read the torment in his expression.

"I can't, Natani, not now."

"Why? What's changed?"

"You're the Chief's wife now. Before, you were just you."

"All the more reason to keep going, don't you think?"

"He would never stop hunting us, ever." His words were like a pinprick to my lungs, tiny but enough to drain the air from inside. I felt hollow again. "We are almost there," he said, his voice angry.

We came to a section in the forest were the earth had been pushed up by some magical force. Layers of different colored soil lay like ribbons stacked on top of each other. Parts of the earth had been dug out where Abanea wanted to work. She had settled in and started collecting the clay. The other three men set to work and filled the baskets they carried. We scooped up the earth until the baskets were full and our arms were coated in grey slurry.

We took a small break, cleaned off the clay, and prepared for our return. While we rested, I sat secretly memorizing his neck and chiseled jawline. How was it possible to desire and hate someone so much at the same time?

Colbryn took a water skin from his waist and handed it to me. I sipped and returned it and watched him raise his head to take a drink. It was like watching a panther, wild and beautiful, strong and mysterious, yet dangerous. How could things ever work between us? It was torturous. Although I loved being with him, seeing him, and speaking to him. I knew I'd still take any opportunity given to me to leave.

Abanea babbled on beside us about something, but my mind was lost in the look and feel of his body, tracing back over every word that had been spoken earlier. When the baskets were filled, we joined the back of the group this time and stayed well behind the others. His long hair blew against my cheek; it seemed that every eager touch was also laced with sorrow. The silence between us was painful, knowing that comforting words could make things between us worse. He swung the strap that held me to him from one shoulder to the other, but not before our faces brushed in a stolen kiss beneath the silky curtain of his hair. Once on the other shoulder, I leaned and whispered into his ear.

"What was that?"

"Like I said before, a perfect fit." I smiled and laid my head against his massive shoulder.

The trees parted, and though we were still far from the cave, it loomed above us once again. I couldn't believe I was going back. The thought made me gasp. Even in the daylight, the screaming face was a foreboding darkness on the horizon.

"Like something out of a nightmare," I said, more to myself than to him. He, too, looked up.

"Yes, nightmarish, and I am forever marked as the ghoul of that dream," he sighed apologetically.

"Just the ghoul taking me back to the demon," I clarified.

"Oh, Natani you break my heart, and I deserve it."

We climbed the path in silence. Why couldn't Colbryn just keep running and take me some place far from here, someplace safer. Part of me was angry that he would even return me to this place. Once inside we were helped out of our slings. My legs gave way, and he grabbed me just like the first night he had brought me to this dreadful spot. We stared at each other for a brief moment. I hated and loved him at the same time. Abanea broke our stare; I was afraid she might be reading into things.

"Wasn't that fun?" she spouted.

She had no idea, I thought to myself. I looked back at Colbryn, and he flashed a sad smile. He had gotten to say the things that were eating him up inside, but knowing the feelings were mutual only made it worse. Our forbidden passion was officially chained beneath a veil of secrecy.

Despite everything, we had been together for the whole day; the separation now was bittersweet. He picked the leather slings up and with one last glance headed off into the darkness to another part of the cave. He left me to churn the cold earth with Abanea.

We started processing the clay as soon as we got to the potting room. Abanea had me working on crushing the clumps but my mind was somewhere else, and it wasn't just because of Colbryn. It had been happening more often, as if I couldn't control my thoughts, as if someone or something was taking over.

"Once this settles out, we will pour off the excess water and knead it until it's ready to use. We can use up the clay we already have until this is ready. Natani, are you listening?"

"Oh yes, right, kneading it until its ready. Wow, processing clay is harder than I thought. I thought you just took it out and started making something with it." She just laughed, and I was glad my lack of knowledge distracted her from the fact I wasn't even paying attention to what she had been saying.

"Didn't you make things in your tribe, or did you get special privileges because you were a Chief's daughter?" That was the one question I had been asked the most in my life and the one question I hated most.

"No, no special privileges." I smirked at her accusation. "Grasses are more readily abundant in the plains where I am from, so we weave most everything."

"I see. Well it takes a little more work, but these will last longer."

As she spoke I was reminded of the vision of the smoke rising from my village. The burning baskets and mats my mother and I had worked so hard on ignited my thoughts.

"Come on, I am starving."

Tetoway's and Eba's voices greeted us happily from the door. "Did you two have a good time while I slaved away here?" Eba joked.

We left to eat and settle in for the night, but I planned on getting an early start to the chores tomorrow to make it up to them and to hash out all the thoughts in my head.

****

I got up before the others to start on the spring cleaning in the Sun Hall. I was sweeping together a pile of leaves when something caught my eye. I noticed a series of jagged rocks leading up to the top of the wall that were concealed by old vines and a tall tree. I investigated closer and after checking to make sure no one was watching, I took the chance and started to climb up. If you're caught you will be punished or at least have a lot of explaining to do, my head warned me, but I needed to take the chance. It was early morning — surely no one would be coming up here for a while? It took some struggling, but eventually I got to the top. The first gaze over the wall was thrilling. I could see the vast, rugged landscape outside. I could see where we had traveled. I could see freedom.

Looking down, I saw a river ran gracefully along the foot of the mountain. I couldn't tell how many feet the drop was — 40, 50, 60? I wondered whether I could survive a jump and whether I would hit the river or the shore. A leap would be risky, but the chance was worth it. Death would be instant, and freedom would be worth the price of death. As I was gazing out, awed by the vastness, a noise caught my attention. Concealed by vines, I froze in place. If it was the Chief, I'd be better off just jumping right now. I looked back over the ledge to get a better feel for how hard I would have to push off to clear the rocky ledge and shore. *You'll have to jump hard*, my head confirmed.

Looking back, I realized it wasn't the Chief. It was Pinnoteh, and she was sneaking into the mushroom garden. I waited for her to get behind the wall so I could climb down unnoticed. I got down more easily than I had gotten up and reached the ground in time to catch her coming back out of the forbidden room. When she saw me, she stopped and quickly tucked something behind her back.

"You should not be in there, Pinnoteh." I told her.

"Fine." She glared back at me as she tried to go around.

"What do you have in your hands?" The adrenaline was still pumping through my veins from discovering my new escape route out of the Sun Hall. I didn't want to have to be dealing with her right now.

"None of your business," she snapped back.

"I think it is. You can show me, or I can call for help." She glared and threw the pouch at me as she turned and headed for the door. A figure met her there; it was the Chief. Pinnoteh gasped and froze at the sight of his intimidating figure. I had just picked the bag up when he came over to me. Grabbing the pouch, he eyed the mushrooms inside. His brows cinched together, and his long nails encased the bag angrily in a clinched fist.

"Are these yours?" he asked, holding up his fist. I shot a look at Pinnoteh and without thinking of the consequences, nodded yes. His hand shot out with lightening speed and grabbed my arm. His long nails dug into my flesh. He pulled me out the door. Pinnoteh's eyes were still full of guilty terror. I was forced into a chamber that I had never been in before. Two guards followed him, and I wondered if either one was Colbryn.

"Send for the head scout," he told one. "Strip her, and string her up." He ordered the other. I was too frightened to speak. My dress was ripped off to my waist, my hands were forced and tied over my head, and the rope was pulled until my toes no longer touched the ground. I dangled helpless in the dark. It hurt; my arms felt like they would soon rip from the sockets. I hung like a gutted dear, the dim light of the cavern provided no comfort. My back was to the door, but I recognized the voice immediately. It was Colbryn; I could feel my body relax.

"Yes, Chief, you called for me?" His voice made all the pain go away.

"Ten lashes," the Chief spoke, and a cracking noise popped beside my ear. My body stiffened again. This was going to hurt. I prepared myself. Every muscle in my body tensed, but I wasn't going to give the Chief the satisfaction of hearing me scream. Ten, that's not so many. I could handle that I thought. The first snap planted itself in the small of my back. It stung like a hornet, and I could feel the blood running down my thigh. I only remember counting to five, and by the fifth crack, I must have lost consciousness. I woke up to Eba dabbing my back with ointment and humming to herself. My back was on fire, and the warmth made every pulse feel a hundred times more powerful. Tetoway walked in.

"You just can't seem to stay out of trouble, can you? Why on earth would you want to steal mushrooms in the first place?" I just lay there and was thinking the same thing about Pinnoteh. Was she using them? Did she get them for Colbryn? That had to be it. I felt better immediately.

Eba had finished wrapping the bandages around me so I would not soil my dress. She just shook her head.

"Colbryn was very upset when he carried you in. He had no idea it was you, not that it would have changed anything. He still would have had to do it. I have never seen a live man so white. You shouldn't be too upset with him." The look in her eye was serious, but I knew there was nothing that could make me mad at Colbryn. She pulled the bandage tight.

"Ouch, OK, OK, that is more than tight enough! I'm not mad at Colbryn. I know he had no choice. The whole thing was embarrassing, and I prefer to forget about it." My cheeks flushed knowing Colbryn had seen me naked, limp, and bloody.

Eba huffed a bit. "Embarrassing? You're back looks like ground buffalo, and you're worried about being embarrassed? I don't think he minded that part; if it makes you feel any better, you were covered when you got here." Eba still seemed genuinely concerned, but a glimpse of warmth sparked in her eyes.

Hours passed, and my back was beginning to feel better. I knew at this rate the cuts should coagulate by morning and I'd be healthy enough to try the wall again. I headed to my chamber to sleep when a figure reached from the darkness and pulled me into a small hall. It had to be Colbryn. I fell up against the rock wall, which sent pain racing through my back again. I gasped, and the figure grabbed me.

"I am so sorry. Please, please, forgive me, Natani!" It was Colbryn. No one else says my name with such fluid tones. "She didn't mean to get you in trouble; she thought they would please me." His deep whisper pierced me deeper than the whip but comforted me more than any medicine. I knew

I wasn't mad at him. But I did have questions, and answers would be nice.

"So she was getting them for you?" I whispered, though I had assumed this much. He was talking so fast I could hardly keep up.

"Yes. I didn't ask her to; she didn't think anyone would find out. I am going to tell him the truth right now. I just wanted you to know," his voice was shaky as though apologizing was pointless — which it was. I didn't need to hear the words from his lips because I already knew what was done was done.

"I had no idea that was you until I cut you down. I would have been softer. In fact, I would have refused. I didn't even know the reason for the lashing until Pinnoteh admitted to me later what had happened. I am going to the Chief to set it straight so he will know you had nothing to do with it. Hurting you was the last thing I ever wanted to do."

I looked back at the sorrow in his face. The hall was dark, but my eyes were adjusting. I could see the deep lines between his brow, his eyes sunken in the shadows, his mouth pursed with anger.

"No, you can't. If you tell him, that makes me a liar. What do you think he will do to a wife who lies to him? I'm glad you didn't know that it was me. If you had known and refused the Chief, he would have wondered why, and we don't need spying eyes. You have to treat me just like anyone else." His expression changed. He closed his eyes and raised his head up. He didn't say a word, but I could tell by his expression that he agreed with me. Tears of frustration filled his eyes and slid down his face. It was strange to see such an impenetrable soul fall weak at my expense.

"I don't have to forgive you because I never blamed you; it wasn't your fault," I said softly. He looked at me, but my words didn't bring him comfort.

"I just wish I could make this better somehow, this place, this situation, this life." His face was pleading.

"You saved my life, remember. You make this place bearable for me." He put both hands to my face.

"I am the reason you are here in this horrible place, and what I have done is unforgivable. For whatever it is worth, Natani … you have my heart, my soul, and it is you that swims through my blood. I will always have you with me." All I could do was stare back into his black eyes. His words had a paralyzing effect on my soul, and I stood motionless as my blood began slowly flowing again. I watched him back away from me and disappear into the shadows like so many times before. He was gone. I slid further back into the darkness and tried to compose myself. This was not love; this hurt too much. If it was love, I didn't know if I wanted any part of it.

I headed back to the wives' room but wasn't ready for the lecture I was going to receive. The three of them sat together; it appeared they had been talking about something. I got the feeling it was me.

"So we've been talking and just can't figure out why you would want to take the mushrooms, Natani. Is there something going on with you that you would like to tell us? We don't keep secrets from each other." Eba asked as they all sat waiting for an answer. I questioned what consequences would come from confiding the truth to the wives. Six eyes were burning at my conscience. I hated telling on Pinnoteh, but not as much as I hated the wives' disapproval.

"I got up early, so I thought I'd get a head start on cleaning when I noticed Pinnoteh in the room. You told me no one else was allowed, so I confronted her. She was defensive, but Pinnoteh is always that way. It took me some time to get her to confess what it was that she had in her hands. She handed me the mushrooms and headed for the door at the same time the Chief entered and found me with the sachet in my hand. I just reacted. When he asked if they were mine, I just said yes. I'm not sure why. I guess I didn't want Pinnoteh to get in trouble."

"You have done more for your friend than she realizes. You got whipped, but she would have been put to death. It is made quite clear when they arrived here the consequences of going in there, not to mention taking anything." Tetoway said sternly.

"We will need to have council with her tomorrow so she knows the seriousness of what she has done. The Chief must not know, for your sake," her eyes shot to me like an arrow. "Do we all agree?" Tetoway added.

Everyone shook their heads, but I was still stunned by the severity of stealing mushrooms. It surprised me that the punishment was death. I had saved Pinnoteh's life, and knowing that she would have been killed had I not lied made me feel nervous, and oddly, somewhat powerful.

"Well, it's nice to know you haven't completely lost your mind," Abanea smiled.

"Is it just me, or does it seem odd that Duran has some sixth sense about you, Natani? He came looking for you when you got lost, then that time you went to see your friends, and now. He seldom goes to the Sun Hall, and why so early? I just think it's odd." Eba's words made my heart stop. I could feel my face get hot as that realization hit me.

"Is he spying on me?" I asked in shock. Did they know something I didn't?

"I don't think so. I just think he is more aware of you than the rest of us maybe." Eba shrugged.

"I could do without that," I said, smiling on the outside but terrified on the inside. Could he know about my feelings for Colbryn? If the Chief knew everything, I'm sure it would mean death for one or both of us. The thought sat like a heavy weight in my throat for the rest of the day.

CHAPTER EIGHT
Fortune

I could tell evening had arrived, not by the light of the day, but because it was the time in which chores had all been completed, dinner had been finished up and there was nothing left to do but sit around the fire with Abanea, Tetoway, and Eba. They made me feel like we were one happy family, a family with a strange, dark secret, one that would come in the night and loom in our minds during the day. I looked forward to laughing and joking with each of them as it helped offset the moments I dreaded so much.

Since I had been here, Eba had become very talented at making herbal tea concoctions. She knew what herbs to collect when she went on clay runs and was quite good at mixing various remedies. She would try them out on us to see how well they worked. I had been memorizing her technique in hopes of having gained some useful knowledge to take home.

Her concoctions were always a surprise. I had learned ginga root for digestion, rockrose for cough, june flower for headache.

We were enjoying her latest brew, which was supposed to have a numbing effect on my back pain, and was working quite well. I asked for another cup when Abanea turned to me.

"So, Natani, tell me again about the disk hanging around your neck? Can I see it? " I was hesitant to remove my pendant, but I knew I could trust Abanea.

"I showed it to you when we made my bowl, remember?" I said trying to remind her so I wouldn't have to take it off.

"Yes, I know, but I've been trying to remember where it was that I saw that design. I swear it looks familiar." I handed it to her.

"You said that your mother gave it to you and that your grandmother gave it to her, so where did your grandmother get it?" Her eyes squinted curiously as she stroked the smooth stone.

"I guess her mother gave it to her. I don't really know. It's just always been around." She turned it over and studied the back.

"Well the bear and eagle are easy to make out, but the bird could be any kind of bird. And I'm guessing this is a cougar and that is a wolf or a dog." She looked up, quite proud of herself, as we all burst into hysterical laughter for no good reason.

"What kind of tea did you say this was?" I asked Eba. "Umm, numbing tea." She spoke with a strange quirkiness to her voice that got us rolling again. "Here, give it to me — I have better eyes than you, Abanea." Eba could hardly control her laughter as she grabbed the pendant.

"I beg your pardon, I can see just fine; it's just that it's not clear." Eba handed over the pendant.

"Oh, it's beautiful." Abanea took another sip of tea. "Umm, I'm going to guess wolf, cougar, and crow." She made a beak out of her hands and squawked and caused another wave of laughter. I watched as my pendant passed from hand to hand. I didn't like it being on display, especially in our state of semi-intoxication.

"Ooo, maybe it's a sacred spell — wouldn't that be neat?" Abanea swirled her arms through the air before rolling over backwards. "Are you sure you didn't sneak some peyote in this tea, Eba? This stuff is making us wild."

"Nope, but it is a secret ingredient," Eba blabbered, practically drooling. She sounded so intense, and the laughter rose to a higher level. I was afraid someone would complain about the noise and end our fun.

"Speaking of spells, Eba, you need to do that bone and rock thing for Na-tani; you know, the one you do that tells the future." Abanea looked at me and raised her eyebrows up and down. I snatched my pendant back and was glad to have it around my neck again.

"She is really good; she predicted you would be coming to join us. It's kind of creepy if you like that sort of thing." Eba got up and was soon back with a small cylindrical basket that had a thatched lid. She handed it to me.

"Okay, so what do I do with this?" I was hesitant and intrigued at the same time; it was a strange combination of feelings, but I figured it was because of the tea.

"It's easy, you shake the basket and say, 'Spirits reveal my future.' Silly, I know. Then take off the lid and spill the contents on the floor."

"What if it's bad, and I wish I hadn't known?" Besides, I couldn't imagine a good outcome of running away with Colbryn, and that was what I hoped my future to be.

"Oh, go ahead. None of ours said anything too bad," Eba screeched excitedly. I shook my head hesitantly and spoke the words.

"Spirits reveal my future — wait!" I stopped. " Where did you learn how to do this?" I asked suspiciously.

"The Shaman in my village taught me. He said I had a real gift. Now just do it!" Eba commanded in her sweet tone.

"OK, but no making fun of my future," I added with a chuckle.

"No, no, go on." I got as serious as I could under the influence of the tea. I said the words, popped the lid, and scattered the contents on the floor. The bones and small pebbles twirled around, bouncing off each other and coming to rest between our feet. Eba leaned over the items in a profession-al manner, mumbled something I couldn't understand, and then scooped the items up, put them back in the basket, and handed it back to me.

"Try it again — this time do it right."

"What? I thought I did do it right; what did it say?" I demanded.

"It said your nose is going to grow really big if you don't do it right!" The other two fell back with laughter. I grabbed the basket with real determination this time.

"I didn't think this was something you had to practice for? Spirits reveal my future." The items came out in about the same pattern as the time before. Eba studied them again, scooped them up, and put them back in the basket.

"Well what did it say?" we all asked eagerly. She looked up seriously, and I didn't like this sudden change in her eyes.

"The same things as the time before; you must not be doing it right." She smiled, and the others laughed.

I rolled my eyes. "Fine, don't tell me!"

Tetoway laughed. "I think that is enough excitement for one night; my side is hurting from laughing so hard. Eba, this is a very good tea, and I can't wait to see what kind of dreams it gives me." She hugged everyone, and we dispersed to our separate chambers after a quick and sudden end to our night of fun. But I was left wondering what my fortune had really said.

My head was swimming with bears, birds, rocks, and wolves all mixed together. I lay in a dreamlike state, but needless to say, between the images and the discomfort of my back, I didn't sleep very well.

The next morning I was still exhausted but awake. My eyes were still shut when I overheard Tetoway and Eba talking.

"You saw something last night, didn't you?"

"Yes, it's not good; we will all need to keep an eye on her, even more than we have, if that is even possible." Eba was whispering.

"What do you mean 'not good?'"

"Pain, suffering," she paused, "I saw a lot of pain and suffering." Eba pinched her lips together and made a strange face.

"Oh poor thing, wasn't the whipping enough? Is there anything we can do?" Tetoway asked.

"Short of killing her, I don't think so. It's all tied together with the medallion that she wears. It would take someone who knows more than I do to sort it all out. It's creepy, really; it seems to be some kind of test. The finger bone was tip up which means there is a Spirit force at work. Maybe she is possessed?" Eba spoke and her words seemed to have vapor around them. I could almost see them dissipate into the air.

"I doubt it. She's a little headstrong but not possessed." Tetoway was searching Eba's eyes for more information.

I ducked behind some baskets. They had to have been talking about me. I got up and joined them as they each turned away suspiciously. "So what were you two talking about?" I tried to act casual and not seem too interested. "Oh, just one of the other wives is having a hard time. We need to keep a close eye on her." Eba was too transparent; I could tell she wasn't telling the truth. I just shook my head. "What's to eat?" I smiled, changing the subject.

After breakfast, Eba put fresh ointment on my back. "Do you feel up to another outing today?" I could actually feel my face light up.

"Outside?" I questioned with disbelief.

"Yes, if you don't think it will hurt your back?"

"Would it be the same as before ... with Colbryn? You know, because I really should talk to him and let him know that I have no hard feelings towards him for the whipping." I almost hesitated too long when saying his name and hoped she didn't think anything of it.

"If you want, I can see if he is here." The thought of spending the day with him set my heart soaring. Even if he could not come, I still wanted to go, but he would be a bonus. Eba came back a short time later. "It's all set up; we are ready when you are."

"Of course, are you kidding? I'm ready now." My day was definitely looking brighter. "So what are we getting today?"

"I need some things for the celebration, and it looked like a beautiful day to be out; so let's get out of this place."

Two men were waiting for us, but this time Colbryn had a worried look on his face. I had expected a secret smile at the very least so I asked, "Do you have something else you need to do — am I taking you away from something?"

"No, I was just worried about you, with your wounds and all; are you sure you are well enough to do this?" I looked away, thinking how to sound convincing without sounding completely bereft of good judgment.

"I am fine, really." I didn't care if every gash in my back opened up — I wasn't going to pass up a chance to leave the cave. Eba spoke up as I climbed into the sling. "Then let's go."

"Are you sure you're alright?" he kept asking.

"Yes, I wouldn't miss this for the world."

We traveled a lot farther than we did last time. The sun on my back was making the ointment burn as it settled in the valley of every gash, but I ignored the pain. It was too beautiful of a day, and I wasn't going to let on that my back was hurting.

"Shh!" One of the men ahead of us stopped and put up his fist. We stopped suddenly and crouched down amongst some wiry bushes.

"Quick, slide off my back," Colbryn ordered in a stern whisper that I wasn't used to hearing. Eba was some distance from me, but I could see the concern on her face. Her eyes were wider than usual, below a creased forehead that before had always been smooth. This must be bad, I thought to myself. I was touching the ground. I knew Colbryn wouldn't have put me down if it hadn't been necessary.

"Follow me," he whispered again. We crawled away from the others for a distance under the cover of rough brush. Sticks and rocks were poking into my knees, and I was glad that today I had worn buckskin pants under my dress. After moving some distance away, we stopped at a large tree and hid behind the thick trunk. I couldn't stand the suspense any longer. "What is it?"

"Raiding party; stay still and be quiet. I will try to lead them away." He crawled off without even looking at me. I could tell that his eyes were locked on whatever the threat was. My view of him was swallowed up by the forest, and I sat staring out into the branches above me and listening for any movement. I wasn't afraid; I knew whoever was in the forest with us was not going to fare well. I fought with the irritation coming from my wounds. The ointment had softened and was now running down the small of my back and causing everything to itch. I went for a quick scratch, and that's when I heard them. There were several men coming my way. I froze in place, but that didn't save me. I felt a hand grab my arm from behind my back and yank me to my feet. As he pulled, I felt the wounds on my back stretch as I let out a yelp.

"What do we have here?" I looked into the smiling face of a horrid-looking man. His face paint was jagged and uneven, his headdress sloppy and unkempt. The others whooped and hollered in response. "Where did you come from, little Dove?" His face was just inches from mine, and his breath was like rotting deer meat. It made my stomach turn.

"Looks like she has had a good lashing." He pointed to the spots of blood that were seeping through my shirt as he examined me from head to toe. The man leaned in even closer. "What are you doing out here?" His eyes were big and threatening.

"Running." I said looking him in the eye.

"Where is your village?" I pointed in the opposite direction from my companions and hoped it would lead them away. He gave me a quick smile and brushed the back of his hand across my cheek. "I will see you later! You two, tie her down so she can't get away, and we will come back for her later. Just remember, I saw her first, and I expect her to be here when we get back." He whirled a sack over his shoulder and bound off into the trees.

The thought of him coming back for me turned my stomach, and I had to bend over to keep from vomiting because of his smell. The two other men tied my hands and feet a little tighter than I thought necessary.

"You must be a wild little thing to have deserved a lashing like that — did ya kill someone?" One man poked at my shoulder with his knife while the other laughed.

"No, I saved someone." I'm not sure why, but I enjoyed telling them this; I felt kind of like a warrior.

"Oooh, she saved someone." They laughed again.

"I'd say a cute little thing like you could use some saving of her own." His face was sweaty, and when he leaned into mine a bead dripped off the tip of his nose. "I could save you; I could cut you free and take you off. You deserve better than this, and I can give it to you." His eyes scanning my body, I leaned into the tree as far as I could. Despite his vile appearance and rank smell, I briefly considered that running off with him might be better than returning to the mountain and to the Chief.

"Alright," I replied without hesitation. I wondered if Colbryn was listening? I hoped he was. "I'll go with you if you are man enough to free me and take me with you before your friend comes back." My words were meant for Colbryn to hear. I wondered if the jab would irritate him into taking this guy's place and getting me away from here. It worked, sort of. From behind a tree with silent steps, Colbryn appeared, and with a swift slice of his knife, he silently laid the man down. Behind him the other man lay motionless as well.

"Funny, Natani. That was real funny."

"He was going to take me away from here. He could have cleaned up nicely," I stated, reaching for the man's knife with my foot. Colbryn took it from me and threw it into the base of a tree.

"I hate to tell you this, but your new boyfriend would have been dead before nightfall, then after I brought you back, I would be lashed for letting him take you." He grabbed my arm, and with one fluid movement, he cut the ropes that bound me. Once again we were moving through the forest. When we were a safe distance, he stopped.

"Are you alright? Do you need to rest? Let me see your back?" His eyes filled with concern as he eyed the darkening blood marks on my dress.

"I am fine," I said smiling back at him.

"Can you go a little further? I can carry you if you like?" The thought was appealing.

"I am OK, really. I will go as far as we need to. What about Eba? Is she close?" I was thinking that we should have met up with her by now.

"No, they headed back before we did. They rushed ahead to catch up with the one who headed off towards your so-called village." We walked until it started to get dark, and then he gathered wood for a fire. I could have kept going, but Colbryn seemed insistent on a break. It did feel good to sit down. I leaned against a log to stretch my back and flinched a little with pain.

"Does it hurt much?"

"It's fine," I lied, trying to sound light-hearted.

"You lie. May I see it?" I turned away from him and raised my shirt exposing my back. I could hear him breathe in deep with disappointment. He put some water on a cloth and dabbed it to my skin.

"You don't lie very well." He pulled my shirt down, and I turned back to him.

"This is not your fault, really." His brows pulled together.

"I should have known that perfect body was yours. Even then, I thought it was a sin against nature to put marks on something so beautiful." I could feel my cheeks flush, and I looked away.

"You must be getting tired of seeing me without clothes by now," I laughed, trying to lighten the mood the best I could.

"Yeah, it's a real pain." He too looked away, lost in thought.

Before he could say anything, I changed the subject. "You were amazing today. The way you took care of those men seemed effortless." He shrugged his shoulders.

"Unfortunately, it's not my first time." His voice was low and regretful.

"Did you have a choice?" My question was more of a statement.

"Well, I couldn't very well go back without you. It is in my best interest to return you to the Chief," he said with a smile.

"Is that all it was? Oh, that's right; it's all about impressing the Chief. See, I haven't learned to be a kiss-up like you yet," I grinned.

"You know better than that," he said, turning to look at me.

"See, I am a good liar," I said with a smile and trying to lighten the mood with my humor.

We stared at the fire and watched the sparks drift into the darkness. The coolness of the dark sky was setting a chill upon my neck.

"Tell me, why you don't leave? Why didn't we just leave the other day when we were getting clay? You're fast. You could outrun the wolves, so why do you go back?" I had to know.

"Natani, I can't just leave. There are many reasons — mainly because it's too dangerous. The Chief would never stop looking for me. I've heard too many stories, seen too many people try. No one has ever been successful. Once you have been chosen and have become what we are, a Chosen One, there is no turning back, no going back to the way you once were. We are addicted to the mushrooms. They make us powerful, and without them we are weak. Eventually the addiction takes over and draws us back to the cave. There is no mercy given — just the final relief of death that is delivered by sharp teeth. There isn't even a need for the wolves to look for us. It's pathetic, but we come back willingly." His smile faded, and his brows pulled together; he appeared to have sensed something.

"Quick, get in the tree!" He jumped up and pulled me to my feet. It was then that I heard the foamy snarls coming through the forest. I could feel my eyes expand in surprise and take in every movement. He hoisted me up with little effort, as I sat staring down from the safety of the branches.

"Aren't you coming, too?" He looked up to make sure I was high enough.

"I'll do better down here." Picking up a half-burnt log in one hand and his knife in the other, he stood waiting. The barking and snarling grew closer. I had never seen the wolves, just the imaginary picture I pieced together of them in my mind from all the stories. I imagined them to be beastly creatures with large foaming fangs and wrinkled-up noses. The first one came through the trees and leaped at Colbryn viciously. He knocked it down with the log, and it lay kicking and twitching. The second one he caught with the blade of his knife, but the third circled him cautiously. It eyed me and then him, and then it charged. Much to my surprise, it was quickly over. The sound of whimpers went silent. Suddenly, we heard voices.

"Colbryn, is that you?" A voice came from the woods.

"Over here." Two men walked into the light of our fire. Their bodies, bulbous and strong, resembled Colbryn's. They greeted him warmly.

"Hey, Stone, Asis." Colbryn said. He seemed happy to see them, and I assumed they were his friends. He kept such a strict demeanor in the cave that it was nice to see him relax.

"What, you only sent three? I am disappointed." He smiled to the one I thought he called Asis.

"Didn't want to waste any more on you. We sent the three oldest ones because we knew what would happen to them." They laughed.

"You didn't find Natani?" one asked while scanning the darkness. Colbryn smiled and pointed up at the tree. I felt ridiculous. He looked up and smiled awkwardly.

"Hi, Natani, good to see you again. I hope the wolves didn't scare you too much." I recognized him from the well. I hated that he had to rescue me again.

"Just a little," I huffed. "May I come down now?" Six arms rose up and lifted me from the branch. "Careful of the back!" I screeched.

"What about the other two? Is Eba safe, or did you send the wolves after her as well?" I couldn't help but sound snide.

"The others are safe and sound; we just didn't know about you two. When they got back and you weren't with them, the Chief wasn't happy. He wanted us to bring more wolves, but we knew three was waste enough."

"I killed the two men that had Natani — thought I would get her back before you sent the wolves," Colbryn sneered.

"Sorry, we thought it was the fastest way to find you." They both smiled.

"Yeah, well, good thing she wasn't alone," Colbryn answered in irritation.

"You know the rules as well as we do, so don't make us out to be the bad guys here." Asis shrugged his shoulders.

"Yeah, just because I know the rules doesn't mean I like them or care to understand them." Colbryn's voice was full of displeasure.

Asis and Stone shared their food and water with us, and we all sat around the fire like old friends. How odd, I thought. When we get back, Colbryn and I will go back to playing our parts and acting like we barely know each other. We played our parts so well that no one would ever guess I would give up my life for this man if he asked me. I curled up by his side and closed my eyes while they talked into the night.

The next morning I woke to a gentle shake. "Sorry, Natani, but it's time to leave," he whispered. I looked into his eyes and tried to read whatever information he might have for me but found nothing. "I will need to carry you from here." He turned and bent so I could climb on his back.

"The others are gone already?" I was surprised we weren't all sticking together.

"They are ahead of us just a ways, but we will catch up." I loved hearing his voice first thing in the morning. I clung to his back with my face against his neck. He walked without saying a word until our time seemed to be wasting away in silence.

"Are you mad at me? Did I say something to upset you?" I had to ask because the quiet was killing me more than my back, which began to hurt as a sharp pain radiated from the base of my neck.

"No, you know, it's not you. Taking you back is just hard for me." I could hardly hear his words. My head was dizzy, and tears started running from my eyes onto his shoulder. The throbbing in my head suddenly made it impossible for me to think. It was all I could do to keep from falling off and rolling on the ground in pain. Why was I suddenly so hot?

"Natani? Natani, are you alright?" Colbryn's voice was loud and scary, but all I could do was let out a screech with my hands cupped tightly against my head. I tried to answer, to open my eyes, but all went dark.

When I woke up, I was in the cool darkness of the cave. I could tell by the taste of the air. I was cradled in Colbryn's arms. It was exactly where I had hoped to be.

"It's hard to focus. Are we back already?" I could only whisper because the loudness of my own voice pulsated through my head. He didn't answer, but I could hear Eba's voice.

"Put her here, and roll her on her stomach. Colbryn, take your knife, and cut the shirt up the back and to the shoulders." I could hear them speaking, but it was like I wasn't there. I felt like an observer. My blood-soaked shirt had dried to me. The ointment had formed a sticky glue, so pulling it off was excruciating. It was the last thing I remembered before waking up for the third time in one day, this time hungry. It must be morning, I thought. I tried to get up, but I couldn't. My arms and legs felt like they were being held down, so I moaned.

"Natani, are you awake?" I could hear Eba's voice in the other room.

"Oh, thank the Spirits, she is going to make it!" I felt a warm hand on my forehead and opened my eyes. Three beautiful faces were looking down on me and smiling.

"How come I can't get up?" I groaned.

"Don't try, just lie still. You have been very sick," Tetoway said, with a worried look.

"We didn't think you were going to make it there for a while. You had us worried sick!" Eba said scoldingly. They all looked so tired that I wondered how long they had been fussing over me.

"How long have I been sick?"

"Three days. We have been pouring elixir down you everyday, changing the wrapping, cleaning your back, and keeping salve on it nonstop. I think the infection is almost gone, but it was pretty nasty when you got here."

Tetoway sounded proud of their efforts.

"Wow, for three days! But ...." It seemed like just last night that I had been sitting around the fire with Colbryn, Asis, and Stone. "Sick from what? I remember having a really bad headache, but that is all that I can remember." I had never really been severely sick before so it kind of scared me.

"We think it was from an infection. I'm sorry, Natani. I should have never have asked you to go with me. That was the last thing you needed to do with a back as sliced up as yours was." Eba grabbed my hand and clasped it in hers, with a look of desperation in her eyes.

"I'm fine really, just hungry and thirsty. Stop fussing over me. It seems like that's all you three do." I smiled, and they laughed.

"Yeah, Natani, you're a real pain in our rears — you know that!" Eba laughed, handing me a warm cup of tea. "Here, try this. It's a new blend we have tried out, and I think you will like it." It smelled like roses in summer with a hint of honey and lavender. The smell conjured old family memories as I closed my eyes and took a sip.

"Mmm, I love it already. Thanks, Eba." I sat thinking, and it dawned on me: If I had been asleep for three days, then the Spring Celebration was only two days away.

"The celebration is in, what — two days!?" I sprung to life, thankful that I hadn't missed it.

"Yeah, you have to get better, or else you're going to miss it," Eba said with a smile. I hoped she was joking because I wouldn't have missed it for anything.

"Oh, no! My chores, the cleaning, preparations, the bowls, all the things I was supposed to do to get ready. None of it is done, I've let you all down!" I had let myself down, too, because the one thing I had looked forward to was making the bowls and being a part of all the planning.

"Not a problem; we made Pinnoteh do all of your chores. We thought she owed it to you." They were all smiling. I wanted to laugh at the thought of Pinnoteh doing my chores, but I knew it would hurt too much.

"She did everything except the mushrooms," Eba said with a sneer.

"She even did some of our work, but we aren't going to tell her that," Abanea laughed. "It's been fun ordering her around," Tetoway added. "Well I feel much better then — thank you."

"You can do the Summer Celebration all by yourself if it will make you feel better," Eba added.

"Yeah, now you are pushing it just a bit, but on a serious note, thanks all of you for taking care of me." I was appreciative of them, and it was nice knowing that they were there for me.

"Of course, even though it's my fault you got sick in the first place, I should have never taken you out so soon." Eba filled my cup. I could see through the swirling steam that her lips were pursed together.

"I'm sure I would have been fine if it hadn't been for that rancid man yanking me by my arm. I'm sure that's when everything opened up." The event sounded worse than I remembered it.

"What? Colbryn never mentioned another man. I just thought you two got separated from us?" Eba's eyes got big.

"No, I was hiding in the bushes. Colbryn left me to go distract them away from you, but a man grabbed me by my arm and yanked me to my feet. I was tied up, and then Colbryn came. Before I knew it, the men were dead. He killed them, and he also killed the wolves. I really don't know what I would have done if he hadn't been there."

"Wolves! After you?" Eba shouted.

"Yes, geez, news doesn't spread as fast as I thought around here. Three wolves came, and I hid in a tree while Colbryn killed them. They were followed by two of our men. I believe their names were Asis and Stone. So see, Eba, it's not your fault. I am getting tired of everything happening to only me. One of you needs to attract some trouble once in a while." I laughed, but I was serious.

"Well, we are seasoned and have learned how to avoid that stuff. You, too, will learn." Eba smiled a petite grin and brushed my stringy, dirty hair from my face.

"You do keep things interesting around here," Tetoway laughed.

"We're just glad to have you back," Abanea said with a sincere smile.

"Yes, it is so dull around here without you!" Eba added.

"I am glad you're happy to have me back. I know I've already been a big enough thistle in your side, but I have one more big favor to ask."

"Of course, what do you need?"

"Well, I am starving, and I really need a bath."

"Oh, that's easy," they all laughed. While Eba and Abanea got the food and water ready, Tetoway knelt down beside me with a vacantly serious look on her face.

"Colbryn has been here several times a day checking on you. Do you want me to send word that you are awake?" I thought about that for a minute, and as much as I would have liked to see him, I figured it would be in my best interest to act like I didn't.

"I'm sure he has better things to do than check in on me." I smiled a casual grin as she smiled back at me. I knew it was probably the answer she wanted to hear.

"Good answer, but I saw the look of concern on his face when he brought you here. He feels responsible for what happened to you." I was surprised she seemed to be pushing this. Was she searching for something, or was it a trap?

"I know, but he shouldn't. I tried to explain that to him. You do whatever you think is best." She gave me a curious look and left.

"There wasn't time to think about the ever-growing difficulties of the love triangle I was in. There was only one thing on my mind, and that was a soothing, hot bath. I could almost feel the residue from the past three days caked up on my skin. I reeked of ointment, salve, sweat and tears. I needed to soak, to relax, and maybe then I could think about Colbryn and Pinnoteh.

Abanea and Eba helped me to the bath and unwound the bandages. I could tell everything was pretty well scabbed over because when I stretched or bent over, it was tight. The steam rose from the stone bath and dissipated in the cool damp air. I breathed in the sweet vapors. Tetoway had sprinkled the water with scented Eucas leaves, and it was heaven. Easing into the water was tricky. The temperature was warm and comfortable until it hit the wounds, and then it hurt like venom.

"Augh! Oh, aughhh! It hurts badly, maybe pour some cool water in?" I stood naked with only my legs submerged, too afraid to sit. To my disappointment, the hot soothing bath was now turning into a chilled, uncomfortable one. The cooler water felt better on my back. I sat in an exhausted daze despite the large amount of sleep I had gotten. Eba returned with some bread, fruit, and a slice of cured meat. It tasted amazing, better than anything I had ever eaten. Tetoway washed and brushed my hair while I sat straight and taut to keep from bending my back. For a moment I actually felt pretty special with everyone tending to my needs. I knew it wouldn't last, but for the moment, I was enjoying every second of it.

CHAPTER NINE
Spring Celebration

I got my strength back quickly over the next few days with the help of Eba's tea and ointment. We were all sitting, having our evening chat, discussing what was left to do, when Abanea glanced at me. I could tell her mood was shifting.

"What? What is it?" I asked, not allowing the strange glance to go unnoticed.

"I have some bad news for you, and I was thinking of how to tell you." I couldn't imagine what it could be. They had never had trouble telling me bad news before, but Abanea was the most sensitive of the three women.

She looked down and then continued. "I went to get the bowls today, and the first one you made was broken." There were a lot of other things she could have told me that would have been worse, so the news was almost comforting.

"The one that has the pattern of my necklace?" I touched the pendant to make sure it was still there.

"Yes," she said sadly.

"How do you think it happened? Do you think someone did it — maybe Pinnoteh?" I hated to accuse her without knowing, but she was the first and only person to pop into my mind.

"I don't know. There is no way to prove it. She had plenty of opportunity while she was down there doing chores. I asked her about it when I found the bowl, but she denied even seeing it. You're not too mad, are you?" Abanea's face was so serious that I couldn't help but to break out into laughter, which I think astonished her even more.

"Ha, ha! Abanea, I'm not mad, as long as you will help me make another one. Is there enough clay?" I smiled, and her face warmed to its usual glow.

"That's the Spirit. I was just sad because it was your first one, and you worked so hard on it. It was so beautiful that I saved the pieces. We can piece it back together, but you are right that it might be easier just to make a new one," she smiled back.

Broken pieces and fragments pasted together in mismatched ways — that was exactly how I felt on the inside and the outside.

We were all excited the morning of the celebration. Even though the festivities didn't start until evening, we were all busy early. The day promised to be sunny but had a chill still in the air. Men were carrying wood to the Sun Hall for the fires, and Colbryn was one of them. I was resting by the pool when he approached. "Good to see you up and around again." I hated that I loved seeing him so much.

"Thank you, and thank you for saving me again," I said, trying to sound light and happy. When he wasn't around, I thought of all the things I wanted to say to him. But in times like this, when he was in front of me, those things seemed to disappear.

"You had us all scared." His eyes searched mine, and I knew he had been worried for me.

"You know me, always knocking on trouble's door." I shrugged as he squinted at me.

"Everything looks very nice. I know you four have put a lot of work into the celebration," he said. I could tell he was making small talk.

"Well, from what I hear, Pinnoteh did a lot of my work." He turned and gave me a surprised look, which I found strange.

"I wasn't aware of that." He bit his lip in a nervous gesture.

"Yes, she filled in for me while I was sick. I thought she would have told you?" The lip thing was contagious. I was doing it, too.

"I haven't see her much, but I am glad she could make amends in some small way. She owes you more than just a few chores."

I smiled. I liked that Pinnoteh owed me. I would always have that over her. It made up for the childhood resentment she held towards me.

"Did Asis and Stone find the rest of the raiding party?" He looked thankful to have something else to talk about.

"No, they followed a trail for a day, but when it went cold, they came back. I'm sure they are far gone now." Just then, someone called his name, and he turned away.

"I had better get back to work. See you tonight." Then he was gone. I got busy again making sure we had all the props for the games. Everything was ready, so I went to rest. It was my job to explain the games and their rules, which made me the one to judge the winner. This was good and bad. It would be fun, but I wasn't really feeling up to all the excitement.

It was strange being in charge of everyone's activities. Enough time had passed that my friends now had new friends. It seemed like a great tribe, but I was still just an outsider. Everyone came and was having a good time. I watched as Tecka and Ottowa played the games. They laughed and ran around like the three of us used to do, but now I was sort of an outcast. I hated that I had to be secluded from everyone. It didn't seem fair.

The games went pretty well. They started with the rope pull, five men and five women on each side, and everyone seemed to enjoy themselves. The rug game was a different story: twenty women and only nineteen rugs. When the drummer stopped, they each had to find a rug. Each time he stopped, I took a rug away, and someone lost. Midway through, there had already been a few contestant pile-ups. When it came to the last three contestants, I was afraid of a fight breaking out, so I declared them all winners. The last game was a simple one called Hide the Rock. Most of the tribe formed a large circle. One member stood in the middle while everyone else tried to hand a rock to his or her neighbor without the person in the middle seeing. They were all surprisingly good at it. When we took a break, I saw Pinnoteh standing by herself, so I approached her.

"Thank you for taking over for me while I was sick. You helped out a lot, and it looks very nice." I was feeling generous and in a good mood, so I decided I would smother her with kindness to irritate her even more.

"I didn't have a choice now, did I?" She gave me a hard look as she walked away. She stayed by Colbryn's side the rest of the night, and they seemed to be enjoying themselves like all the other happy couples. Pinnoteh had her arms around Colbryn, and he was laughing. They looked happy. I don't know why it was so hard to watch. I wanted him to be happy even if he couldn't be with me. My strength started to wear out, so I asked Abanea to take over for me. I went to rest, so I could gain strength in case Duran allowed everyone to leave the cave for the ritual.

Once back in my room, my nerves kicked in. The contrast from excitement to silence and from watching happy couples to being alone in the darkness was just too much, and sadness swept over me. Hot tears ran down my temples and into my hair. I ran my fingers over my shoulder to comfort myself. Rough scars were forming on my once-smooth skin, and the jagged scabs were still clinging. I was startled by an unexpected noise at the door. I turned to see a figure standing in the opening. My first hope was that it was Colbryn, but then I realized it wasn't. The Chief's deep voice ordered me from the darkness to get undressed. The blood drained from me, and I went cold. I obeyed because I had to. He was more violent than usual, as though his anger over something else was being taken out on me. I allowed my mind to go blank. It would be over soon. It will be over soon, it will be over soon, it will be over soon, the words repeated in a comforting dance within my mind. When he was finished, he dressed and left without a word. I lay there numb, thankful he had gone. As I got up, I had to peel myself from the blankets. That's when I realized that he had re-opened the wounds and that I was bleeding once again. Damn it!

I thought and staggered to my feet. I wrapped a blanket around me and went to find Eba. My knees were unsteady, so I leaned up against the wall to support myself. The one person I didn't want to see me like this came by. Colbryn smiled.

"Looks like the evening is a big success." He was happy, and I was glad. It was a rare sight, but I just kept walking with nothing more than an "uh huh."

"Natani, are you all right?" I felt him grab my arm through the blanket and stop me.

Green spots started forming in my eyes. I had felt this feeling before, and I knew it was only a matter of time before I passed out. "Would you find Eba for me?" He nodded, and I turned to go.

"Natani, you are bleeding again. Let me help you to your room." He grabbed my arm and led me back. "What happened — did you fall?" The blood on my bed and clothes made it obvious.

"I just need Eba!" I pleaded again.

"Let me see your back." He reached for the blanket. I was naked, so I jerked away.

"No, I will be fine, just go get Eba, please." I knew she would be able to help me. Colbryn left my side in an instant. I was glad to not have to answer him with details. "What has happened?" Eba asked, wisking frantically through the door.

"Nothing, I just need some ointment and tea." I tried to smile and look calm, but I still felt dizzy and couldn't open my eyes. It was the best I could do.

"Sit, sit, sit." She examined my back and turned it away from Colbryn, who was still standing in the shadows of the door. "How did this happen? You have knocked off some of your scabs with quite a force, Natani."

"I fell," I answered while glaring up at Colbryn.

"Without your clothes?"

Colbryn pointed accusingly.

Eba stood up and turned to him. "Colbryn, this does not concern you." Anger and frustration reached his face. It was obvious he was trying hard to hold it in.

"Only an animal wouldn't be able to wait until she was better!" He kicked the blankets across the floor.

"He has just as much right to her as you do your wife, whom by the way, you need to go see right now!" Eba's words shot back as she left and walked him out of the room. I could hear their voices, and then Eba was back with some tea. Between the tea and the ointment, I was feeling a lot better, but I hated feeling weak.

"Thanks for coming and fixing me up." I smiled at her once again through the steam of my much-needed tea. I knew I didn't have to explain to her. I was glad our friendship was reaching that point.

"Happy to do it, Natani. It's getting a little wild out there, so I was glad to get away."

"I think everyone is having a good time," I said slowly to see if she agreed.

"It is the best celebration ever, as far as I can remember anyway. Everyone is having so much fun with the games. This is just what everyone needed." Eba turned to me pursing her lips first. "Colbryn is a little more concerned for you than he needs to be." I felt like her words were meant to send a message, but I pretended to not catch on.

"He feels terribly responsible for what happened to my back, Eba. It is just kindness." I had hoped she would be convinced.

"Even so, it could get him into a lot of trouble, the type of trouble we don't need around here. Do you know what I mean?"

"I understand. Can you tell him I will be fine tomorrow? Do you know if everyone is getting to leave the cave at dusk for the ritual?" I wondered if she knew.

"I don't think so, we have never all be able to leave. I have a feeling its all just false hope, Natani. I think with the raiding party still out in the woods, there won't even be a chance" She cocked a smile to the side of her mouth.

"What, the Chief is scared of his own medicine?" I knew if the Chief had heard me say that I'd be spending another three days in the pit, but I couldn't resist drawing attention to the irony of the situation. Eba gave me strange look but said nothing. I was disappointed about not getting to leave the cave, but I was also a little relieved. The healthier I was, the better my chances of a successful escape. I had some more healing to do. Plus, I'm sure the wolves would have smelled the blood on my bandages from miles away. In this state, I would have been an easy target.

"I will tell Colbryn that you are fine now, just tired." She smiled back, and I could feel my eye lids getting heavy. I don't even remember falling asleep.

Everyone was already up when I awoke. Tetoway was the first to speak. "Everyone had such a good time last night, Natani. They can't wait until the Summer Celebration."

"And we owe it all to you, Natani!" Abanea added.

"I didn't do that much. I was sick, remember?"

"It was the games that made it so much fun for everyone, and they were your idea." she smiled.

"Thanks, I really appreciate the credit even though I didn't do much. So what are we doing today?"

"Glad you asked," Abanea chimed in. "It is time to move the mushrooms to their summer garden, but I don't think you need to be doing anything."

She picked up the bloody sheets from the night before and glanced over to Eba. I wasn't sure how I wanted to respond, but Eba saved me.

"Just a little extra wash to do." Eba took my clothes from Abanea's hands and headed on as normal.

"Please, I'd love to help. Can I at least come and be in the Sun Hall with you?" I knew if I were alone that the Chief might come and repeat the night's events.

"I think that would be OK." Abanea waited to see if Eba was going to agree. I was relieved she said nothing.

"We will get the ground ready. You shouldn't be bending over until your back heals. While we are doing that, you can get the spores ready to transplant. Both gardens will be in use until we are sure they take, just as we did when we moved them into the cave." I could tell Eba was unsure about me helping, but she went about telling me my duties anyway.

The path to the indoor summer garden took me through the mountain and past the dwellings along an upper passage that allowed me to look down into the village. Walking by it every day flooded me with mixed emotions. I was envious of the happy couples, sharing their lives with each other, seemingly oblivious to the lives they left behind, and I couldn't stop wishing that I were like them. There wasn't much point in dwelling on something or someone I would never have. All the same, I knew I would miss this trip when the garden was moved back outside. From time to time, I would see Colbryn talking to his friends or doing some simple chores. I even saw him a few times with Pinnoteh. I missed him with every fiber of my being. The restless yearnings I had for him were only growing. I started thinking of ways to meet him secretly, but then Tetoway's words would resonate: "Death to you both." The days passed. Sometimes our eyes would meet, but I would just keep walking like a banished castaway. I wondered if I haunted Colbryn as much as he haunted me. Occasionally, he would nod, and I would smile. Thus, we went about our days. The moth to the flame, a distant flame.

CHAPTER TEN

Scars

It had been an uneventful day, as so many were now. We sat around the fire and drank Eba's tea. At first, I didn't notice the look frozen on her face.

"Eba, Eba, what is it? Are you okay?" I hadn't seen her look this way before.

"Eba?" I touched her shoulder, and her trance broke with a sudden jerk and gasp.

"Something … something has happened." She frantically scrambled to stand up.

"What, what has happened? Why are you worked up?" I reached out to calm her, but as I did, three men were suddenly stumbling through the passageway. I immediately recognized two of them from the tribe, but the third man was slouched over. As I looked more closely, I realized that bright red drops of blood were cascading off of the tips of his hair like crimson pearls and pooling on the floor. Abanea gasped in horror.

"It was a bear attack. It's very bad!" The man spoke in a cracking and frantic voice and was losing control. We all jumped up. Tetoway cleared a bench with one swipe, and everything on it now twirled across the floor. Eba put down a clean rug. Everyone else sprung into action, but I just stood there. I didn't know what to do, and I was still processing things in a frozen stupor.

"Put him here!" Eba screeched. The two men carried him in, and I could now see that they, too, were covered in blood. The wounds were bad, so bad that I could almost see the man's soul drifting out. His leg was broken, one side had two deep slash marks running down his thigh, and there were numerous bite marks over his entire body. But worse of all was the large flap of scalp that hung to one side. His entire face had swollen to twice its normal size. Tetoway looked at him, and I could already see the look of defeat forming in the wrinkles of her face. She brushed the hair from her eyes with the back of her hand to avoid the blood on her fingers, but she was now covered in it, and it smeared in her hair anyway.

"This is beyond my knowledge of healing." She spoke in abandoned hope. There was silence except for the gurgling moans of the man faintly rising from the floor. Everyone stared at each other in horror. Were we just going to stand here and watch him die? I had seen people die. I had watched old members of the tribe rise to the Spirit land many times. But they were old, and there was nothing more to be done for them but bless them on their journey. This was different. This man was not old, and he needed help. Something moved within me, and words formed and took flight from my mouth as if something had sucked the air out of my lungs and made sounds beyond my control.

"I have seen it done," were the words that came out.

They all looked at me with questioning eyes.

"Tell us what you need?" Tetoway's voice was frantic. I wasn't used to her seeming more helpless than I.

Had I really said that? Was I volunteering to fix this unfixable man?

"Um, um, I need sinew, a bone needle, a small flame, a tender reed straw, the medicine pouches, several wraps, and Tetoway — the tea, you know which one." Everyone dispersed all at once. I knelt beside the man. I could smell the blood, the scent of the bear, the earth, and they all told a gruesome story. I prepared myself mentally, trying to remember the correct steps my mother took to heal a woman who had been attacked by a mountain lion. I was surprised how calm I was staring at the man. I guess I knew anything was better than nothing, and I knew I wasn't going to do nothing. This man deserved a chance. One by one, everyone came back with the supplies. I had never seen so much blood; it just kept coming.

"Just start," Tetoway shouted, breaking my trance. I knelt down and spoke in the deepest, calmest voice I could.

"My friend, we are going to help you. If you can hear me, this is going to hurt. I need you to let your body go loose — your arms, your legs, your mind." As I spoke, I could feel warmth radiating from my palms.

"I don't think he can hear you, Natani," said a voice from somewhere; I barely heard it; I was just going through the steps I remembered.

"If you can hear me, move your lips." Nothing happened. I wondered if the man was already dead.

"It's important that you remove your mind from the pain. I will summon you when it is time to come back. When you hear me, say, 'Medicine cloak away, soul now awake.' Tetoway, the tea now."

I tied off the leg where blood was flowing the most. "We have to realign the leg if we are ever going to get it to stop bleeding." The two men helped. One held his chest under the arms while the other one pulled the leg straight. I stabilized it with sticks, cleaned the gashes, and sewed up the edges as I went. I started stitching his scalp back on after Abanea washed it with warm salt water. Cleaning and sewing, we then moved down to his side. I was thankful he was still unconscious. My mind drifted to the poor man's wife, who needed to know what had happened. I turned to one of the men and asked if she was coming.

"She is on her way," the man answered.

I continued, but the face was beyond recognition. I worried how his wife would react when she arrived, and I wanted to have him sewn up as much as possible before she did. I worked the best I could and continued sewing and wiping. The sewn gashes were cauterized with the rock edge and flame. The smell of burning flesh made everyone back away, but I held tight and worked as fast as I could to stop the bleeding. Then, I packed each with resin salve and pine and wrapped it tight, hoping this was the mixture my mother had used.

A scream shot from the doorway; it was Pinnoteh. Why was she here? I was irritated that she would act so badly in front of this poor man. She knelt down beside the man and just screamed — it was horrifying. I stood back and watched as the man began to move. He was shaking and moaning.

"Pinnoteh, calm down. Why are you so upset?" I reached for her. She leaned into me with all her fury and struck me across the face.

"Why do you think I am upset!?" she screeched. I could hear everyone gasp. I was stunned and confused. I got up and slowly backed away.

"But that's not … that's not …" The realization hit me harder than Pinnoteh had, but I couldn't say his name out loud. I couldn't say anything. My heart stopped, and I felt my palms go cold. The blood on my arms was drying and pulling the hairs on my skin. Everything seemed like it was in slow motion. The man I had been working on, the man that lay on my floor ripped to pieces was Colbryn. I could see everyone else putting it together, but no one wanted to say anything. I felt sick to my stomach. The smell of blood and burnt flesh now reached my nose, and I felt like I was going to pass out.

"Natani, Natani, sit." I could hear Abanea at my side.

Pinnoteh continued to cry hysterically.

"Please take her out. She's making it worse," I ordered the men, and they agreed. With a man on each of her arms, Pinnoteh screamed and thrashed about. I could hear her voice finally fade off into a deep cavern.

I regained my control and looked back at the helpless man in front of me. My hands began to shake. Thankfully, all the stitching was over. Eba came back into the room with an ointment she had just mixed.

"What was that all about? Thank goodness you removed that woman; she was not helping one bit. If she thought he looked bad now, I would hate to think what she would have done if she had seen him before he got here. Who is he by the way?"

Abanea answered. "It's Colbryn, Eba." She was silent and stunned.

"Oh, no!" They all seemed to care for him, just not as much as I did.

"Oh, no … no, how, but how?" was all she could murmur. She just sat down and handed me the ointment in a cold stone bowl.

"Please go ahead and apply it," I asked. I knew she was dealing with the shock, but I couldn't do anymore. I couldn't touch him.

"After sewing him up, you're suddenly squeamish?" There was desperation in her voice. I didn't want to explain my sudden hesitation, so I took the container and went to work again. Abanea and Tetoway cleaned up and finished washing off the dried blood. We all stood back looking at his helpless figure in front of us.

"We have done all we can do; it's out of our hands." Eba said.

"Natani, you did a wonderful job," Tetoway said. "I have never seen anything like it. If you hadn't been here, he would be dead for sure."

"He is not out of danger yet — far from it. Eba, would you mix up some of that tea that you gave me for my fever and put some extra kuva kuva and valeoan in it to help him sleep?" I asked.

"Good idea. We might have to start calling you the medicine woman around here, Natani." The truth was I hadn't even thought about what I had done. I just somehow knew what to do. The other two looked at me and said they would take over my chores so I could stay with him. Then Eba helped me, and we worked to get some of the tea down his throat.

"I think he is resting better, and his breathing is more even," Eba stated.

"Yes, now that the worst is over, we need to wake his Spirit back up so it can begin healing."

"OK, what's going to happen when you do?" I sensed a nervous tone in Eba's voice.

"Well, I'm not sure. I have never done this before, so anything could happen. He might suddenly be hit with all the pain, he could die, or he could just keep sleeping. I'm not sure." I took a deep breath and prepared to say the words.

"OK, I'm ready, just get it over with." Eba felt the need to brace his shoulders.

"Medicine cloak away, soul now awake." We both sat motionless waiting for something to happen.

"Well, nothing happened; he is still breathing?" Eba whispered.

"It's a good sign," I whispered back, not really knowing. "I would hate to think how much pain he is in. Eba, would you go with me to see Pinnoteh?" I wanted her to know that I didn't mean anything by making her leave. She had the right to be upset. It just wasn't the time or the place. I knew she truly cared for Colbryn. I just hoped she would be able to be there for him now.

"That is a good idea. Sure, I will be glad to go. I'll tell one of the others to watch him while we are gone." Eba didn't say a word as we made our way down to the village, and I was glad. When we got to Pinnoteh's tent, several women were standing around.

"She is sleeping. We gave her a tincture to calm her down, and it knocked her out," replied a woman at the tepee door. We went inside. It was strange for me because I knew this was where Colbryn slept. It was their space. Pinnoteh was sleeping. I wondered if I should just let her sleep and deal with this in the morning. I knew it wouldn't get any easier, and I hoped that her being drowsy would work in my favor. I gently shook her shoulder, and she woke startled. She rose up onto her knees, and I could see her face was red and swollen from tears.

Jumping up, she looked from one face to the other.

"He is still alive. We thought you would want to know." Eba reached out for Pinnoteh's arm in a compassionate gesture. Pinnoteh jerked her arm back and with one step forward slapped me hard across the face.

"What right do you have to order me away from my husband?" She yelled.

I was getting tired of Pinnoteh's fist on my face, and one of these times she was going to really regret her inability to control herself. Eba stepped between us and got right in Pinnoteh's face.

"She had every right; you were out of control. She should have you killed for that. I know I would have!"

"It is alright, Eba. In the state you were in Pinnoteh, it was necessary to have you removed. If I had not done it, one of the others would have." I tried to sound compassionate.

Eba piped up. I could tell she was running on high anxiety from the day because she usually didn't make confrontations.

"Until you are able to control yourself, and I don't just mean around your husband, do not come to visit. That's an order. We will let you know when a convenient time for you to see him is." She grabbed my arm and pulled me out of the tent. I had more to say to Pinnoteh but knew our visit was over. The shock on the women's faces outside the tepee made me look to the ground. When we were well away from them, Eba turned to me.

"Why do you put up with that horrible woman? I would have given her to the wolves long ago. I guess someone will need to take care of Colbryn. Hopefully, she will be capable of at least doing that?" Her words were angry, angrier than I was. Part of me sympathized with Pinnoteh.

"I know, I have always disliked Pinnoteh. I guess the fact that she is one of the only members of my original tribe here makes our conflict seem comforting. We fought then, and we still fight now. At least one thing hasn't changed since being taken to this place." It was true; our inability to get along was the only thing that had remained the same. Even my best friends had changed, but the hostility Pinnoteh and I shared was a constant and bizarre comfort.

Eba just grunted, smirked, and looked away.

When we got back, Abanea was lying on a mat next to Colbryn.

"He is still breathing," she whispered, her voice slow and smooth.

"Here, Natani, you look like you could drop. What happened to your face? It's all red."

"She was attacked by that vicious wife," Eba blurted out.

"Doesn't she know that if it hadn't been for you, he would be dead right now?"

We just shook our heads, too exhausted to respond. The day had been long, and I knew I wouldn't be doing much sleeping that night. Adrenaline was still pulsing through my veins. Knowing that Colbryn was in so much pain and fighting for his life, I knew I'd be awake in case anything happened.

"Well there isn't anything left for us to do tonight, so let's get some rest and hope the Spirits don't take him overnight. Who's going to stay out here and tend to him?" Abanea looked from Eba to me to Tetoway. No one spoke up.

"I can for tonight." My voice was rough and shaking, but I wasn't sure why. I knew I wouldn't be able to sleep next to Colbryn's mangled body. But he could be dead by morning, and this might be all the time I would have.

"OK, thanks, Natani." They were as exhausted as I was and wasted no time retreating to their rooms.

Silence.

I took a slow deep breath.

We were finally alone, and I checked his forehead and wiped his hands with cool water. The candlelight glistened off the damp wounds as I sat watching his chest rise and fall with each breath and thinking that at any moment now I might see it stop. If he did live through this, would he be the same man he was before? Would he still be allowed to be a part of the tribe if he wasn't strong and could no longer fight? I laid my head on the floor next to his.

"Colbryn, once you asked me to stay with you. Please, I am asking the same of you now. If I have your heart, you have to keep it beating for me." I fell into a restless sleep. Dreams of angry bears ripping flesh made me wake suddenly gasping for air. Wheezing gasps were the only sound coming from Colbryn; he was struggling with each breath. I touched his face, but he was still unrecognizable. How could this have happened? Colbryn was the strongest of them all. His skin was burning, and a fever had started. I gave him more tea. Drop by drop, it seeped between his still beautiful lips. I dabbed his body with cool water in hopes of lowering his temperature, but I couldn't tell if it was doing any good.

Eba woke me the next morning. "Go get something to eat, Natani. I will take over for now. You need to get out of here for a while. Go do your chores or something." It took me a minute to wake and process everything. She read the look on my face as everything came back to me.

"Yes, Natani, if he has made it this long, he has a good chance." I was so relieved. I don't know what I would have done if he had died in the night, and I had woken up to his cold body at my side. I followed Eba's orders and went to hurry through my gardening duties.

I hurried through my chores so I could keep a close eye on Colbryn's fever. That evening, we cleaned and changed the bandages. Wrapping his massive thigh and arms was oddly thrilling. Some of the swelling had gone down in his face, and he was starting to look more like himself again. He opened his eyes for a short time, and I thought I would cry. It was like looking at someone through smoke when you just faintly see their expressions.

"Colbryn, can you hear me?" A deep moan came from his throat, and a tear rolled from his eye.

"Don't speak, just rest. You are going to be just fine — just lie still." I tried to reassure him.

"How bad?" he asked anyway in a weak voice.

"I said not to speak." I couldn't help but smile at him. Even though he was in so much pain, I could still read the humor in his eyes.

"Nothing a few days rest won't take care of." He gave me a meaningful look.

"OK ... you're pretty rough off, if you really want to know. Your leg is broken, you have two deep cuts down your side, and several bite marks here and there. Oh, and a few stitches on your scalp," I added as an after-thought. He smiled without success. I bent down to him.

"The main thing is you seem to be doing just fine. You will be happy to know that the men are curing the hide and have saved you the bear's skull. All in all, I would say that you came out quite well. When you dance with fire, sometimes you get burned." He looked at me and tried to smile. "I have something for you to drink. It's pulped mushrooms for strength, Yarrow for your fever, Devil's claw for the pain, and Passionflower to help you sleep. That doesn't sound very appetizing, does it?" I laughed.

"Passionflower sounds appropriate," he smiled. "Seriously, Natani, I owe you my life, I ..."

"Thank me later; save your strength right now. Here, drink." I handed him the tincture, glad it wasn't me who had to drink it. He got it down with some food and was asleep in no time. I felt liberated and accomplished for the first time since I had been here. The feeling was great.

Colbryn became my full-time patient. I almost felt lucky to be the only one who knew the simple medical tricks because no one tried to step in. I was proud that my mother had taught me so many things, things I had thought I had forgotten. I wondered where my mother was now. Was she with my father and brother? Did they start the tribe over in a new location? Did they think of me? I missed them more each day, and it reminded me of the promise I made to myself the day I arrived: *Don't get comfortable here, and escape as soon as the opportunity presents itself.* I was not going to break this promise no matter how happy I was right now. I had Colbryn to myself, and it was blissful — as blissful as it could be, but it wouldn't last. I washed him, fed him, and slept by his side. I was even feeling sorry for Pinnoteh, just a little. Eba must have sensed something because she cornered me in the garden the next day.

"Natani, I think it's time for you to stop sleeping beside Colbryn, now that he is out of danger,"

I looked at her surprised.

"I am not hurting anyone," I questioned her.

"Yes, you are. If the Chief finds you there, what do you think he would do? It won't be good. Use your head, please."

I felt like someone had taken all the air out of me. I wasn't ready to give him up. Other men of the tribe would come up to visit regularly. I recognized Asis and Stone, so I sent them to tell Pinnoteh that she, too, could visit, but she never did. I wasn't disappointed. The men would carry him out to the Sun Garden because the other women didn't mind. A nervous feeling kept growing inside of me. Eba was right that I needed to be careful. I would do everything I needed to do to keep him near me, yet far enough away not to cause problems.

Tetoway announced that night that the men would be going on another raiding trip. New brides would be brought back, and we needed to start thinking of the wedding dinner, as though it was a happy occasion. The thought of more poor girls unaware of their fate sickened me. I couldn't do anything to stop it from happening, and I hated that.

"Let's play games like we did at the Spring Celebration! What do you think, Natani?" Natani, did you hear me?" Abanea poked my shoulder.

"I am sorry. My mind had drifted . . . yeah, that sounds great. What do you need me to do?" I wasn't in the mood to plan parties.

"You can get things organized and help Abanea make some bowls like last time. It would be nice to have one for each bride as a gift, if you can do it."

A gift? I thought. Their lives are being taken away from them, and I am in charge of making them a stupid bowl as a gift? The thought irritated me more and more.

"We have enough clay. With Natani's help, we should be able to do it in time." Abanea smiled. This was going to mean less time spent with Colbryn. I knew they meant well by the idea, but for me no gift would have made me happier here. I guess my fate was a bit different though. Ottowa and Tecka did seem happy, perhaps happier than I had ever seen them. The unhappiness seemed to be limited to just me.

That night when it was time for bed, I made a production out of going to my chamber. Once the fires were out, I snuck back to Colbryn's side.

"It's just me," I whispered. "I just wanted to make sure you were alright." Feeling in the darkness, I found his hand.

"I am fine. I haven't had a chance to thank you for saving my life." He squeezed my fingers.

"Well, you saved me several times. It was the least I could do. I sort of owed you." I squeezed back.

"No, any of the men could have rescued you from the pit or that raiding party. I heard their voices — Eba's, Tetoway's, Abanea's — I heard them say they didn't know what to do. I had let go of hope. I was dying there in front of everyone. But you, you stepped in when the outlook was grim, when no one else would and you saved me. Natani, I just wish. . ."

"Shh," I interrupted him. "I just wish this time had been as much fun for you as it was for me." I finished.

"Fun? You have had fun cleaning my disgusting wounds and feeding me like I was a helpless old man? You have some strange ideas of fun." His voice was sarcastic, and I was glad to hear that.

"Sorry, but it has been fun for me taking care of you. You don't know how much I envy Pinnoteh. If she knew, maybe she wouldn't hate me so much."

"The things between you two go deeper than just me, Natani. I have been lying here for days thinking of ways to get us out of this place. There has to be a way, and I promise you I will find it. There is nothing in this world I am more sure of than the fact that we are meant to be together."

Before I could answer him, we both noticed a soft glow coming from the hall. I got up to see who it was and came face to face with Duran.

"There you are," he growled.

"I was just checking on Colbryn." I whispered softly making it sound like Colbryn had been sleeping. The back of his hand struck my face before I could react.

"I don't care what you were doing. All I know is, once again, you were not where you should be!" He grabbed my arm and dragged me back to my chamber. I could only guess what thoughts were going through Colbryn's mind having to see that and being helpless to do anything about it. I lay there huddled in a ball, after Duran left, too ashamed to face anyone.

The next morning, I woke to the sound of many voices in the next chamber. I jumped up to see several of Colbryn's friends huddled around him. Asis and Stone were there. One had brought a pair of sticks to put under his arm so he could walk. They were moving him out the door.

"Where are you taking him?" I asked, a little louder than I had intended. One of the men I didn't know turned to me.

"Back to his wife. She is ready for him." Colbryn gave me one quick glance. I could not read the expression on his face. Soon everyone was gone. I ran to the garden and balled up in the darkest corner. I was unsure what to do with my anger.

I fixed him up to send him back to her! I thought. The voice in my mind, the one I heard down in the pit, shouted back at me again.

He was never yours ... never will be yours. You can't do anything about it. He doesn't belong to you! Tears slid down my face. The voice was right… He wasn't mine and never would be. That was fact, and I simply couldn't bear it. He was the only thing that made this place tolerable, and without him I was better off dead. As the tears ran down my face, darkness filled my mind every bit as dark as the pit. The only difference was that I had hope down there, but here there was none.

In that moment, I could feel a change in my body. It was as though an invisible darkness had cloaked me. My eyes even seemed to glaze over as though staring out from the darkness was more comforting than the light, like a wild animal, exposed. It was then I realized that I could not survive in this place any longer. I was trapped in a world not of my making, and I couldn't stand it. I was sick of being cornered, held here without my consent. I had to get out. I was tired of promising myself freedom and doing nothing about it. I was at a breaking point. I could feel the resolve racing through my veins. If I stayed, I would do something stupid, and Colbryn would die. Or he would do something heroic, and we both would die. The only solution was for me to escape.

Escape, Natani.

Escape.

Escape.

Escape.

CHAPTER ELEVEN

Wild Skin

My eyes locked on the rope we used at the last celebration. Remembering the rock steps behind the tree and its overhanging branch, I realized that I could lower myself down to the small ledge and jump to the river from there. I convinced myself that this would be fairly easy, but in reality it was probably suicide. Wiping the tears away, I felt surprisingly better. I had a plan, and I would go tonight. I headed back still wearing my newfound wild skin.

My sister-wives were very quiet all day long. Were they avoiding me? I couldn't tell. Maybe they sensed that something had changed in me. Maybe they were wondering how I was going to react to Colbryn being sent back to Pinnoteh. After chores, I cleaned up the area where I healed Colbryn. He had left a skinning knife behind. It brought back memories of that gruesome night. I had taken care not to hurt him as I tried to remove it. I washed off the dried blood and oiled it for him. Looking at it now, it seemed so precious to me. I held it to my chest thinking that I could use it as an excuse to see him one last time, but what would that accomplish? What would I say to him with Pinnoteh standing there? Have a nice life? I can't stay here without you? Please don't forget me? No, I decided just to keep the knife as some small part of him that I could take with me. I now had two precious items that were a part of me: the pendant around my neck and Colbryn's knife, which I would wear around my waist. We sat around the fire that night while a storm raged outside. Eba went to check on the garden and came back soaked.

"I guess it doesn't matter," I thought to myself. Whether I was going to be wet from the rain or river, wet was wet. We were all subdued from the day's events, but the anticipation of my impending escape jittered through my arms and legs and left me restless. It was a lot different in the wives' chamber without Colbryn because he had been our common focus. We had all worked towards getting him healthy, but now that he was gone, we all felt as if something were missing.

"It's sure quiet around here without Colbryn," Tetoway broke the silence.

I thought I was the only one who missed him, so I was glad to hear that we shared the same feelings.

Eba added: "I just hope that woman is smart enough to take care of him properly."

"We will all need to check in on him from time to time," Tetoway nodded. Hearing that made me feel much better. Even though I wasn't going to be there, they would be looking out for him.

I wanted to say goodbye to them and tell them that they had become my friends and that I would miss them. I hated that I had to leave them behind in this place. I wondered if they would be punished for my escape. Would Duran beat all of them? But I couldn't think about that. I couldn't let it change my mind.

We hugged good night and went off to bed as usual. As I was lying in the dark waiting for them to fall asleep, my thoughts turned to Colbryn again. I pictured his face and felt the touch of his skin. His last words to me were full of so much hope, but I knew there was no way he would be able to leave the mushrooms or the cave. In the end, he was even more a prisoner of this place than I was. Images of him swirled in my head. I will never be free from the pain of loving him, no matter how far away I am, but for now I tried to shut away these thoughts. Right now I had one goal, and it was my only focus.

I was anxious to get my plan in motion. My wild skin crawled, and feral blood pumped through my veins. I was, for the moment, no longer a woman. I was a trapped animal that had gone mad, and my frenzied thoughts of escape had taken over. I arose and slipped into my knee-high moccasins, and without even the slightest sound, I was on my feet. If all went well, I would be floating down the river. If not, well, I just wasn't going to think about that. I wondered if tonight Duran would be coming to my chamber. I needed to move quickly. I knew the wild trance I was in would not allow me to be submissive tonight. If found, I would fight to the death.

The cave chambers were dimly lit, but I reached the door to the Sun Hall by memory. I had gone over this route in my head many times. My heart was beating so hard. The large wooden latch was damp and cold against my burning palms. The darkness continued out into the Sun Hall. The rain was light, but the lightning was charging the air with a static energy that seemed to warn me. With each burst of light, I made my way to the rope and then to the stone steps. I took a deep breath and let the cool rain clear my head and heighten my resolve.

Go, just go. My mind kept saying.

I went. The stone steps where slippery, and the moss peeled off under each finger hold. But I dug my nails in and clambered like a wild cat. I stopped at the top, took one last look at this beautiful oasis, remembering how I felt the first time I saw it. Now dark, it was as though the flowers had faded and died, and now I was seeing it as it truly was — a facade. "Good-bye, Colbryn." I tied the rope to a branch and trusted that it would not break as I slipped my body over the edge. I had a great distance to go to get off the sheer mountain cliff, but each step and each inch was only that much closer to freedom. I lowered myself down, losing strength as I went. My arms were shaking, the rope was wet, and my hands slipped a little with each new grip. I could feel the blisters forming, but I had to hold on — not much farther, I promised myself. I reached the end of the rope, but to my surprise it did not reach the ledge. Damn! I had not planned for this. I dangled several feet from the overhang and swayed out over the cliff and back against the rock. I didn't have enough strength to climb back up. I was stuck. Dangling at the end of a rope with thunder cracking and lightning falling all around me, I suddenly realized this wasn't such a good plan. My fingers were giving out, so I held my breath and just let go. This might be the end, and if it had to be, I was okay with that.

The air around me was cold. I couldn't see the ledge except when a flash of lightning lit the sky. Was I going to land on it or go over? My legs hit the rock surface with crippling force. It hurt, but I was alive. I clung to it for a few minutes and was afraid to open my eyes. I forced them open, and the lightning lit up the sky again giving me a good view of the river still far below. I had fallen with only inches to spare. I could barely make out a large form floating down the river; it was a tree moving in the swift current, and it was headed this way. With a little more luck, I figured I would be able to swim to it once I hit the water. But do I jump before it gets to me or after? I had to decide quickly. I knew I didn't want to land on it, so maybe I should wait until it passed? *Go, just go.* My mind was on repeat. I didn't hesitate. I just jumped.

down

down

The fall took an eternity. Did I jump too soon? Was I going to hit the tree? Was I going to hit the shore and miss the river all together? Maybe I should have jumped out further. Should I hit feet first? It was going to hurt but how badly? Would I be knocked out? I had time for a thousand questions to scream out in my head, but I had no answers. My thoughts flashed to Colbryn. Warm and lying next to Pinnoteh, he was now so high up in the mountain.

Bam

I hit the water with enormous force. I wondered if my legs were even going to be able to kick. They stung with pain. I was still conscious, but I floated motionless for several moments. Was I okay? The mountain water racing around my body was so cold. I knew I had to start moving, or else I would freeze. Colbryn wouldn't be coming to rescue me this time. I was finally free, and I had to make it on my own. I started moving, fighting my way to the surface. I came up gasping as the water pulled me violently along. I could see the tree; it was huge, much bigger than it had looked. It was moving fast ahead of me, and I struggled to catch up. Branches underneath the surface threatened to tangle my legs, but I managed to fight my way to the trunk and climb up through the roots. As the storm raged overhead, I caught my breath and had my first taste of freedom.

Sometime during the night, the rain stopped, and I fell into an exhausted sleep straddling the trunk of the tree with the last remaining energy I had left. It carried me along the river. I didn't have a clue where it was going and I didn't care as long as it was away from the cave. The mountain loomed behind me. I could barely make out the ledge of the Sun Hall from where I jumped. Its appearance would have been barely noticeable to someone who didn't know it was there. From here, it looked so far away. I couldn't believe I had started there and was now here, moving swiftly away. I had done it. I had escaped.

******

I woke to something tugging and clawing at my shoulder. When I opened my eyes, I saw a huge crow picking at the colorful beaded trim that adorned my dress.

"Shoo!" I screamed, but he didn't react. He tugged for another second or two and then flew off, but not before stealing a shell bead. I broke off a branch of the tree and chucked it at the crow, who was perched at the top of the branches watching me. He leapt off squawking, as I watched my beautiful bead plummet into the river. He circled, cawing obnoxiously in protest before settling back into the branches.

The sun warmed me, and I felt better than I had in a long time. Freedom was beautiful. The dewy reeds along the shore glistened as birds and frogs danced alongside its flooded banks. The crow, however, wasn't going to let me enjoy it for long. Its honking cries continued, so I sat up to throw another branch and hoped that maybe this time I could knock him into the river. The sound of raging water became louder, and I was suddenly made aware that my obnoxious friend had been trying to warn me. I could see the river in front of me, but up ahead it looked like the bottom of it had just dropped out and nothing but air filled the space. The growing roar was beginning to drown out the crow, and I knew I had to do something. It flew off to the north bank, and I decided to follow. Diving back into the cold water was unbearable. I came up gasping, and the sting of the icy water took my breath away. Fighting once more with exhausted arms and legs, I made it to shore just in time to see my tree — my canoe to freedom — stop briefly and then disappear over the cliff.

The shore was muddy, but the water was so high that I was able to grab onto tree branches to pull myself out. Collapsing into the grass was such a wonderful feeling. I had missed the forest, the trees, the animals, the fresh air. It was all such a wonderful contrast to the stone fortress in which I had been imprisoned. How long had I been there? Time had stood still inside those walls.

I stripped off my clothes down to the bandages that I still wore and wrung the river water out the best I could. I hung everything up in hopes that a little morning breeze might dry things off. The soft green shoots of the grass felt like silk upon my bare skin. I ran my fingers under the bandages and felt the raised scars that ran down my back. These weren't the only things I had taken from the mountain, but they were a permanent reminder of the events I endured there. Those events had broken me, but they also made me something that I didn't know I could be ... strong.

I wanted to stay and regain strength, but I knew I had to get moving. The peak of the mountain was still protruding from the horizon like a knife in my side. It was early morning; now would be about the time someone would discover me missing, so I knew I needed to go. Pulling on my damp clothes, I headed out.

Walking through the forest after being in a cave for so long made me feel very exposed. I started heading towards the sun, which seemed to be the same direction my crow friend was going. He would appear, squawk at me, and then disappear again. My stomach began to growl. Why didn't I bring some food along? Maybe I didn't think I would make it past the jump, or maybe I should have planned this out better, I thought. It didn't matter because I was free. All other obstacles were insignificant.

The day warmed up, and I started to get use to the openness of being outside. The landscape was strange to me: hills, rocks and trees hid an occasional deer that ran in terror from me. Flocks of turkeys bolted into the sky and caught me off guard. Since being in the cave, my forest intuitions had weakened, and I tried to remember the words and teachings of my father.

Shadows grew longer as I came to a large stream. Walking along its banks, I came upon a small bear that had just caught a salmon. When he saw me, he dropped it and stared. I wondered if it was still with its mother, so I approached cautiously and waved my arms until he ran up the hillside. What luck, I thought. I picked up the squirming fish and hung it over my arm with a makeshift cattail rope and quickly headed off before the bear returned. I was still exuberant from the escape, and I realized that I had been wearing a smile all day. I was free, and now I was going to celebrate with a salmon dinner. I found a good spot to make a small camp hidden from view. Putting together sticks and dried fronds, I started a fire. Cooking the fish like this brought back so many memories of my mother doing the very same thing.

The small fire made me feel warm and comfortable. I was finally able to fully dry my buckskin moccasins. The fish was cooked until the pink flesh fell from the bone. I ate the entire thing, and it was the best fish I had ever eaten. I sat wondering if this might be a good place to spend the night, but noticing the funny gray-purple sky to the south, I reconsidered. A storm was brewing, and I didn't want to spend another night wet. Walking along the bank, I heard the first rumbles of thunder as I saw a rocky shelf sticking out from the hillside. Climbing up to it, I scooped out the soft, loose dirt underneath and stacked rocks along the outside to keep the rain out. Just in case this was a mountain lion or bear shelter, I kept Colbryn's knife in my hand. I got the place feeling cozy just as the first drops started to pelt the ground around me. Full, dry, and safe. All in all, I would say my first day of freedom was a great one. Even with the flashes of lightning and thunder, I slept hard and sound.

Another bird noise woke me that morning, but it was a sweet chirping song. I stretched, accidently knocking some of my stone wall out. When my eyes finally focused, there in front of me was the prettiest yellow bird I had ever seen. "Hello, little friend." It flitted around, pecking at the ground and singing to me. I left the safety of my shelter and headed out. I paused to see if I could hear the faint howling of wolves in the distance, but whether they where ones sent to hunt me I did not know. I wondered how far and how long Duran would search for me. Surely by now everyone knew I was missing. I wondered who first put it together: Abanea, Eba, or Tetoway? Maybe the Chief came late in the night to find me missing. The thought made my stomach turn. The strange yellow bird reappeared, and it seemed to be going my direction. I was thrilled to have such a pleasant traveling companion. It helped me feel less alone.

The landscape started to change. Mountains became hills, hills turned to rises, and trees gave way to meadows. "Beautiful, beautiful, beautiful!" I felt that for my entire seventeen years of life, I had taken everything for granted — literally everything. I was caught up in my own insignificant needs and what I thought mattered, but there was this whole other way of looking at things that I had been oblivious to. Like a slap in the face, I felt like I was finally waking up to something important and becoming aware of something greater. The eerie calling that had always taunted my soul seemed to be satisfied for the moment.

I walked all day. The sun was on its lateral descent when I came to a small stream scattered with trees. Sadly there were no bears to give up their catch, so I gathered enough wood for the night. I built a makeshift shelter of sticks to protect me and a small fire to keep me warm. I climbed inside and listened to the crickets singing to each other and an owl hooting in the distance. The sounds lulled me to sleep.

My eyes had just closed when I heard a whining sound. It sounded like a dog, maybe a wolf. Could they have already found me? Had the wolves traveled this far? I froze and listened for any movement. Staring out from my blind of sticks to the fire, I wished now I had built a stronger shelter. Reeds snapped across from me as I made out the faint outline of a large animal staring back at me. My heart began pounding. Was this one of Duran's wolves? A bear? A cougar? Its eyes reflected off the fire. The site was alarming to say the least. It moved slowly, bobbing its head up and down trying to get a better look at me. When it moved, I could tell it wasn't a cougar and wasn't gnarly enough to be one of Duran's wolves. It looked like a wolf, but its eyes were a light-blue silver color, which made the pupils appear in an odd but striking way. Its fur was shades of brown, and it had white legs and a white muzzle. It was far too elegant to be a wolf. My hand went to Colbryn's knife, and the other reached for the longest stick I could find. His piercing eyes watched me curiously on point before relaxing and sitting down. He didn't seem to threaten me in any way, so I relaxed just a bit. Was he going to sit out there until I went to sleep and then pounce on me? I didn't have enough strength to keep traveling if I didn't sleep, and I knew I wouldn't be able to with the creature staring me down all night. I decided if there were going to be a fight, I'd rather get it over with, so I decided to confront it.

"Hey," I spoke out loud, my voice shaky.

"Hey, you!" It didn't move.

"Hey, you with the creepy eyes!" Its ears perked up, and it grumbled a bit. Apparently, I had irritated it with the comment. I was on to something. If I pissed it off enough, it might strike, and I could have the safety of the shelter over me and the knife ready to stab it. I just needed to get it to attack. I tried to growl at it hoping to sound like I was ready to challenge.

"Grrrrr, rrrr ... ruff ... ruff!" Oh, geez, what was I thinking? I don't know how to speak wolf. The creature crawled a couple of feet closer and lowered its head. I could see now it was definitely not a wolf and did not seem threatened by my menacing growl.

"You wanna fight? Huh? I have my dog-killing knife right here. It's big, bigger than you, so you just go on and see if you can get to me. Grrrrrrr …" I threatened it with the meanest voice I had. I even terrified myself a little bit, but it didn't move. It just laid his head down on his paws and closed its eyes. This was a smart dog. He was playing tricks with me, and he was going to wait it out.

"You sly little turkey. You're going to wait until I fall asleep and get me in the back aren't you? Well, I have news for you. I have a nasty, gnarly, tough, scarred up back, so before you do, you should think twice about that. Oh, and don't forget about the dog-killing knife I have. It's right here, and I'll cut you … dead … really dead!"

Despite the threatening tone, my words didn't seem to bother the creature.

"Well if you don't kill me, then it will be nice to have the company." I said this more softly, hoping that maybe he just wanted a warm place to sleep. Could I be that lucky?

I lay down too afraid to close my eyes. I needed some rest, but the large dog didn't seem to be in any hurry to leave or to attack me. I was stuck in a waiting game, so this was going to be a long night. The flames from the fire reflected off the stripes of the dog. He looked so gentle and soft but not to be fooled with. I knew he had a mouth of ivory teeth. I wondered how far away Duran's wolves were. Would my companion of the darkness help distract them if they reached me in the night? I stayed awake until the moon had passed over three quarters of the sky, but that's the last time I remember checking. Sometime after that, I must have fallen asleep. Luckily, the morning came, and I was still in one piece, no large dog to be seen. The sweet yellow bird that had been my traveling partner was again greeting the day with such glory and racket that the whole forest could hear her singing her heart out. On a rotten stump not too far from me was the black crow as well. He sat motionless as though carved from wood and watching my every move. I welcomed their company and wondered if they would continue to follow me.

Another day passed, and my stomach was empty. I was going to need to find something soon, or I would be forced to turn on my feathered friends and have roasted crow for dinner. The morning dew dripped off the ferns as I walked through the forest. My moccasins were wet again, but the rising sun warmed the chill of soaked buckskin. The forest was alive with movement, squirrels, birds, and bugs. All of nature moved around me. Another day and I was so thankful to be alive and free to enjoy it. I had been so caught up in my life as the Chief's daughter, and my only worry had been finding a Brave to marry. I had changed a lot from those days. Looking back, I hardly knew the old me. I felt bigger now, stronger. I had once relied on my parents for everything, and somewhere through the Hell I had been forced into, I discovered that I could and did have the power to rely on myself. I had lived up to that promise I made. I had freed myself. I had left a piece of my heart behind in that screaming mountain, a piece that was never mine to begin with, but also a piece that I was strangely glad to leave behind.

I looked up, and the crow was threading in and out of branches and diving toward a thicket of blackberries. Luck was with me. The blackberry bushes looked to be a gift from the Spirits. Their sweet, juicy texture was delicious. I had forgotten how wonderful wild blackberries had been to eat right off the bush. My hands were stained by the time I had eaten all I could hold. Both birds pecked at the berries. They, like the wild dog, had seemed unusually friendly towards me. I threw a berry at the crow. He flapped and launched his big body out of the way and returned to the bush with a loud caw directed straight at me. I couldn't help but laugh at him. Had I been apart from nature so long in the mountain that wild creatures now seemed like friends? I thought about naming them. The little yellow bird would be Shosong which meant song of the sun, and the crow practically screeched his name every time he squawked. "Cawttwa!" I squawked back laughing. Why were they still with me, I wondered? Full and tired, I continued. We headed with the rising sun at my back, and I hoped this direction would take me to more familiar territory.

I could see through the tree line that patches of meadow were opening up onto the prairie. It would be easier traveling through the grass, but I felt a sense of added safety within the cover of the rough forest and continued traveling within its branches. The sun was overhead now but added little comfort. There was a heavy weight in my stomach, and the berries were not agreeing with me. Why had I stuffed myself so much? This was not pleasant traveling. My stomach reacted badly to the berries, and I became sicker with each step. I spent a few minutes hovering over a hollow trunk. I didn't want to waste energy vomiting, but I felt better afterward. Hopefully that trunk wasn't some little creature's home; otherwise, it was in for a surprise. Afterward, I lay in the tall grass, weak and thirsty. I couldn't see the yellow bird or the crow. I wondered if the big dog was anywhere near. For the first time, I felt terribly alone.

I closed my eyes. I had to hear his name — it had been trapped in my mind now for two days.

"Colbryn!"

I shut my eyes and pictured him.

I opened my eyes and wondered what he was doing right now. Was he happy that I was free? Was Pinnoteh taking care of him? With her there to take care of him and me out of the picture, I was sure their bond would grow. The same frustration I felt back at the cave came back to me, so I got up with new determination and started walking.

Up ahead, I could hear the mighty crow, and I followed. Stumbling occasionally due to my hunger, I still managed to keep up. With the sun getting low, I came across a creek bed with plenty of running water.

"How stupid of me not to have brought a water skin." I needed to start thinking like a Brave. I needed to be a better planner, a better trapper, a better warrior. These things would be essential as long as I was on my own.

Gathering dried grass and buffalo dung from the prairie, I started a fire. I figured it would make me feel better, and it did. The sun was a finger's distance to the horizon. Night was upon me, and I knew it would be another hungry night. I decided that tomorrow I would wake up and try hunting like a Brave. I knew I could. I had watched the Braves do it many times. I'd be OK even if I only caught a mouse, and at this point, I would eat anything, as long as it wasn't another blackberry. Sitting gazing into the fire and listening to my stomach grumble, I heard a distant bark. I reached for my knife when the striped dog appeared from behind a tree. I gasped startled. It could have pounced and been on top of me before I could have even reacted. Instead, it stood a fair distance away, its ears rotating right to left scanning the forest noises. He stood, questioning my reaction with his wild eyes. I didn't move. In his mouth hung a limp, lifeless rabbit. He dropped it by the fire and backed away, letting out a low whimper.

I couldn't believe my eyes. This was such unusual behavior. Was he actually giving me the rabbit? I had a hard time wrapping my brain around this; was this wild animal trying to help me? He easily could have killed me already, so I didn't think this was a trick to get me to leave the fireside. I had never heard of wild dogs acting like this, but I was very grateful.

"That has to be the nicest thing anyone has done for me in awhile." I smiled but quickly snapped my lips together wondering if flashing my teeth at him might be read as a threat.

He sat and panted while I skinned and squared the rabbit. I rambled on about my day while he sat several feet away attentively watching me roast the meat.

"Did you belong to someone once? You seem unusually friendly." He just looked and cocked his head. In a silent way, it did seem like he understood me. I wished that he could answer back. The fire sparked and popped as the rabbit roasted. I hoped that I wasn't attracting other animals with the smell of cooked meat, but at least the dog was here.

"You need a name. I think I'm going to call you Dune, after the sand dunes of Little Sorerra desert. What do you think about that name?" He lifted his head and then lowered it onto his dirty paws and snorted puffs of dust into the air.

"You love that name? Well, great, Dune it is."

The rabbit was a bit tough, but I ate it anyway and started to feel like my old self again. I tossed Dune his own half of the rabbit, which he swallowed up in one gulp. Full and tired, I put myself in the hands of the Great Spirit and went to sleep. Tonight I wouldn't worry. Perhaps I was being too trusting, but Dune did not appear to pose a threat to me. I closed my eyes and once again began feeling that weight in my stomach. The stress of the past few days was surely affecting me. I hadn't eaten a proper meal since I left the Dwells, and sleeping on the cold ground couldn't be helping either. My stomach rumbled again. After a few hours of sleep, I woke up. The rabbit wasn't sitting well with me. I sat up feeling sick. Groaning, I got to my feet and went to the creek shore. The cool water on my feet calmed my need to heave, but as soon as I stood to head back to the fire, a wave of nausea forced me to my knees. Yuck. Once I emptied my stomach, things improved. Why did this keep happening? I needed the strength, and losing another meal was going to set me back. I was already feeling weak. I needed to find a village.

Looking to the distance, I could just make out a line of purple gray that was either mountains or clouds. I decided to wait until the first light of dawn to break over the horizon and then head in that direction. The night was peaceful, and I got some much-needed sleep, though still hungry, and woke to another beautiful morning. I was sad to discover that Dune was gone and my new friends Shosong and Cawttwa were nowhere to be found.

I headed out on my own. Flat grassland made for easy walking, and an occasional stream helped keep me hydrated. By the time the sun was overhead, I could tell that the line of purple gray that I had seen during the night was definitely mountains. I continued towards them. As I walked,

I scared up some turkeys. I knew that catching one would require more energy than I had, so I sadly watched them disperse into the underbrush. In a clearing, I found some Yucca plants. The flowers, though dry, where better than nothing and didn't require an exhausting hunt. I chewed the flowers, hoping there were at least a few nutrients left in their white petals.

As the sun sank again on my third day with no real food, the weakness in my knees was beginning to affect my travel. I sluggishly stumbled from tree to tree, my mind jumping from thoughts of my mother's flatbread and wojapi pudding to roasted quail. The light now dim, I knew I needed to get some shelter, but the thought seemed too difficult. I gave in and collapsed into a ditch and was unable to move. This seemed as good a place to sleep, stay, and die; I was past the point of caring. Even Colbryn's voice couldn't encourage me to make a fire, care about food, or even get out of the ditch. I lay there motionless staring up at the stars that glared back at me. A noise came from within the trees — it was Dune. He showed up at his usual time, but even he could see that I was a lost cause and left. I closed my eyes and listened to the night sounds, not caring what could reach me or crawl over me in the night.

CHAPTER TWELVE

Ya' 'Were Yintra

"Well Put! Are you just going to stay in that old ditch all night?" I was suddenly jolted awake by a harsh demanding voice. Hovering over me stood an old woman. A dried toad swung from around her neck. Her face reminded me of cracked clay baked by the sun, and she had a voice that was equally appealing. In her hand was a torch, and by her side stood the biggest ram I had ever seen. I blinked, thinking this was just an illusion, an effect from not eating. Surely my dying brain had made her up, but then she spoke again.

"Come on, come on, dinner is waiting."

The magic word "dinner" reached my ears. Eager but slow, I tried to get up, but in my condition, getting out of the ditch took some doing. Gathering up what little strength I had left, I crawled out on all fours and raised to follow the peculiar woman. I hoped after all this effort that she was in fact going to have something to eat waiting, wherever it was she was taking me. She waddled fast through the dim evening light, and I staggered to keep up through the thicket of branches. Finally the congested clump of trees opened to a clearing where a welcoming fire was blazing.

"Sit down, sit down." I wondered why she said everything twice like that?

"Who are you?" was all I could spit out.

"I have been waiting for you for two days, two days. What took you so long? Humph?" She grunted, never looking at me when she spoke. Instead, she stabbed at the fire with a stick, causing the logs to shift and the embers to tangle and twist like little rising comets.

"You were waiting for me? You must have the wrong person. I don't even know you." What was she talking about? No one knew I was going to try to escape the mountain.

She handed me cheese and milk. That's when I noticed several other goats, smaller than the first, standing behind her and staring at me just outside the reach of the firelight.

"The Spirits told me to be watching, watching for you," she answered as she sat down.

"Spirits? The Spirits tell of greater ones than I; I'm sure you have me mistaken for someone else. I do appreciate your hospitality, though." She was old and clearly a little out of her mind. I tried to sound as polite as possible.

"Hmm, really? And yes, yes you are polite." Her words squeezed out of her lips with a scratchy gasp.

Had I said that out loud? "Well, I have been sick and had a hard time getting food on my own." I didn't feel like having to explain myself to this old woman. I just wanted to eat in peace.

"Hard time finding, finding food, or keeping it down?" She asked, questioning me in a way that seemed like she already knew the answer.

"Well, I've been sick," I admitted again between bites of my creamy cheese; it was delicious. She broke out into a low chuckle that grew with every jiggle of her layered belly.

"Sick? Put! You're not sick, not sick child . . .you're ya` `were yintra." Her eyes widened as she leaned closer to me pointing to my stomach speaking in the old language.

"Ya` `were yintra?" I peeped, choking as I spoke.

"Yeah, you know: bat in the cave, eating for two, full moon rising..." she sputtered on.

"...Yeah I know what ya` 'were yintra means." I stopped and stared at her confused. I could feel with distinct clarity the last bit of cheese as it slowly slid down my throat.

"Thought you would have figured that one out yourself," she smiled back. I just stared into the fire feeling like the air had been knocked out of me. I couldn't speak. In fact, I could hardly breath. *Breath, Natani, breath,* my mind had to remind me. Could this be true? It couldn't — that would mean that I was carrying the child of a monster, Duran's child. She finally broke the silence.

"I can see you are confused. I probably let that out of the bag too quickly. I tend to get ahead of myself a lot. My name is Pontotok. I've known that you ... well, someone, would be coming. It took longer than I envisioned, but under the circumstances I can understand."

"Known?" How could she have known, I wondered? My heart was racing with anxiety and dread from what she had told me.

"I am a Spirit reader, talker, seer, whatever; whatever you want to call it, it is of many names."

"Sort of like a Medicine Yechi?" I choked out, trying to steady my breathing. "We had a Medicine Yechi in our village, and he was wrong all the time." I could not relate this Spirit reader to anything else I had been around.

"Oh Put! Medicine Yechi? Ha, Medicine Yechi's are amateurs. Oh my child, the vastness of the things you do not know. Perhaps they will reveal themselves to you, now that the Prophecy is in rotation. All in due time." She poked the fire again.

"What? I'm not following. What Prophecy?"

"Yes, safer that way — best to ease into the dealings of those that move but cannot be seen. Something is in store but is not made clear all at once. I am just glad you are safe here with me at last. Golden Boy and I were getting antsy." She pointed to the enormous ram and smiled back at me with her discolored teeth and changed the subject before I was ready.

"I think you have already met crow and yellow bird, right?" she asked.

"Oh, Shosong and Cawttwa? They are yours?"

She shook her head. "They don't mind those names, so I can live, I can live with it."

"Is the large dog yours, too?"

"Dog? Adoetae? No, no, he is not a dog. Well, he is, but he is not mine. He's a Sibahé. I just asked him to look out for you and to keep an eye on things to see if anyone would be following. You've eluded the wolves, the bad ones at least ... for now anyway," she added.

"Sibahé?" I questioned.

"Sibahé, you know, snow-type dogs?" She twirled her finger through the air in a strange gesture.

My head was spinning so fast that I worried that I would pass out and land head first into the fire. I eased back into the grass just in case. None of what she was saying made any sense. I mean, yes, technically I could be pregnant, but surely she was just misinformed. Surely she had mistaken me with someone else. I couldn't be pregnant, and if she were right, and I was pregnant, well ... I just jumped off a mountain cliff into a freezing cold river and haven't eaten for days. The baby wouldn't have been able to withstand all that. My mind flashed back to Tetoway's voice telling me the stories of the babies, how they would be taken and never seen again.

Images of the Chief made my skin crawl and the hair on my neck stand on end. I didn't want any reminders of him or that life to follow me. The scars I had endured were bad enough. How would I live attached to something that was a direct bloodline to such evil? My eyes started welling up when I thought of the unwanted child I might be carrying. Ruins, I could be in ruins. Reading my mind, Pontotok spoke.

"It's all right now dear. We are going to take care of you. First things first, we need to get you feeling better." I turned to her, wiped the tears from my cheeks and hoped she hadn't seen them. I hated feeling weak in front of people I didn't know.

"Are you sure about the baby? It couldn't just be something I ate or drank?" I asked, trying to convince her.

"No, no dear, it's as real as I am sitting here. You need lots of rest and some good food, and you will feel so much better. I will tell you all about it once you are back on your feet." She got a blanket and covered me up like my mother used to do. She was right. This was all too much for me to take in right now. I closed my eyes and didn't wake again until I heard Cawttwa crowing the next day.

****

I rose to the new morning as bits and pieces of the previous days' memories came to mind, a parade of fragments and emotion. Pontotok was busy cooking at the fire. She looked different in the daylight — older, weaker. When I sat up, she smiled and handed me a bowl filled with goat's milk.

"Drink this, and we will see if it stays down." I did, and it tasted good. I sat in silence examining my skin to see if anything had changed, a hint perhaps that I was in fact pregnant? This was the first issue weighing heavy on my mind this morning. Luckily, everything looked the same. For now, I was still convinced I was the same old me.

"You won't find it written on your skin, my dear," Pontotok shook her head at me, which made the toad around her neck dance back and forth.

"So how much do you know about me?" I was almost afraid to hear what she was going to say.

"Most of the important things." She nodded.

"My name is Natani, and I was taken from my people by the Chosen

Ones." I felt the need to introduce myself.

"Yes, I know. Is that what they are calling themselves these days?" She turned to me, a look of disgust on her face. "They are parasites, living off other people. Put! They contribute nothing — only taking, only taking, leaving heartache, and suffering behind. Chosen People my foot! Put!" She threw a stick, and the goats bucked out of the way.

"Well, they do choose the people they take," I said to clarify, but not sure why I did.

"Yes, only the best of the village. Whenever the tribe wants to grow, it raids young girls like you. The men are only taken in the winter. How do you think that leaves the village?" She was right. She handed me a bowl of cooked wheat and honey and then sat down by me with her own portion.

Shosong flew down by my leg and started to peck.

"So, Cawttwa and Shosong — you said they were yours. How did you train them to follow me?"

"The birds are part of the Spirit world, like Golden Boy. The Spirits communicate with them and with me, and they knew where to find you." I knew the Spirits interacted with animals, but I had never had them react to me before. I sat in amazement of the little birds and expected them to begin speaking.

"But how do they get chosen over any other bird or goat?"

"All animals have a Spirit to be respected; some are just enchanted. That's the way it is." She spoke as if talking about the Spirits was an everyday occurrence.

"And the dog?"

"No, Adoetae is not part of the Spirit world." She seemed to have stopped repeating words, for which I was glad.

"Then, how did it know to follow me?" I questioned.

"Hmmm, well I told him to."

"So the Spirits told you and the birds that I was coming, and you told a dog, which isn't your pet ... and they all followed me to this place where you found me? That just sounds ridiculous," I shrugged.

"Yes, the Spirits spoke to me. They said to come here and wait for you. Much seems ridiculous until you understand the Prophecy," she grunted.

"Why? What Prophecy and what business do the Spirits have with me?" I was determined to figure out this case of mistaken identity. I was just a simple girl trying to get back to her people. I was of no interest to the Spirits no matter what Pontotok thought she knew.

"I don't know yet. They tell me as it is needed. You already know what you need to know. In fact, you already know it all; you just don't know that you know." She chuckled. "When you are feeling better, we will go back to my summer hut. Eat up, Natani, you must become stronger than you are. Chief Duran has not stopped looking for you, and I doubt he will." As she spoke, she wove her hands through the air like she was catching mosquitoes or feeling for something.

I felt a nervous pressure in my stomach. The day seemed so much more ominous knowing that that horrid monster was out there somewhere in the forest looking for me.

"Can the Spirits talk to me? Did they talk me into leaving?"

"No, they have no power that way. They simply report the events; they don't cause them to happen."

"You said you had been waiting for me for two days? It took me two days to prepare to leave, and two days from when I left to get here." How could she have gotten the word so fast?

"Could you explain just how that works because you found out about the same time I made up my mind to go."

"If I had to guess, the Spirits informed me the very moment in which you first stepped off the mountain. There is much in this world that is beyond my explanation, but that does not make it any less real, Natani. The Spirits communicate in a blink what it would take days for us to relay by travel."

"I am not a dumb girl, Pontotok. I know there are many different Spirits, but please, what Spirits are these that speak to you?" I tried to not sound doubtful of her gift, but I needed an explanation.

"Well, the main ones, the Four of Four. There are the four Spirits of the Cycle: Spring, Summer, Fall, and Winter, which are also the Spirits of Life: Birth, Growth, Fulfillment, and Death. The four Spirits of the Sky: Moon, Stars, Sun, and Weather. The four Spirits of Natural Life: Animal, Plant, Earth, and Water, and the four Balance Gods: North, East, West, and South. They all have their own separate traits, but the Four of Four are capable of sending messages and occasionally toying with energy." She finished drawing her diagram in the dust and looked up grinning.

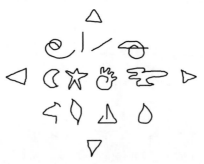

"So what, they are just always telling you things at random times?" I asked.

"Oh, no, it's not like that, not like you're thinking. It's more like being able to read the energy that they put off; it's hit or miss."

I finished eating my cheese and a hunk of bread that Pontotok had put on a plate. I felt like I had grown up oblivious to the powers around me. I remember the elders and my parents speaking of them, but I never really tried to understand or take them seriously. I had been taught strict respect of animals and the land and to work hard so we would be blessed with a healthy crop and abundant rain, but I figured that was all that really mattered.

"So where do the soul Spirits fit in, like when you die and ...?"

"...Yes, when you die, your soul Spirit rises to the Spirit lands. It is taken there by Akuwa the Spirit of Winter and Death, but sometimes, before this can happen, the soul Spirit is captured and not allowed to move on. That is what Duran is doing in the mountain."

"Collecting Spirits?"

"Yes, I've known about it for years, and it's a sad and sickening thing. I'm convinced it has to do with the Prophecy and with you."

"Me? I don't have anything to do with capturing negative Spirits."

"No child, with saving and putting an end to it somehow. Duran collects the negative Spirits, and they get trapped in the mountain. Maybe 'collect' is the wrong word; 'use' may fit better because somehow he is benefiting from them. For a long, long time, the negative forces have been building, and the time to stop its spread has been foreseen."

"Foreseen by whom?"

"There is an imbalance. The Prophecy speaks of this; it has been dormant for a very long time, but now the imbalance has begun setting everything in motion."

"Alright, but what I don't understand is why do the Spirits care about what happens to me?"

"You are a very important part of this, and that is enough for now. Take your blanket, and rest under the tree. I am going to milk the goats and clean up."

"A nap?"

"Yes, dear, the Spirit of Birth told me to tell you." Her crafty smile could not hide the humor in her voice or the mischief in her expression. I couldn't help but roll my eyes.

"I doubt that, and I doubt I'm even pregnant, but if you want me to go lying around all day instead of helping, I will sure do it," I jumped up and headed off. Pontotok left me with more questions than I had started with. I lay down under the tree with visions of Spirits zipping in and out of things. The images were hard to ignore. What had I been living with in that cave? Were they the voices I heard coming from deep below the pit? Still so many questions.

I awoke to hear Pontotok talking to a male voice. "Do not get attached to her. She carries another's heart, and do I need to remind you she is the wife of another?" She sounded irritated.

"Then why did you send me to watch over her?" the male voice almost shouted back.

"You know why, but I am telling you right now that Natani is not the answer for you."

The voices paused as I sat up to see where they were coming from.

"I think you are wrong," the male voice finally answered.

I looked again but only saw Pontotok picking herbs by herself just inside the tree line.

I fell back asleep and woke later in the afternoon feeling great. I had slept for the better part of the day, which surprised me, but the extra sleep had been beneficial. Looking around, I was by myself, so I decided to get up for a drink of water. I headed to the camp where Pontotok had boiled a pot of water and reached for a bowl when a strange man came up beside me. Startled, I jumped, threw the bowl of water, and stumbled over a log into a couple of resting goats before catching myself.

"Sorry, I'm so sorry." He smiled, chuckled softly, and tossed down two rabbits freeing his hands, to help me up. He was very attractive and had a strong build. My guess was that he was around my age or a little older.

"Hello," he said with a smile. "I am Adoetae, a friend of Pontotok."

"Adoetae? That's funny — I thought she said that was the dog's name?

He smiled. "Sib, Sibahé," he corrected me.

He paused as I tried to decipher what he was telling me. "Not just a dog, that sounds, too ... mmmm, mutt-like. We are Sibahés from the cold, and yes, I am one and the same." He smiled and held out his hand.

"What? Oh, I get it. You are just as crazy as she is — what no shrunken head or dried mouse to hang round your neck? Why does everyone have ridiculous stories? I thought I left all the crazies back in the cave." I shook his hand anyway and smiled.

"Well, you can think I'm crazy if you want, Natani, but it was great seeing you again. I will be back later. Will you tell Pontotok that Adoetae came by?" He snuffed, "I actually prefer Dune, though." He smiled, ducked into the woods, and left me with a frown frozen on my face. My knees felt weak again, so I knelt and got another bowl of water. I could hear Pontotok whistling an old melody in the woods. Eventually, she popped out carrying a cloth of berries, mushrooms, and some more herbs.

"So why didn't you tell me Adoetae was some kind of shape shifter?"

"Shape shifter?" Her voice got high-pitched, as if she were making fun of me. "Adoetae is no shape shifter." She knelt unwrapping the berries.

"Well, he was a dog — a Sibahé — a few days ago, and now he is apparently a man. How do you explain that?

"Well, if that's how you put it, then I guess you're right. He has two shapes:

a dog shape and a man shape" She laughed. "I prefer the dog shape myself. Oh, look! I guess you and I will be having rabbit tonight." She snatched up the rabbits and held them up admiringly. "I'm guessing you didn't catch these. Has Adoetae been around here?"

"Yes, and I think he is coming back, so there will be three for supper." I was amazed at how calm she was about my little discovery.

"Oh." She sounded disappointed. "I should have known."

"Known what?" I was getting tired of having to piece together Pontotok's perplexing, riddle-like way of communicating.

"Known he wouldn't stay away." She sliced through the rabbit and gutted it with ease. "Oh, a juicy one." She drifted her focus back toward the rabbits.

"So he really is able to change?" I still couldn't believe she was holding back from telling how Adoetae was able to change into an animal.

"I will let him tell you about that. You go gather up some firewood, and then go sit and be still," she answered.

"Sit and be still? I've been sleeping all day. I feel like running circles. Thanks, but I think your taking this pregnancy thing a little too seriously."

"Hmphf," was all she grunted as she continued to dress dinner.

I stood in the woods and gathered twigs and sticks for the fire. Through the trees, the fire where Pontotok stood looked so warm and safe. But everything else was falling dark, and the wind blew a coldness that reminded me of the mountain. Part of me wanted to turn around and just start walking, to leave Pontotok and head for home. I wanted my old life back. However, I knew if I left, I would be on my own, and even though Pontotok seemed a little crazy, she was knowledgeable and nice enough to provide me with food and safety. I would only stay long enough to regain my strength, and then I would return home, to what was left of my old life. I headed back with my bundle of sticks. The night sounds seemed to die off the closer I got to the fire.

"Here, I'll take that. Now, you sit and erase those thoughts." She touched my head when she spoke. I wondered which thoughts she was referring to, but I didn't ask.

"You leaving," she replied.

I couldn't help but smile. I'd been caught.

"Hey there." Adoetae was standing beside me before I had even heard anyone coming.

"Must you startle me every time I see you?" I asked, glaring.

"Sorry." He sat down across the fire. Pontotok and Adoetae were quiet, and the crackling of the flame seemed to be a large wall between us all. Pontotok threaded the rabbits on shaved birch branches and laid them across the fire to cook, the juices making strange sounds as they fell to the coals. I finally decided to break the silence and ask what I figured both of them were waiting to hear.

"Well?" I started.

"Well, what? He can't read your mind," Pontotok spurted out.

"Yeah, well, what?" Adoetae peered at me with his dark eyes.

"Well, are you going to explain to me how you do it, or do you think I'm gullible enough to believe your stories about changing into a dog?" He huffed, sat back into the grass, and twirled a dried weed between his fingers.

"Sibahé, remember?" He paused and stared at me as though he were able to look directly into my soul. "Why do you doubt me. Have I done anything to make you question my truthfulness?" he asked with a smirk.

"Hmphf, exactly. I question you because I don't know you. Where I come from you have to earn trust." I returned the same half-cocked grin.

"Fair enough, hmmmm, explain ... well, in brief, I come from the Horticans tribe. It is very old, and there are very few of us who still remain. We used to be a great tribe, a large, strong tribe, but that all changed when the amulet was found."

"Amulet?" I asked.

"Yes, my great grandfather lead a hunting party into the Absaroka Mountain range, to the place where the snow line falls off. They were hunting caribou. The legend says that on the morning before they were to leave, they killed four large caribou and were taking them back down the mountain when a bright reflection beamed out across the canyon. My grandfather tried to get other men to go with him to discover what the object was, but they were all too tired from the hunt and wanted to get back to camp. My grandfather, despite being turned by the other men, abandoned his caribou and set off alone. When he came to the spot where the reflection had been, there was nothing he could find except a deep cavernous hole. He stood upon the ledge of the mountain and watched as the clouds moved across the sky, and when the sun appeared once more, a blinding light came from deep within. My grandfather climbed into the pit, and there at the bottom lay the amulet."

"What, what was the amulet?" I couldn't stand all the waiting.

"It was a transparent rock that looked like a human skull carved out of ice." He turned to me almost shaking. I could tell he didn't speak of it often.

"A silver skull?"

"Let him tell the story. Here, have some." Pontotok handed me some meat and a bowl of milk to shut me up.

"Yes, and once my great grandfather returned to the village, all the tribe's people had heard of him abandoning the caribou and were very angry because it was winter and there was very little to eat. The Chief's son came out and was so mad that he attacked my great grandfather. He hit and killed him in front of the tribe and his son, my grandfather. As he lay dying, he took my grandfather's hand, placed it on the pouch that held the skull, and said before his last breath "protect." Many of the tribe died of illness that winter and blamed my great grandfather and family for the fact that there was not enough food. The Chief's son knew more, though. Somehow, he knew my grandfather had something, something of power, something that had been found in the mountain. He convinced others in the tribe to kill my family to pay for the lives of those who died to find and possess whatever it was that had been found. The legend has it that when they surrounded the tepee the night of the ambush, all they found were large paw prints in the snow leading to the mountains.

"The skull has given men of our family the ability to take the form of the Sibahé; it has allowed us to keep the amulet safe for many generations." He paused, and then looked back at the fire. "There, how's that for trust? Now, you know my biggest secret." Adoetae seemed sad, or perhaps just deep in thought. I got the impression something weighed on him. At this point, I wasn't sure what to say or how to act.

"So how do you think the skull got there?" It seemed to be the most appropriate question.

"There are stories of silver skulls in ancient legends brought to earth by Storm People."

"Yes, I've heard legends of the Storm People but never about the skulls. How many are there?"

"No one knows. We don't share our story with just anyone, so the legend remains just that, a legend." Adoetae poked at the fire with a stick until the tip flamed. Pontotok was asleep against a tree, the bottoms of her shoes practically worn through.

"So why did you tell me then?"

"Pontotok told me somehow my story and yours are tied together. They have been for a long time. Now that things are in motion, our paths have been united, and we are both warriors in this storm, Natani. It is still a bit too far for any of us to see it coming, but it is."

The fire was dying down, and the glow of the coals reflected a warm perfection off Adoetae's skin. I couldn't take my eyes off him. I was trying to see a hint of wild Sib in his eyes or the color of his hair.

"If you're watching to see if I will change in front of you, you'll be watching a long time, and your staring is making me nervous."

"I'm sorry, it's just that I can't believe that you are the same furry friend I named Dune." I grinned. The words coming from my mouth sounded strange to my ears.

Pontotok interrupted our gaze. "You might as well tell her the other stories as well."

"I thought you were asleep?" I asked, but all she did was grunt and close her eyes again.

"Don't you think that's enough storytelling for one night?" Adoetae stood, stretching his calf muscles.

"Tell me which other stories?" I insisted.

"It has to do with the necklace you wear." Pontotok spoke with her eyes still closed. My hand went up to it, and I tried to explain.

"It's just a simple piece of jewelry. I don't know why everyone is so interested in it."

Pontotok's head popped up. "Who? Who has talked about it?"

"My sister-wives asked me about it one night."

"What did they say?" She asked curiously squinting.

"One of them had seen it before but couldn't remember more than that."

Pontotok was silently contemplating. She then turned toward the fire and asked, "What did your mother tell you about the medallion?"

"Just that it was her mother's and her grandmother's before that. No one remembers where it came from, it has always been passed to the first daughter." It was then that I felt a small jolt in my stomach that took my breath away. As I reached to my side, Adoetae gave me a strange look.

"Would you two please tell me what is going on?"

"One question first. Did Chief Duran see that?" Pontotok asked.

"Yes." That brought back that awful memory of my first night there. I had all but tucked it away in the deepest caverns of my mind.

"How did he treat you?" she asked, almost whispering.

"Well, it wasn't pleasant. I'd rather not go into detail. I'm not saying anything else until you two tell me what is going on." Everyone sat silently thinking and trying to piece everything together. The fire had died down so much that the warm golden hues of the flames had changed to a deep, red and were now glowing mounds of sparkles. I threw another log on top, and it sent embers dancing wildly into the sky. The movement broke their deep thoughts, and Pontotok looked at me with large eyes.

Stars were twinkling in the night sky, and I felt as far away and alone as they were. It was as if I were looking down at earth, watching from a cold, distant place, and waiting for someone to finally let me be a part of what was going on.

Adoetae started: "We are both a part of the Prophecy."

Pontotok turned toward me. "Your role is unclear. The true meaning has been lost in the ages, which is why we are all waiting on signs from the Spirits. But I think you are either the eagle or the dove."

Adoetae started pacing behind Pontotok.

"But I have no magical power. I just have an old piece of jewelry. If I were part of this, my mother would have told me. I would know somehow. Don't you see how this doesn't make any sense? Pontotok can read Spirit energy, Adoetae," I faced him. "Apparently you can turn into another animal, but I'm just me and I'm barely good at that. This is all very interesting, but you have the wrong girl."

"You don't understand just how old this is. No one could predict when the unbalance would happen and set the Prophecy in motion. The Prophecy and legends have been lost, and little is spoken, if at all," Pontotok explained. "Natani, how do you think I knew where to find you?"

"That could be pure coincidence!" I had heard all I wanted to hear. I had been caught up in the stories allowing myself to believe–I had wanted to believe there was something special about me. I had to face reality, the sober grounds of truth. I was carrying an unwanted child whom I would have to explain to my family when I got home. I had lost my best friends and didn't even know where I was. I had heard enough, so I got up to leave.

"Natani, I know about Colbryn." Pontotok whispered.

I stopped. Had I mentioned anything to her? Perhaps I had said something in my sleep. There was absolutely nothing I could say. Emotions were running out of control in my mind. The stress of not knowing what was happening to me, the events that had lead me here, and now the images of Colbryn and of my unborn child all collided within my soul, and I felt as though shards of unanswered questions were piercing me from the inside. Tears rushed to my eyes.

"I can't talk about this anymore tonight." I turned, stumbled into the darkness, and tried to find some kind of comfort in solitude. When I thought I was well out of sight, I collapsed on the damp ground, and tears welled up in me from depths I didn't even know existed. It felt good to cry. I didn't know which of the recent happenings I was crying about, or if it was all of them. Perhaps I was indeed pregnant, and the stresses of that were affecting me? I tried taking long, deep breaths, and let the cool night air dry my tears.

"Hey, can I join you?" Adoetae appeared from the woods out of nowhere. I quickly tried drying my eyes, but I couldn't hide the frustration on my face.

"Sure, if you want," I spoke, still trying to compose myself. I hated looking weak.

"She's a little abrupt with her words sometimes. You can't blame her. She's just, hmmm, a little more calloused than most." He smiled.

"I know, I'm learning quickly, but it's just a lot to take in. It's kind of overwhelming." I hated trying to defend my actions. "I'm not mad at her, I just don't believe what she is saying."

"So this Colbryn ..." Adoetae paused after saying his name.

I wondered if he was waiting to see how I would react before continuing. I knew the question would be a hard one.

"... You loved him?" I had never discussed Colbryn with anyone before, and no one knew my feelings for him. Admitting my feelings out loud now seemed to be a forbidden confession.

"I did." The hesitation and regret in my voice was obvious.

"Did he not share your feelings?"

"No, he felt the same, but I was already chosen as the Chief's wife. He was forced to pick someone else." Adoetae did not respond but just let the wind carry my words away as I sat wishing I could reach out and bring them back.

"You are strong then."

"How do you figure that?" I asked surprised. He waited a moment before responding. I could tell he was drawing from something in his mind.

"You cannot adjust the direction of the wind, but you can adjust your direction in relation to it. That way, it's not blowing in your face and making each step harder. You chose to turn and go, and I admire you." His words blanketed me with much-needed comfort. It was the first time I had been affirmed in the decision I had made. I finally faced him with my tear-chapped face and smiled. The wind was fittingly blowing at my back.

He laid back and faced the stars that had started speckling the sky. I pulled my knees up to my chest and sat facing out into the vastness as well. Instead of desolate silence, a power blew through the air strong enough to carry a soft melody from somewhere far, far away.

I felt Adoetae's finger press against my back in silence and trace the thick raised scar that showed on my unconcealed shoulder blade. I flinched away from his touch. I wasn't sure how to read it. I had been self-conscious about my scars, and they were an everyday reminder of my wounded past. I was already feeling vulnerable, and now I felt too exposed. Instead of making me feel shameful, Adoetae's words had made me feel liberated, but right now, I needed to be alone. I got up, headed back to the fire, and left Adoetae lying in the grass.

When Pontotok saw me, she stopped and headed away from the light of the fire. She met me halfway and threw her arms around my body in a way I had not expected from such a coarse woman.

"Can you ever forgive me for pushing, for pushing you too far? I didn't want to bring up Colbryn's name, but I didn't know any other way to convince you. I am very sorry." She released me from her tight grip.

"It's OK, really. It's clear to me that there is a lot I don't know, and you were only trying to help me see the clear picture, which is what I have wanted all along. I think the emotions just got the best of me. It was a lot to take in." I tried to smile but felt a little embarrassed about my outburst. "I'd just like to go to bed." I headed for a warm spot near the fire and lay with my back to Pontotok. I was not going to speak or hear about Spirits or Prophecies anymore tonight.

****

Adoetae came strolling into camp early the next morning. I was still lying down when I noticed him sitting on a stump and helping himself to a bowl of milk.

"Sorry about last night. I should have kept my hands to myself. It's just sort of in my nature to be protective, and I hate to see, well, pain."

"External pain only hurts for a little while," I responded, sitting up.

"Sure, it does," he shrugged, making a strange gesture with his eyebrows as if he didn't agree.

"Internal pain hurts a lot more." I was sure of this.

"You mean being heartbroken? Are you referring to Colbryn?"

"Just in general." I paused, but he didn't say anything. I wasn't sure why he felt the need to mention Colbryn again. Adoetae seemed caught between two thoughts.

"I understand. I've been there. Memories are still very powerful. I just didn't want you to ...."

Pontotok interrupted with a boisterous "Breakfast is ready!" She came walking up with berries and a few eggs, though I didn't know how she'd found either.

"Natani, do you feel strong enough to start heading home? We could head out today."

Home? The word seemed foreign to me now. Regardless, I knew that was not my home that Pontotok was talking about. We were headed for her home, another unknown place, but this time at least I was free — sort of. I would go with them until I was convinced I had no part in this.

"Yes, Pontotok, I do feel strong enough to travel." I was glad to be going, to be getting farther from the mountain and from the evil eyes of those who were looking for me.

I didn't have anything, so I helped Pontotok. Adoetae was gathering the goats, so I sat and watched. He moved with a strong animal-like grace, and I wondered if the goats could sense the Sib in him. He was a truly beautiful man, and I was surprised that I hadn't fully noticed until now. His hair was long but tied back with a coarse leather band. His eyes were wide set and flanked by chiseled cheekbones. They where lighter than most. Instead of the dark brown, they were a silver-blue that was haunting in certain light. I allowed myself to entertain these thoughts — harmless right? I wondered if he had a wife; was she as beautiful as he was? The sun was rising quickly, and I heard Pontotok shouting. So I got up to see if she needed help.

"Oh, Put! You give me that back!" Pontotok was whirling around with a stick pointed at the treetops. "You sneaky trickster. I saw you take it; now give it back!" This time she pointed with her crooked finger and shook it violently. I couldn't help but laugh. Sitting high up in the safety of the tree was Cawttwa the crow, with a silver bangle looped around his beak.

"He doesn't seem to mind well, does he?" I laughed approaching them.

"Oh, he is a sly one. You have to watch him or else he'll take everything you own. I have half a mind to catch him and tie him up, he makes me so mad." She shook her head with her hands on her hips in defeat.

"Let me try," I smiled.

"Give it a shot — he won't listen." She shooed her hand at me and turned away.

"Cawttwa," I sang his name. "Cawttwa, my dear corvid, you taunt her so; won't you drop the bangle that you have in tow?" I made up a pleasant melody to sing the words to him, but he just stared at me with black, motionless eyes. I looked back at Pontotok with a half-cocked grin. "I tried." Her eyebrows lifted, so I turned back in time to see Cawttwa glide over me and drop the shiny, silver bangle into my open hand.

"Well, look at that." Pontotok was as amazed as I was. I turned, feeling pretty proud of myself, and held up the bracelet.

"Well, it's yours now. He obviously didn't want me to have it." She was still shaking her head.

"Thanks, Cawttwa!" I called out to him while admiring the bangle on my arm. He was a few paces away watching from another treetop. I couldn't help but chuckle a little to myself. Maybe it was coincidence, but it was nice thinking Cawttwa saw me as a friend.

Pontotok rolled her large pack onto her back with a wheezy grunt and cinched it down with leather straps. I wondered how such an old woman could wrestle a tepee pack onto her back and still manage to stand.

"Humphf!" She grunted. I smiled and grabbed a bundle of her remaining items, and we set off, heading away from the little camp that had become familiar. We were now, once again, venturing into unknown territory — well, unknown to me. Pontotok and Adoetae seemed to know where we were headed, so I just followed in anticipation. It was nice having them to travel with; it would have been a challenge to travel, hunt, cook, and protect myself with the condition I was in, even though for the time being, I looked the same as I always had. I had not factored a pregnancy into my escape plan. I was grateful for all that Adoetae and Pontotok had done.

"You're welcome," I heard Pontotok say from several feet behind me. Was she hearing my thoughts again?

"So do you hear all my thoughts or just some of them?" I asked, needing to know if it would be possible to censor what she was hearing.

"I don't hear any of them actually. It is just a feeling. There is energy in emotion, and it radiates from people just like Spirits. It can be passed, felt, captured, released, and so on. The closer you are to me, the stronger I can feel it; the farther off you are, the more it dies off. I just felt what you were thinking — you are appreciative of us." Adoetae looked at me but didn't say anything, only flashing a quick half-smile from the corner of his mouth before looking away.

"Great, I will have to watch that. Can you feel Adoetae's energy, or is this something that only plagues me?" I asked, trying to pry into her special little power.

"Unfortunately, yes," she grumped.

"Well why don't you ever speak back to him like you do to me?" It was only fair to be let in on his thoughts as she was exposing mine.

Pontotok laughed. "You're better off not knowing. That would be a lot of energy to talk about, and I'd never get anything done." She laughed again. Adoetae had disappeared when I turned back around.

The weather was enjoyable — warm but not too hot. We walked for most of the day under the cover of trees, stopping briefly at the streams to drink and cool my now swelling feet. The goats moaned and bayed at each other, traveled at inconsistent speeds, and stopped to chew branches every few paces. Pontotok would yelp at them and hooves would bear down into the dirt sending them galloping forward to the next tree. The forest was quiet and peaceful; its energy was positive. I tried my hand at absorbing it and vacated my mind of thought so it could enter. The forest was the perfect place to think — only I didn't want to think. I had exhausted all thought as it was, and for now, I just cast my fate with those of my traveling partners. Later, as the sun began tucking itself in the trees and casting dark, striped shadows across us all, Adoetae reappeared carrying berries to eat and a turkey for dinner. The goats wagged their tails and surrounded the plump kill.

"Let's stop here for the night. We will build a fire, eat, sleep and be ready, be ready again by morning." Pontotok was repeating things again; it was strange, but I was getting use to it. I hoped that she couldn't hear my energy.

Adoetae prepared the bird as I watched.

"So did you catch that as a ... Sib or as a man?" I asked, breaking the awkward silence that had been between us the entire day.

"Just because I can, doesn't mean I take advantage of the ability. I am still very much a man, and yes I trapped the turkey as a man." He smiled, but I saw it more in his eyes than anything. Did he find my question a little insulting? I was getting a strange vibe from him and couldn't figure out the reason.

"Well, I didn't mean anything by it. I think it's pretty amazing what you can do." I responded, hoping to soften his mood.

"Yep, becoming a furry dog is pretty amazing." He replied almost sarcastically.

"No, I meant finding berries, trapping and killing a turkey, and still managing to keep up with us without us even knowing you are around — that is what's pretty amazing." I winked, finally breaking through the tension; he smiled, then laughed, throwing himself off balance, and having to steady himself.

I stood and walked away, proud that I had fixed our little awkwardness with my humor.

"He likes you, you know," I heard Pontotok say as I came to help her with the goats.

"Adoetae?"

"Yes, he was very concerned about you last night." She never looked up from milking the goat. I sat down next to her not sure what to say. After a long pause, I felt it appropriate to ask about the conversation I had overheard them having.

"I heard you two talking the other day and wanted to ask you what that was all about?"

"Oh, you heard that did you?" she paused. " I told him not to get too attached to you because I knew your heart already belonged to someone else."

"Oh, that's what you meant?" My heart did belong to Colbryn, but I didn't have his, not free and clear anyway.

"I haven't told Adoetae anything else about you other than you are Duran's wife." When she said that, my stomach clenched. I would need to lose that title. "I just don't want to see him hurt anymore. His wife died giving birth, and his son is all he has. He took it very hard, and he even left the child and his tribe for a time to seek solitude and answers from the Spirits. It's been a difficult journey for him, but I believe he is on the downward side of that mountain." She pulled her cloak tight around her shoulders, so only her round head popped out of the top.

"So you two are good friends then?"

"The Spirits cross our paths often, and now since we both got wind of the Prophecy, we have been searching for the others in the Calling. It is a good partnership …" — she thought for a moment — "… or friendship," she concluded.

"You were right to discourage him," I replied.

"I am afraid you are the one who has to discourage him," she grunted.

"I will do my best," I told her.

I decided to be helpful and start building the night's fire so that we could cook the turkey. I went to the forest to collect wood. Much of the forest was dead, so I quickly had a large pile. Few of the trees still held onto their dried leaves as they shook and rattled up in the treetops. Once again I was alone. I sat on a fallen tree trunk and rubbed my hand over my stomach. Had this small bulge always been there? Perhaps all the goat cheese and milk was taking its toll on my figure? I was still refusing to truly believe I was pregnant. I wondered what Colbryn would think if he knew I could be pregnant with Duran's child? I wondered if he would be mad? Perhaps

Colbryn was too busy healing and falling in love with Pinnoteh to even be bothered by thoughts of me. There was no way for me to know. One thing I was sure of and would never second-guess was the decision to leave the mountain and Colbryn behind. I was glad and knew I had that strength inside of me. I was braver than I had thought; perhaps there were things about myself I had yet to discover. I headed back with a pile of sticks jutting out from under my arms. Adoetae had already started a small fire. It was smoldering and wafting out puffs of smoke as he fanned it trying to get it to grow.

"Oh, good, just in time." He reached for the kindling I had found.

"Glad to be of help." Was that the best response I could come up with.

I sat watching as Adoetae got the cook fire blazing. Pontotok's words echoed in my mind: "You are the one who needs to discourage him." It was nice knowing that Adoetae liked me even though he had not actually confessed this to me. So far his actions had not crossed any lines, and I hoped that they wouldn't because I knew it would be hard for me to confront him and I didn't want things to become awkward between us. Even though I had only known him for a few days, he had already become a support to me, and that was something I didn't want to jeopardize.

Pontotok came and joined us at the fire. I wondered if she had read the conflicting energy in my mind. I quickly focused my thoughts on the turkey roasting on the spit turning over the fire. Turkeys were not common where my tribe was from, so I looked forward to the meal with great anticipation. Adoetae finished flipping the meat and finally broke the silence.

"So, Natani, what was it like being in the Dwells? I have only heard fragments of stories but never a firsthand account." Adoetae asked between chugs from his water skin.

"Well ..." I sat thinking for a moment. My life in the Dwells seemed so distant now, like another life altogether. I think that was my mind's way of trying to move on. I didn't even know where to start.

I told them about the screaming mountain face, the bats, the mushrooms, and the pit. I enjoyed telling them about the Sun Hall, though I didn't want them to think it was as nice as my description suggested. Luckily the turkey was ready to eat, so I took the distraction to compose my mind. I knew they would want to know about Duran, but I didn't feel comfortable saying his name out loud. Adoetae handed Pontotok and me a generous portion of meat. I ate it with goat cheese and some creamy maize paste. It was delicious. I wanted to just close my eyes and enjoy my meal in quiet, but Adoetae was quick to resume the discussion.

"And Duran?" he asked. When it came to Duran, I wasn't sure what to say. My time with him had been masked in denial. I was already denying that the events with him had happened, that time and the pain it caused me would forever be part of my soul. I hated having to remember the events of those nights, and I was also hesitant to say much about Colbryn. He, too, was something I needed to resolve in my mind and recall at will. So I was brief and vague and quickly changed the topic of conversation to my escape.

"It was perhaps the single most terrifying event of my life thus far." Remembering how I felt riding down the river on the tree trunk made me smile with accomplishment. "Thanks to Cawttwa's warnings, I am actually here today." Looking back, I'm amazed that I survived. Cawttwa sat frozen, hunkered down in the treetops above us, a ball of black within the night. I wondered if he knew just how important he had been to me?

"The mushrooms — were they all you had to eat in the Dwells?" Adoetae asked.

"No, they are only for the men. They make them strong, stronger than most. The men are addicted to them." I responded.

Adoetae leaned forward towards me. "Stronger? How much stronger exactly?"

"Oh, I don't know; it's hard to say, maybe twice as strong as you?" I smiled wondering if he'd take offence to my comparison.

"So the addiction is what binds them to the cave and to Duran?" Adoetae asked, squinting.

"Yes, probably. It is interesting, very interesting," Pontotok said, scratching her burly eyebrow with a fingernail.

"Didn't the Spirits tell you about them?" I asked, wondering why this was new news to them.

"No, they can't see anything that happens within the mountain. It wasn't until you hit the water that they knew you were coming. He, too, is protected, but only by the mountain." Pontotok tapped her foot in nervous thought.

"So what would happen if someone left the cave?" Adoetae asked.

"He would send out the wolves to kill the escapee. He sent three wolves after me for not returning on time when I left to get supplies; it was one of the two times I was ever allowed to leave the cave. But luckily I was with someone that knew how to kill them." I didn't want to go into detail about my time with Colbryn in the woods. I was trying to keep him out of my mind as much as possible. I glanced over at Pontotok, and she gave me a knowing nod.

I could tell that Adoetae and Pontotok were digesting all this information in their minds because they sat deep in thought. I finally had an opportunity to finish my meal, so I welcomed the silence. I felt better after sharing with them what I had been through. I felt proud of what I had done, but telling the story out loud also made it more real. I knew remnant memories of the cave would be on my mind all night.

The remainder of the meat was hung above the fire to dehydrate for the journey tomorrow. I helped Pontotok clean before being the first to settle into my blanket. I knew that traveling tomorrow would be long and exhausting, and a belly full of warm meat beckoned me to sleep.

CHAPTER THIRTEEN

Summons

The night did not start as I had hoped; bad dreams interrupted the restful sleep I had anticipated. I dreamt I was back in the pit, in its consuming darkness. Hands were touching me, coming from every direction, holding me down against the cold rock floor. It felt like I was drowning. I could still breathe but was struggling under the weight. I could hear Duran's unmistakably evil laugh getting louder and coming closer, and the pressure on my chest was crushing me until finally I screamed and sat up gasping for air.

"Natani, Natani, it's OK — it was just a bad dream. You're safe. Take a deep breath." Adoetae's words were so comforting to my ears. I was soaking wet from sweat, tears, or both. I cupped my face in my hands, and Adoetae put his strong arms around me in comfort.

"I am sorry." I tried to sound casual about it, but I was extremely embarrassed.

"It's alright, just a bad dream, huh?" He held my face between his hands to make sure I was OK. Pontotok, lying beside me, never flinched, and I was glad I had not woken her as well.

"Just a bad dream," I convinced him. Had he been beside me the whole time?

"Just try and get some more rest. We should be home tomorrow if the weather holds out. You will have a more comfortable place to sleep then. For now just dream of ..." — he thought for a moment — "... cuddly puppies," he winked at me.

"Alright," I whispered, lying back down and closing my eyes.

It wasn't long before I drifted off to sleep again, but instead of puppies, I dreamt I was flying back up the river to the mountain. The rope was still hanging from the branch as I sailed through the Sun Hall, down the corridors, and into the wives' chamber. There were Tetoway, Eba, and Abanea sitting around the fire that I had enjoyed so much. Their faces were serious, almost void of any expression. I wanted to make them laugh but knew I couldn't. Something drew me into Duran's chamber. I didn't want to go, but I had to. Standing at the doorway, I noticed that the walls of his chamber were moving. Black and gray shapes clinged and crawled all over it. They were arms and legs of tribes people, and the vision sickened me. He was sitting on a thrown made of people, their faces haggard and tired, their backs breaking under his weight, their eyes vacant. The Chief held my broken bowl in his hands. When he looked up, he could see me standing there, so I bolted. I flew away as fast as I could. Heading down to the village, I thought I would see Colbryn for a moment, one last time before I left. He was sleeping soundly, alone in his tepee. He was so beautiful, just as he had always been. I crawled under his blanket and was lying on top of him and stroking his hair. The corners of his mouth turned up, so I kissed them. To my surprise, he said my name. Everything seemed so real. I could taste, smell, and touch him. We caressed each other like we had never done. Our emotions had been building for so long, and in this moment, we were finally free to be with each other. His breathing became deep and hard, and I could feel his heart pounding in his chest. He rolled over on top of me. The weight was so real, pressing my back into the bear fur mat. He whispered my name, and I could have died happily right there. I had missed him more than I had even known. "Colbryn," I moaned.

The flap to the tent opened, and in walked Pinnoteh holding a bowl of food.

"Colbryn!" she yelled, dropping the bowl. Nuts and gooseberries scattered, rolled, and settled into every crevice of the rawhide blanket like anchors trapping me beneath it. I ripped free and vanished up to the top of the tepee and listened to Pontotok and Adoetae yelling at each other. I flew down the dark caverns, shot out of the screaming mouth, and felt higher than I had ever felt before. As I flew away, I had the urge to return to the mountain and be with Colbryn again. Circling around the mountain, I saw the river, trees, and plains zipping below me. I looked down and saw Pontotok and Adoetae calling for me to come down, but why would I want to be down there when the sunshine up here was so warm and felt so good? I smiled and shook my head. I wanted to go back to the mountain again.

Blackness.

"Nothing like a good whop to get her back," I heard Pontotok grunt angrily. I awoke in an instant with the side of my face stinging. Cawttwa was flapping hysterically beside my face, and Golden Boy was kicking up dirt as he stamped the earth beside me.

"Owww! What did you do that for? What is it?" I asked as Adoetae and Pontotok hovered over me with surprised expressions on their faces. Pontotok spoke first as she shook me.

"Natani, where have you been? Tell the truth — it's very important!"

What was I guilty of? It was just a dream after all.

"I was dreaming of ... the mountain. Why do you look so upset — did I say something?"

She looked at Golden Boy, and he pawed the ground and swang his huge, thick horns from side to side. She then looked to Adoetae.

"Is this bad? What happened to her?" The tone of Adoetae's voice scared me.

"I think he tried summoning her." Her voice was frantic and harsh. "Did he see you?"

"It was just a dream. Let's not make too much of it, please." I pleaded.

"Did he see you? Duran, did he see you in the dream?" she barked again.

"I don't think so ... well, maybe?" I lay there feeling too good to be upset. I could tell Pontotok and Adoetae were irritated that I wasn't taking the matter as seriously as they were.

"I was afraid of this. I should have warned you. It will just make things that much harder, a lot harder. Put!" She stood and wheeled around, causing the dusty floor to follow her cape into whirls of dust and debris.

"It was only a dream," I tried to explain.

She looked at me. "How real did the dream seem to you?"

I smiled. "It was very real," I admitted guiltily.

"That wasn't just a dream, Natani." She tapped the wrinkle between her eyes in a nervous thought.

"I'll say." I smiled back still rubbing my face.

"Natani, that was Duran summoning you back to him!" she screeched. " He needs to think you are dead, but you can't be dead if you go trotting back to him when he calls! If he saw you, you no longer have that working to your advantage. If he summoned you and you saw him in the dream, then he knows you are alive!" I could tell she was furious with me.

"I am sorry. I didn't know."

"I know you didn't know, but this has put us all in danger. If he thinks that you're alive, he will continue looking for you." She stormed back to her bed, covered up, and ignored me. I looked helplessly at Adoetae, and he gave me a sympathetic look. I lay there thinking on what I had done. What on earth had I done.

We got an early start the next morning. Pontotok woke me up before the sun had even started to rise, and I could tell she was trying to suppress some anxiety and was eager to get moving. The fire was gone, not a trace of the embers remained, and no trace of us ever being there was left behind. Adoetae walked close to me, perhaps afraid my Spirit would mysteriously go off to the Dwells. The good feelings I had when I was with Colbryn had all left my mind. How in the world was I supposed to control my dreams anyway? I was pouting and mumbling to myself when Adoetae spoke.

"I know how you feel. I loved someone like that once," he said without looking at me. "Being willing to give up anything just to see them one more time."

"No, you don't." I felt my brows pinch in defense. "I never got to hold hands, plan our lives, or even share a thought, let alone see him smile in the morning. I never got any of that. I only got to dream, and now I can't even do that. I'm not willing to give up everything. I didn't know what was happening. It was like I was under a spell. I thought it was a dream!" Knowing what had happened to his wife. I didn't want to sound harsh, but it came across that way.

"I am sorry, I was just trying..." He went silent, and I wished I hadn't gotten so upset with him. "I see how it eats at you. I just wanted to let you know that I will be breaking off and heading to my village. I have duties to check on, and my son is there. I am not far away, so if you need anything, just send the old crow — and I don't mean the one in front of us." He shrugged his eyebrows in Pontotok's direction.

"I heard that!" Pontotok yelled back. I smiled, and it helped me out of my foul mood.

"Leaving? But I thought we were all traveling together?" Adoetae's news caught me off guard. I didn't want him to go, especially after I just yelled at him. He had been a great support to me, and I suddenly felt a sadness come over me.

"Yes, for now anyway. You're near Pontotok's camp, and you two will be fine there." Even though the sun was up, Adoetae's eyes haunted me. I feared I wouldn't ever see them again. I reached out to his arm before I realized what I had done. Perhaps it was my subconscious way of trying to get him to stay.

"Thank you for saving me and sharing your food with me. I never would have made it without you." His arm was warm and familiar, and I could feel his heartbeat through his muscle. I realized the lingering touch was inappropriate and let go awkwardly.

"You are stronger than you give yourself credit for, Natani. It's not like I will never see you again. You can save the thank-yous." He then walked up to Pontotok. "Hey, old crow."

She smirked back at him.

"Sorry, I just couldn't pass that one up. Send for me if you need anything," he patted her with a mocking grin.

"Sure, sure, I will wait to hear what the Spirits say. We probably have some waiting time. Never fast are these matters, never fast." She swung her hand through the air and shooed him away.

"I would like to be with you when you talk about the Prophecy if that's all right." he said.

"Yes, yes, let us get settled a little; you can bring us a rabbit or venison." I heard them laugh, and he headed south. I was surprised how I felt when I last saw his dark skin disappear into the trees. Was Pontotok feeling my loss? I quickly thought about other things.

I could tell we must be getting close because the goats ran ahead baying. Golden Boy grunted, and it reminded me of Pontotok. I knew I needed to talk to her to see if I could somehow right the wrong. I hated that I had disappointed her, but I also blamed her for not warning me about the dreams.

"I am sorry about last night, Pontotok." I paused. "I just didn't realize."

"I wasn't mad at you. I was mad at myself for not seeing that this might happen." She answered. "I have a belt for you; it's made from Golden Boy's wool. It will tie your Spirit to you, so the next time you want to go off dreaming, your Spirit will come back to you before it gets too far. I didn't think to bring it when I left, but I will give it to you once we get to the wigwam."

"Why does he care so much about getting me back? Can't he just get another wife?"

"I am sure he wants to show the tribe that there are consequences to escaping. He is not one to show mercy. You know that, right?"

"So I've made him look bad, and now he wants to make a lesson out of me for everyone else?" I guess I already had figured as much, but I wanted Pontotok's opinion.

"Most likely, probably something gruesome."

"Death?"

"Death," she agreed, slowly bobbing her head.

The thought of Duran making an example out of me was terrifying. I wondered if he would feed me to the wolves and make everyone watch as they tore apart my flesh. The sight of my dead corpse would be burned into their memories.

"So what can I do?" I felt a little desperate, like a fugitive on the run.

"We carry on as planned. We can elude him, stay a few steps ahead of him, and hope he gets tired and gives up." I was glad Pontotok wasn't abandoning me to deal with the Chief on my own. I would need her help, and I would need to be more aware, more conscious of the things going on around me. I needed to take advantage of her knowledge, and I needed to learn as much as I could from her.

"So what happens to my body when my Spirit flies off? Is it just an empty husk?" I asked.

"Your will is gone, and you just exist. That is about the simplest way I can explain it. Your Spirit has the ability to go off to places impossible for your body to go to, but when your Spirit is off, your body becomes vulnerable." I looked away, pondering the thought of a Spiritless body.

"So if I had stayed dreaming at the mountain, what could have happened?

"Those that you visit in your Spirit form have the ability to sense you. If your Spirit energy was drawn to Duran, or anyone else for that matter, they can see you as your Spirit form. If Chief Duran saw you, then he will know you are alive. That is why this is dangerous."

"I don't think so, but I did see him."

We walked the rest of the way in silence. I was deep in thought and wondering how long would be long enough for the Chief to stop looking for me. Days, moons, seasons? Would I be running from him for the rest of my life? The thought exhausted me.

When it was just about dark, we came upon a dwelling. It was nothing like the tepees used in my tribe, so I was intrigued.

The side of an embankment had been dug out exposing a rock overhang. The massive stone provided a strong shelter from above. The walls were hewed logs, sticks and rawhide, much like the wigwams in the permanent camp. It had a stone and mud chimney up one side, and on the other was a sheltered pin. The structure was bigger than a tepee but not as tall. Some of the goats called to us from the pen, happy to be home. Cawttwa and Shosong also welcomed us, and I was glad to see them again.

"Aw, Put! Out. Get out!" Pontotok started shouting. A large raccoon and three babies, strolled out unhappy to be evicted. "I leave for a few days, and the critters try to take over!" She paused and looked around. "Well, this is home. I had Adoetae make a bed for you before we left. I think you'll find it satisfactory." She lit a fire in the fireplace, which gave the space a comfortable, homey glow. The stick walls woven in a web-like pattern were impressive, and I wondered if Pontotok had made this shelter herself. Baskets were stored under the cots, and colorful rugs helped cheer the room. Strings of herbs and skins draped and hung from the rafters along with two birdcages. Interestingly enough, there were no doors.

"This is very nice," I told her, happy to have a comfortable place to sleep once again.

"Serves me well," she replied humbly.

We ate some cheese. I sat staring blankly at the fire trying to calm the uneasy thoughts I had been tossing around the whole day. Was Pontotok ready to help me with such a burden? Had the Spirits warned her of the difficulty and danger that would be put on her for helping me? I didn't know if she knew what she was getting into, and I knew that with the days to come, I would become a huge burden to her. That worried me.

"Well, this should be a good bed." She jarred her hand against the wooden post to test its strength.

I watched as she slowly folded herself into a kneeling position on the floor, grunting with every bend. She reached underneath the bed and pulled out a woven straw basket. Inside was a beautifully braided belt the color of Golden Boy. "Put this around you, so I can sleep without having to worry that you will go floating off again in your sleep." She tossed me the belt; it was beautiful, long, and silky with a simple silver clasp. It smelled like a strange sage, but I didn't care. If this was what was going to keep my Spirit from being summoned by the Chief, then I would gladly wear it. I wrapped it around my waist but it was too big, so I looped it over my head and wore it like a sash across my body. I didn't want it working itself off in the middle of the night.

"And keep an eye on it if you take it off. Cawttwa has always had a thing for that buckle. He would snatch it straight off of you if he got the chance." She glared up at him as he perched in the corner among the hoard of trinkets he had collected over the years. Pontotok reversed her moves until she was standing again and then went about her business.

"So now what? Is there a plan?" I asked, wondering what my new role was in this picture.

"We wait, you rest, and the plan comes when it comes," she smirked without looking at me.

Time slowed down greatly at Pontotok's home. It seemed I had hurried to get here just to wait for something. Every time I asked her what our plan was, her response was always the same: "Rest, the more you rest, the stronger you get. The more time passes, the better chance we have that the Chief will give up looking." The plan made sense. I just wasn't convinced that she actually believed it. I could see in her eyes that she doubted Chief Duran would just give up looking for me. I was getting bigger, and that undoubtedly meant I was slower as well. I wouldn't be able to run, and for that reason alone, I was happy to just relax.

Many days passed without a sign of Adoetae, and eventually I stopped looking for him. I was surprised that with all of the effort to find me and get me here, he would just disappear from my life. My pregnancy was becoming more noticeable every day. I had accepted the truth that I was actually going to have a baby, but it wasn't until I could actually feel it moving around inside of me that I actually came to terms with it. I tried not to think about the fact that the baby was Duran's. That thought would just make me mad, and there wasn't anything I could do to change it. What I could change was my focus. I just didn't have the energy for negative thoughts right now, so I tried my best to keep them out of my mind.

I was glad that I had fallen into a routine. I would gather firewood in the mornings, sit watching the goats graze in the evenings, and tend to various chores for Pontotok when needed. Days became comfortable again, as if I were living a new life. Although in the back of my mind, I knew there was much more boiling to the surface that I would need to be prepared for. Everything would change once the baby was born. It was as if I lived at the base of a snowy mountain, and at any moment an avalanche could decide to fall.

CHAPTER FOURTEEN

Magic

One evening I sat brushing Golden Boy's hair. He had finally warmed up to me, and until recently I had avoided him and his menacing head of horns. Beneath his silky coat of golden fur was a stout, muscular body, which I knew should not be underestimated. I was cautious with every stroke. Looking into his eyes, I could tell a spark of majesty resided there. He was in fact, as Pontotok put it, enchanted. He nudged me with his snout and started pawing the ground and shaking his head. This was a reaction I had only seen from him one other time, but being that we were alone, it made me nervous. He stood stretching his head up high and reading scents in the air. He charged away from me and stopped looking back, so I got up and followed until he stopped again at the corner of the goat's pen, where I saw three men talking to Pontotok.

"Get back," I called to Golden Boy while gasping and throwing my body against the pen. I froze in fright, but Golden Boy beat the earth even harder and stepped out from the corner. Pontotok waved us forward and introduced me as her niece Green Leaf.

"We hear you can consult with the Spirits. Is that true?" one man asked.

"Well, not entirely," Pontotok responded.

"Our friend and family member has been missing for a moon now, and we want to know what has happened. We heard you could help us," another man spoke. The third man remained silent and edgy. I wondered if Pontotok was called often on matters of this type? Would she be able to help them?

"Yes, I can help. Come, let us eat first."

They stayed with us for dinner and afterwards Pontotok instructed them to build a huge fire, larger than normal. I sighed, knowing I would have to replace the stack tomorrow, but I was intrigued by the ritual that I was going to get to see. Pontotok turned to the men and asked if they had brought payment. They went to their horses and brought back bags of cracked maize, wheat, and dried fish. I was thrilled. They handed them to me, and I quickly went to store them. I didn't want to miss any of the ritual.

"Do you have the item belonging to him?" Pontotok held out her old, dry hand in anticipation. One man pulled a leather moccasin from a pouch and handed it to her. By now it had turned dark, and the fire provided the only light. She held her arms in the air, his moccasin in one hand, and called his name.

 Her voice became unfamiliar and slightly eerie to me. It seemed to travel, cutting through the air, sharp and crisp. Chanting to the Spirits, she walked around the fire with spastic jerking movements, first facing east, then north, and ending with west. With each step, she asked the Spirits of direction and balance to help find the missing man.

Pulling something from a sachet attached to her waist, she threw it into the fire, and smoke curled into the sky — first an amber hue and then a suspended white fog. It was cloudy at first, but then I could see something. I could see a man standing on a cliff and looking out into the vastness.

I recognized a Bristlecone Pine and a Subalpine Fir, so I assumed that it was somewhere up in the mountains. It was amazing to see. The images were so clear. The other men were bewildered by the image. One man was sweating profusely, streams running down his face and glistening in the firelight. He held his hands clasped tight and wrung them in a tight ball as his foot shook constantly in a nervous jitter. Suddenly, I recognized someone as another man entered the fog image.

It was the sweaty man himself. He walked up to the man and put his arms out as if to embrace him but instead pushed him off the ledge. I saw him fall. It was only a moment, but I saw the look of a friend's betrayal in the falling man's face as it disappeared into the canyon. Everyone but Pontotok gasped in horror at what we had just witnessed. The image suddenly seemed to turn to sand and fall in a sheet of dust into the fire. The other two men jumped to their feet in a rage. Now weeping, the guilty man just sat dazed and stared at the fire. I didn't know what they would do, but I prepared myself to see them kill him. I sat motionless and wondering if I should go inside.

"I had to," the man finally spoke and looked in desperation through sobs at the other men.

"What? You had to? You killed my sister's husband and then took her as your wife!" he shouted at the stricken man. His face was red, and his eyes were bulging. Pontotok stood watching and threw me a glance of concern, so I rose and took a step back from the fire.

"I had to. Didn't you see I wanted her so badly?" It was all he could muster between wheezes. They yanked him up and dragged him to their horses and then rode off into the night.

I could hear the gallops slowly become smothered out as Pontotok began chanting to the Spirits, thanking them for their help, and reassuring the dead man that his death would be avenged. Finally she stopped. I had been staring in amazement. The whole act of calling the Spirits was beyond anything I had seen before. I realized now just how powerful Pontotok was.

"Natani, what are you staring at?" she demanded.

"That was unbelievable. How did you do that?" I sat beside the fire. The remnants of the sand were still glowing white like permanent snow within the embers.

"It is what I do — I thought I told you that."

"Yes, but I have never seen it done before. You are definitely more than a Yechi. It — you — that was amazing!" The words fumbled from my lips.

She sat down.

"Well, thanks, but no, I am not a Yechi!" She rocked back on her stump and rested her legs.

"Where did you learn to do that?"

"From a very old woman when I was very young." She was making the strange motions in the air again as she had done earlier.

"Can you show me my family? How they are doing? Or does the person need to be dead?"

She thought about it for what seemed like a long time before answering. "I don't know if you really want to do that."

"Are you serious? Why wouldn't I want to see?"

"You must have two things," she paused. "You must have something that belonged to that person." Then she stopped and felt the air again.

"Well, my necklace, it was my mother's. What is the second thing I must have?" Could this really happen, could I get to see my family, I wondered.

"You must be prepared for what you might see. Sometimes the truth is not always what we want revealed." What could she mean? Why would I not want to see my family, know that they are safe, and see where they are so I could find them?

"You have your mother's necklace, so it can be done. Just think about my warning, Natani. Think about it."

"Oh, I would love that. I would want to know exactly what has happened!" I knew there was no need to think about it.

"Very well, but not tonight. I am out of energy; it takes a lot of strength." Pontotok felt the air again and then snapped her fingers as they cracked towards the ground. The dirt around the fire rippled up and was sucked into the center of the fire as the flames disappeared and left only a thin trail of smoke to rise from the center. She then turned and headed down toward the wigwam. I didn't say anything. The night had amazed me. I only hoped that at some point Pontotok would teach me her abilities.

Consulting the Spirits about my family was all I could think about the next day as I watched the goats graze in the tall grass. Even Golden Boy could feel my excitement and nudged me every so often to disrupt my deep thought. That evening, I knew I had to ask again. I had to see if Pontotok would summon the Spirits for my family. I wanted it so badly, but I was afraid she would have another excuse not to do it tonight. When we got back to camp that evening, I decided to try asking again.

"So how are you feeling? Do you think we could summon the Spirits tonight?"

"If you have thought about it and really want me to." Without hesitation I started stacking wood for a big fire.

"Natani, what are you doing?" She took the large log out of my arms.

"I'm building a fire, a big one. Don't you needed a big fire?"

"Put! No, that's just for the paying customer."

"Oh, well, do I need to pay you? I don't really have much, but I could come up with something."

"Don't be silly, child. Just sit. So you have really thought about this? You are prepared for what you might see?" she asked again in a serious voice.

"You keep saying that, as though I will see something bad. Do you know something I don't?" This was just a precaution, right? She tells that to everyone as a warning, doesn't she, I thought.

"I've seen it happen more times than not. I just want you to be prepared for anything. You told me the last time you saw your family was the day you were taken. It was a raid, and you saw smoke. I've seen what Duran's men can do, the destruction, the death." Her words scared me. In the back of my mind, I always knew something bad could have happened to my family, but until now I had dismissed it. Knowing the kindness Colbryn had treated me with, I couldn't imagine him hurting the people I cared for. Would I let the possibility of seeing something bad keep me from knowing the truth? If something had happened, then what had been done was done, and I could not change it now. I still wanted to know the truth.

"So are you prepared?" Pontotok asked me again as she searched my eyes for clarity.

"Yes." I was pretty sure I was ready. "I know Colbryn. He would never have allowed the raid to hurt my family. I loved him, and he loved me. He had watched me for many moons. I don't think he would have let anything bad happen." Did I believe the words I was saying? Colbryn was a monster that first day, but he wouldn't do that, not kill. He wouldn't do that to me, right? I had to decide.

"OK, hand me the necklace, and tell me the names of your family." My hands shook as I removed the pendant. Flashbacks of the smoke streams rising from my village appeared in my mind. The shrills, the screams of the other girls, it all played over again in my mind.

Pontotok chanted and jerked around like she had done before. She called to the four directions and then threw something into the fire. Smoke curled up as before, and I watched without a blink as an image came into view.

Oh, let it be a pleasant sight where my mother is cooking for my father and brother. Let me see tepees in the background. Let it be happy, I thought. A familiar sight appeared. It was my village, and it was the day I was taken. There I was. I saw myself being carried away with the others. There was fire everywhere. I could barely distinguish the fog from the actual flames of the fire. A screaming woman came running out engulfed in flames. My face went cold as I realized it was my mother. My father tried to attack but a spear struck him in the chest, and he fell to her side. Then there was my little brother. He was screaming and trying to put the fire out on my mother. They struggled until he was struck silent from behind … no one moved. There, among it all, in the last image was Colbryn, as he finished setting fire to my village.

I realized at some point that I had stopped breathing, and I could no longer feel my heart beating in my chest. My blood slowed to a stop, my muscles hardened, and my mind recoiled into an absent cavern inside my head. The shock of what I had witnessed paralyzed my entire body. Did I just imagine what I saw, or had that really happened? Was my family really … all dead?

"No!" I screamed. "Tell me this is not what happened!" I looked to Pontotok for reassurance, but she just stared at the fire with the same look of horror I had on my face. She jumped up and started chanting again. I still couldn't move.

I could feel the tears running down my face, but I couldn't move my arms. What was happening to me? I wanted to stand, I wanted to run, to seek revenge, to hunt them down, to make them pay, but there was nothing in me. Instead, I slowly got up and walked into the hut. Finding my bed, I collapsed. It was all I could do. I did not cry. I could not feel anything. It was as though the light had just gone out.

Chapter Fifteen
Waking Up

"She has been like that for two days, two days! She won't eat, drink, or talk. She just lies there. I am afraid for the baby." Pontotok's voice was frantic, but it did not affect me. I could hear her, but I did not respond.

"Baby! What baby?" a familiar voice spat out.

"Oh Put, Adoetae! I told you that she is pregnant, that she just wasn't showing the last time you were around. Maybe you forgot?"

"No, you never told me. I think I would have remembered something like that. Let me guess, it's Colbryn's?"

"No, you know whose child she carries." He gave a low growl, and I could hear footsteps shuffling to one side of the room and back again.

"Tell me what happened?" I heard their voices, but I did not respond–I couldn't and I didn't care to.

"Her family ..." the voice hesitated. It sounded like Pontotok's. "... they died the day she was taken, all of them. It was done by those parasitic Bear Eaters. She saw it all. She asked that I show her where her family was. She wanted to call upon the Spirits, and I agreed. I didn't want to because something wrong was in the air. I should have listened to my gut. She persisted, and the fog reveal was horrible, horrible."

"When do you think she will come out of it?" Adoetae asked.

"I don't know."

"I could take her. The pack and I are going to hunt and spend the night by the river. She could get fresh air and relax to help clear her mind. Besides, getting out of this stuffy place would do her good. " Someone's hand was pressing down on my head.

"Humph! Stuffy you think? It's worth a try I guess."

The heaviness of a thick cloud seemed to surround me. Where was I? The sounds all came and went with spastic, vibrating melodies. Where was I? Who was I? Adoetae ... I recognized the voice. I had missed him ... I didn't feel the strong arms picking me up or feel the sun on my face. I did not realize I was being laid on the ground. I knew none of this, but somehow it all happened because when I did wake, I was no longer in Pontotok's hut. I was someplace else. I lay with my eyes still closed, but I was awake enough to hear the movement and sounds around me.

"nnnnn, nn yeerryak"

Something was at my face, its sound a strange sporadic yelp. Despite my curiosity, I remained in a stupor. It was not enough to bring me to full consciousness.

"mmmnnnnn"

It came again now from my feet. Whatever it was, it was surrounding me, or growing. I could feel something breathe on my face, and the breath was small and direct, yet warm. It seemed to bob up and down in hesitation. I assumed it might think I was free for the taking, a nice warm dinner perhaps. I didn't care. Suddenly I felt a thud against my face as a ball of silky fuzz nuzzled into my neck, burying a cold, slimy wet point right up under my chin.

I awoke.

There were five of them, four still staring in various poses waiting to pounce or run, and one was biting at my moccasins. Where was I? A rush of questioning whines started up as the balls of fur closed in on me.

"Welcome to the pack," a voice called to me. It was human, and I recognized it.

"Adoetae?" I asked, my voice hoarse and dry.

"Yes, I'm here. Don't be alarmed; you are in a safe place." His voice was even more welcoming than I had remembered. "Pontotok summoned me, and I was alarmed at the condition you were in. She was very afraid for you as well. We both decided you needed a break, a place, well ... where positive energy flows constantly. This is the place." He looked to see if I comprehended his words. "How are you feeling?"

"I don't know quite yet. I feel like I've been in a cloud, and everything is hazy."

"You have been out for several days." He brushed my matted hair back from my face, his warm hands comforting. I was still confused and trying to piece the information together. I knew I had more questions, but my brain wasn't forming thoughts correctly.

"Dogs?" It took me awhile to make sense of everything. Were these Sibahés? "Sorry, it's taking me a minute to remember things." *Remember*, something in my head told me not to remember, to just go back to sleep and shut it all out again.

"So are you up for being den mother? I figured since you're going to be a mother soon it would be good practice." Adoetae smiled and slid a pillow behind my back for support.

"Oh, that's right" Looking down and remembering my bulging stomach, I was surprised that that fact had slipped my mind.

"I know. Pontotok told me, though now I can see for myself."

"Unfortunately, yes." I took a deep breath and rubbed my temples.

"Can you walk? I have dinner about ready." He held my hand as I stood with my bones aching.

"So is this where you live?" I always wondered where Adoetae's tribe called home.

"Yeah, now it is." He smiled, his familiar haunting eyes calming my soul. I assumed his comment referred to the traveling that Pontotok had told me about, but I wasn't ready to ask him about that yet.

"The silver, is the silver skull here?" I asked, remembering the story.

"Shhhh," he paused. "We don't speak of the amulet." He was whispering and eyeing the Sibs.

"Why?" I whispered back.

"It remains a secret and only a legend for the young until they are old enough to understand. We are sworn and bound to its safety by blood, and for that reason it is just not spoken of. You understand, right?" His voice was nervous sounding, and I hated that I hadn't known the rule before speaking.

"So you don't have to be close to it to change?" I was hoping he would show me the skull, but I didn't hold my breath.

"No, I tried it once. The power reaches as far as about a four-day walk. The closer to the amulet we are, the easier it is for us to change. At this range, it is even easier to live as a Sib than as a human. It is all part of us being able to keep it safe. As Sibahés, we can escape to the mountains to climates much colder than what humans can survive in."

"So your son ... is he one of these?" I eyed them all seeing if I could tell.

"So Pontotok told you I had a son?" he questioned.

"Yes," I smiled not sure if I was supposed to know or if he would be offended that Pontotok had told me about his past. He looked out in silence, and I worried that he felt betrayed.

"You must be a man to make the change. At fourteen to fifteen summers, around the point when the voice lowers, they must deal with two changes, their human change as well as their tribal change. I refer to them as pups because they are recently changed, but in their human form, they are men. Cree is yet a babe."

My heart ached for Cree knowing he no longer had a mother. It also ached for Adoetae, it was obvious that he used his time helping others to forget his loss.

"So where is Cree?" I asked.

"My mother cares for him when I am away." His response was quick and disconnected, and he quickly changed the subject.

"Pito!" he shouted towards the dogs, and one of them came bounding towards us. He was beautiful. I could tell he was one of the largest and had the same haunting silver-blue eyes.

"This is Pito," he smiled. Pito stopped and stared at me with his ears at full attention. "Pito, this is Natani." He knelt down in a submissive position, crawled towards me, and nudged his nose up under my hand. A bark echoed from the distance, and he instantly bolted away.

"He can't talk back ... that must be nice" I laughed.

"Yeah, but it's hard to get through to them sometimes," he shrugged.

The evening light was casting long shadows from the surrounding trees over the meadow where the young Sibs jumped and played with each other. I watched with fascination as they tripped and knocked each other down. They were testing and experimenting with their new bodies, and seeing such innocence and purity within this beautiful place almost caused me to forget the evil that I had grown to know. Adoetae sat by my side, and a large deer was roasting on a spit above a fire. It was really pleasant being here — wherever here was.

"Can you give me a hand?" Adoetae asked. The fire popped and crackled.

He put down an oilskin, and I helped him lay the cooked venison on it. That got the attention of the other five sets of hungry eyes that sat in a row, wagged their tails and waited for permission to eat. "Too hot! Go get a drink, and by the time you get back, it should be cool enough." They took off in a dash racing into the ever-growing darkness.

It was interesting seeing Adoetae in this parental role. I wanted to ask him how caring for Cree had been since his wife died. But the question was too heavy, and I thought the information might come up later.

He cut the back strap for me, diced it into bite-size pieces, and then handed it to me in a wooden bowl. I held it and tried to decide if I could eat it or not. My stomach had been without food for days now, yet the smell of it wasn't appetizing. Adoetae took a large bite of meat, and then started carving up the carcass. I was still holding mine when the first of the pack arrived. Waiting and drooling with anticipation, they sat in a row the same as before. "Alright," he motioned to them as they dug in, each pulling off its portion to enjoy alone. I knew I should try to eat to get some energy back, so I took a bite. It tasted pretty good.

"You need to eat. Pontotok said you haven't eaten in days. Here …" Adoetae handed me more venison.

"Oh, no, I can't. Thank you, though. I can't eat another bite. I think my stomach shrank. Don't worry, I will get it back to normal," I laughed as I handed him my bowl back.

"Well, nothing goes to waste, so just toss it."

"Toss it? But that would be wasting."

"Ha, not here it isn't," he laughed.

I chucked a hunk of meat over my shoulder, and three of the Sibs darted to see who could swallow it first. The remaining ones perked up to see if the game was going to be repeated. I gave another piece a toss and it was snatched out of the air before it even hit the ground. The game lasted until the pieces were all gone.

"You've got village check, and then clean up before you come back. We need to show extra manners tonight." Adoetae spoke the orders and they seemed to understand every word and took off once more into the darkness.

"Come on, I want to fill the water skins and don't want to leave you here by yourself." He reached down and helped me up. "You look good pregnant — a little skinny, but good." I appreciated the compliment.

"What, no torch?" I asked, stumbling into the darkness.

"Oh, sorry, I forget, we see perfectly well in the dark, so I don't think about it ... here." He took my hand. "I won't lead you into anything, I promise." I followed his lead down to the spring and washed up. He filled a water skin, and we headed back, once again joining hands. He held onto my hand long past the point of a clear view of the fire.

"Um, thanks." I tapped him on the back of the hand. "Oh, sure." He finally reluctantly released my hand. When we reached the fire, he rolled out a blanket for me. Strangely, it was several feet away from the fire.

"Am I spending the night?" This concerned me. I knew that pregnancy and sleeping on the ground, without adequate buckskins, didn't mix well.

"Not afraid, are you?"

"Um, yeah, of being in pain in the morning. No offense, but that just does not look comfortable, and it seems a little far from the fire. Are you trying to freeze me, too?" I tried my best to sound neither sarcastic nor whiny.

"Don't worry, I have your best interests at heart." he smiled.

What? I thought. Gazing out into the evening sky, I felt as comfortable as I possibly could given the situation. Adoetae was out gathering more wood, and I sat staring at the fire. *Fire* ... until now I had not remembered, but in that moment, it all registered as clear as day. The images came back.

It was like I was there again, only seeing it now for the second time. I knew what to expect. The visions, as crisp as they had been in the smoke reveal, played now in slow motion across my mind until the last image of Colbryn turned to a sheet of sand, fell, and disappeared into darkness. I came to a sad and startling realization, one that weighed at the pit of my heart. My family was dead, and I was truly alone. I was the last of my family, maybe even the last of my tribe to even exist outside of the Dwells. I sat quiet. I didn't know how to feel other than empty. I had been betrayed by the man I thought I loved, that I thought loved me. It was more than I could wrap my head around. Either directly or indirectly, Colbryn had killed my family. I had been deceived by the love I had felt for him. He was the first person whom I had ever felt that way about, and now, knowing it hadn't been deceived made me ponder: Had I ever really loved at all? He had convinced me that he loved me, and I was so naive that I believed him. I should have known. How stupid of me! There was a vast hole within me, and the love I had felt for him had already turned to a more ominous feeling ... hate.

I wished I had just let him die from the bear attack. It had all been a lie, a trick. For once I was glad that the baby I was carrying wasn't Colbryn's. Duran was a horrible evil man, but at least he didn't directly slaughter my family. And for that Colbryn would ...

"Hey there." It was Adoetae.

"Hey."

"You seem deep in thought. Are you OK?" He sat beside me and stared out at the valley. "I won't push. If you want to be alone, I understand." He rolled up onto his knees as if to leave.

"No, stay. I was deep in thought. I was just remembering ... everything," I admitted.

"Pontotok told me what happened to your family, and I am so sorry, Natani." His voice was compassionate, and I appreciated his genuine concern. "I know it's not much and won't make you feel any better, but I know what you are going through. It hurts, and it's OK to let it hurt. It will pass. It might take many seasons, but it will get better. Their Spirits are all about you and always have been since that day. They were with you in the cave, they were with you when you escaped, and they are with you now. You will never lose them, and you will never be alone — not the way you feel now. You have a baby to think about now, Natani. Just focus on that." He was right about the Spirits being with me. His words touched me, and I felt better, but focusing on the baby did not make matters easier for me.

"The baby …" I paused, not knowing how to express my feelings about the baby without sounding cold.

"The baby?" he asked, seeing the distress in my face.

My resentment worked its way up my throat. I could feel the anger building up inside of me. "This baby is Chief Duran's; I can't just focus on loving it like you say because I don't. I don't love it. I don't even care about it. I don't want to be reminded daily of that man or that place."

Despite the way I felt, I still hoped the baby couldn't hear me. How horrible it would be to not be wanted by your mother. My words were harsh, and I knew that, but I didn't choose this. It just happened to me. I knew it would be difficult, but I hoped that Adoetae would understand. His eyes, however, weren't telling me anything.

"It is more of you than it is of Duran." He spoke softly and looked out into the night. His words hurt. "It is helpless and will need you."

I still saw the baby as a parasite. I knew that Adoetae was going to judge me, and I wondered if I would ever be able to convince him. I felt the need to try.

"But the part that is Duran will always be Duran, and I will have to look at it every day and see the same eyes staring back at me that did those horrible things to my family and me." I seemed to soften him, but mostly I was convincing myself. The pups came pouncing and bounding back, and I was glad for their interruption.

Adoetae wiped away my tears, which had finally welled up enough to overflow from my eyes.

"Time for sleep; we will have an early day tomorrow." He got up and walked a few steps away, where he lay down in the grass. I stretched out on the only blanket and felt guilty for taking it from him. I hated going to sleep feeling the way I did. Our conversation weighed heavy in my mind as I stared up into the stars.

A familiar breathing sound grew in strength from behind me and instantly put a smile on my face.

The Sibs came hesitantly at first, but then I could feel them snuggling into every bend of my body. I realized then why Adoetae had placed me so far from the fire. I wasn't going to need any extra warmth tonight.

"Not too close, guys. She might want to turn over, or breath," he chuck-led.

I fell asleep easily, but it was not a restful sleep. Images of my mother and father tore at me, as well as visions of my brother and the forgotten babies. My chest was heaving, and sweat rolled off my forehead. I couldn't catch my breath. Gasping for air, I felt Adoetae's arms wrap around me and his voice suddenly at my ear.

"Natani, you're dreaming again. It's only a bad dream; you are safe." The look of terror still on my face, I lay down with him and struggled to catch my breath. He comforted me until I fell back asleep with the pups sur-rounding us.

The next morning was the first time I had woken up with a man's arms around me. It was comforting and nice. Through barely opened eyes, I could tell it was just getting light. The kicking in my stomach made my eyes flutter open. Adoetae was smiling back at me.

"Somebody wants you to get up." He touched my stomach, which made me instantly self-conscious.

"You felt that, huh?" I shifted my stomach away from him. He nodded and whispered back in a groggy voice.

"I had almost forgotten how nice this was." He unwrapped his arms and got up.

"Time to get up. I am walking Natani home, and then I'm going to the river. I will be back after that." Despite the wildness in their eyes, the young seemed to understand everything he said as they untangled their long gangly legs from ours, rolled out, stretched and yawned at each other.

We walked most of the way in silence, and I was afraid to ask him what he was thinking.

"I had a really good time. Thank you for everything." I started. "Now I know where to go if I need a soft place to lay my head or if Pontotok's snoring gets any more out of control." I smiled.

"Anytime."

"So what is next?" I asked.

"With what exactly?"

"With the Prophecy, with Duran, with everything. I mean, it's clear to me that something needs to be done, that he needs to be stopped, however that might be. I want to do whatever I can." I knew I couldn't do much, not with this billowing body, but I couldn't just sit back and allow more families like mine to be slaughtered. And I couldn't imagine other girls being raped or more unwanted babies filling that evil mountain.

"I will come to Pontotok's in a few days, and we can discuss everything. I'm glad you are accepting your role now. I thought it would take more to convince you."

"Well, I'm still not sure that I am part of the Prophecy, but that doesn't matter. I have my family's honor to avenge. I should have died with my family. I'm the reason they were killed. I am on borrowed time anyway, so I plan on using it." I took a deep breath. I finally understood what was going to be needed of someone — what was going to be needed of me.

CHAPTER SIXTEEN
Prophecy

When we arrived, Pontotok was making cheese, a welcoming and familiar sight. She stood and hugged me.

"I am sorry, child. I had no idea. If I had only known, only known, I could have braced you." I held up my hands and stopped her apology once again.

"I know, but I needed to find out. I've been living in my own oblivious world for too long, so thank you." Adoetae backed away without a word and headed back to the pack I assumed. Pontotok touched my cheek.

"Put, child! Are you sure you are alright?" she asked.

"Amazingly, I feel pretty good. Plus, I had an interesting night with six men." She raised her eyebrows. I smiled without giving her any more information and went to take the herd to pasture. I wanted to reflect.

As the goats grazed, I realized there was a lot more to think about than I originally thought. Most important, for the moment, was what I was going to do about the baby. One thing was certain: I simply didn't want a daily reminder of that mountain or what had happened at the hands of that monster. I also knew I would never hand the baby over to the mountain, no matter how much I didn't want it, I did not have the evil in me that it would require to do such a horrible thing. I decided that tonight over dinner I would ask Pontotok what she thought.

I couldn't get a grasp on the hole of betrayal left in my heart from Colbryn. There had been so many feelings for him that now were cold ashes scattering in the wind. I wondered if I would ever have the opportunity to confront him, to ask him how he could be so much like Duran, whom we both hated. It was liberating in a way, knowing now what I knew. I had planned to go back to my village after the baby was born, but now what would I do? I had no family. It had bothered me why my father did not come for me, and now I knew why. I also knew he would have if he could, and knowing this took the strain off my heart. It was finally put to rest. I wondered how many others had died in that raid? How many innocent people died every time they went fishing? It made me sick to think about it.

A new sense of determination had been born in me. "If there is anything I can do to destroy that unnatural beast, I will do it, so help me." I spoke out to the Spirits, or the wind, or whoever was listening. Golden Boy bleated out a call in the distance, and I wondered if he knew what I was feeling. A warm breeze blew my hair and kissed my cheek. I closed my eyes and imagined my family surrounding me with their love and support. The baby kicked and brought me back to reality. I put my hand on my stomach.

"Poor little unwanted thing, what is to become of you?" I whispered out loud, my words being carried away in the night air.

That night I told Pontotok some of the things I had thought about in the field.

"So I have done a lot of thinking and ..." pausing to take a breath, "... I do not want this child; it would be best to give it back to Duran perhaps in exchange for my freedom?"

"Exchange! Put! Put! Chief Duran does not want that baby any more than you. Do you know what he does with his children, with all the babies born into the mountain? No, no you don't. They are taken and never allowed to leave those damp caverns or see the light of day. They are collected in the deepest depths of the mountain. They are hidden down there. Their hair never grows, their eyes never fully develop, their skin becomes translucent, and the only language they learn is their own — a combination of moans.

They are Duran's forgotten horrors, a population of abandoned babies. Would you really want that for something that was once growing inside of you, your blood?"

The ghostly images of the babies and children of the mountain haunted me with shame.

"The moans …" I spoke to myself, remembering the four days I had spent in the pit.

"What?"

"I remember hearing moans, an unrecognizable language that would resonate up from below me. I thought it was the mountain talking to me or that I was losing my mind and hearing things, but it must have been the children calling out." I sat thinking for a moment. "I think I might be sick." I had no idea that this had been going on below me. I thought I had been living in Hell, but all the while, I had been far better off than those poor souls. Taking a little baby to that place was beyond what I would be able to do, but that didn't change my mind about keeping it.

"Do you know of a good couple who would raise it?" She looked at me in surprise. I wasn't sure really how to ask a question like this or how she would respond.

"That baby is half you. Are you so ready to give away that half as well?" I had already had this conversation with Adoetae and had hoped that Pontotok would be more understanding.

"I wouldn't be able to look at it without seeing a monster. It needs a mother to love it, and I just can't." I felt ashamed of my words, but they were true and I couldn't ignore that.

"If that's the way you feel, I will see what can be done." Her eyes did not agree with me, but I did not care.

"There is something else I have decided I want to do." I stared at Pontotok with determined eyes so she would see the seriousness.

"What is that, child? I've been sensing something, so you might as well tell me before I figure it out."

"I want to stop him." I stated.

"Who?" She poked at the fire.

"Chief Duran," I stated confidently. "Someone has to, and it might as well be me."

"Oh, well, that makes sense now. I knew it had to be something big like that; the air has been awfully thick tonight because of you." I was surprised at how calm she was. Wasn't she going to tell me that it was a ridiculous idea? That I was too weak to stand up to a monster like Duran?

"Well, what do you think about that? You don't seem too concerned?"

"Concerned? It is just another thread of the weave twisting itself into the timeline; the Prophecy is in motion. We don't know the outcome, but you are here for a reason. I am here for a reason, and you feel the way you feel for a reason. It's all within reason." She motioned through the air, and I wondered what her "reasons" riddle really meant.

"That's it? You don't think it's a crazy idea, and you're not going to stop me?" I was surprised. I had expected something more from her.

"Crazy idea — no, it is exactly what I would expect the Dove to say. Dangerous, yes. I have been sensing something in the wind. There was an unusual downdraft at dawn. Something rode in on it and has been lingering around here." She felt the air with wide scooping motions. "I assumed it was just an unclear message from the Spirits, but I can see now it must have had something to do with this news. There are changes ahead, many changes. He is strong. Many work to help him as you know, but I think with the powers at work, the time is coming to stand up against the mountain." Pontotok sat speaking through the flames of the cook fire, her rough face catching every reflection in the creases and folds of her skin. I was glad she was with me on this. "I had not said anything of the Prophecy to you before because I didn't want it to play with your mind. I wanted you to make your own decision, but now I think it is time you know more."

"Prophecy? Well, you can say it has something to do with the Prophecy, but for me it has a more personal connection." I threw small twigs into the fire and watched them burn.

"We will need to call upon all the Spirits and ask for their assistance. There is no guarantee that they will help, but it is the only way."

"Why? Why wouldn't they help us?"

"They might not even know of the Prophecy. They exist at rest in total balance and wake only when the balance is thrown off. We will need to convince them that the disturbance is coming and that their help can prevent it. If allowed, we will need to harness their energy. It will be more than I have done before, and I must warn you, it does come with risks." I didn't like the uncertainty in Pontotok's voice. I was used to her always seeming strong and brave.

"What kind of risks?" At this point, I didn't care about the risks. I was going to do something whether the Spirits were going to agree to help or not.

"Waking the Spirits before an unbalance is dangerous; unless worthy enough, it is means for almost certain death." Her voice was calm, yet matter of fact.

"Worthy enough — what's more worthy than this?"

"That's not for you to decide, child."

"Well, if we could be killed for asking for their help, let's not waste our lives on them. Let's go straight to the source and go to the mountain." The decision seemed pretty clear to me.

"Oh, Put! We wouldn't stand a chance. Now that Duran has summoned you, he could well know you are alive and be looking for you. The woods are probably full of wolves and Bear Eaters. Plus, the closer we get, the stronger he can feel us. It's not like we can just sneak up on him as we are." Pontotok laughed as though my idea was ridiculous. "You realize don't you that we will be fighting against Colbryn as well — the whole mountain?" She lingered on his name and stared deep into my eyes. I could tell she was trying to read me to see if this news would somehow change how I felt.

"Yeah, he is responsible. He was just a player in that game, but he still played. What happens to Colbryn is his own fate, but in order for this to end, Duran must die." My words felt strong, and she nodded at me in agreement.

"Sounds like you have gotten things in order." Pontotok spouted. I tried to keep my face blank so she would take me seriously. She smiled, and the bags beneath her eyes rose like pillows.

"We have much to discuss with Adoetae. He should be here tomorrow, but let us rest now."

I was looking forward to sharing our thoughts with Adoetae. I had missed his company and looked forward to all of us discussing the plan. I went to sleep, playing various scenarios in my mind.

****

The next afternoon, I sat braiding a leather band when I saw him coming through the forest. His long hair was tied back with eagle feathers that whipped as they caught the air. His dark skin was still a heavy contrast to his silver eyes, and I found myself having a hard time looking away. I smiled and got to my feet to greet him with a hug. I awkwardly pressed my bulging stomach into his rock-solid abdomen.

"Oh good, you brought dinner." I was hoping he would. He held up two venison back straps.

"Well, I knew if I didn't, then the menu would be goat cheese and milk."

He laughed. Grunting, Pontotok took the venison from him.

"Might not have even had that. Natani has about cleaned us out." Pontotok laughed and turned the joke on me. I knew she was just playing, but it did make me feel bad. It was true. I had been eating a lot more than usual.

"It's not my fault; I can't help it." I frowned, a little embarrassed.

"Here, I brought extra just for you." Adoetae blinked his silver eyes, catching mine like a fly in a web. Their haunting addiction causing me to feel uncomfortable as I akwardly break away. He handed me the pouch.

I washed the vegetables and skinned them for boiling. Adoetae and Pontotok carried on with small talk. It was nice having the three of us together again. The potatoes were roasting, and the loin was cooking. Delicious smells wafted through the chilly air. This was one of the things I missed most about home. Despite the fact that I was being hunted by an evil monster and his pack of evil wolves and the fact that I was carrying his evil little child, right now everything seemed perfect.

With our stomachs full, I waited for someone to start the conversation and was glad when Adoetae took the initiative.

"Well, I know we have a lot to discuss." He paused. "For Natani's sake, why don't you tell her what you know about the Prophecy, and we can go from there." Adoetae's voice was like silk. He seemed like such a leader. I wondered if he had always been like this.

"Yes, Pontotok, please, that would be very helpful." I was trying not to sound too excited, but inside I was thrilled finally to be learning about this strange Prophecy that I was somehow tied into.

"Well, the story is based around a collection of negative Spirits. It is very old. For generations upon generations, the negative energy has stacked up like a totem pole just waiting to topple over."

"So when did the Prophecy start?" I asked.

"Well, it's true origin I cannot say because I don't know, but it must have started somewhere around here. Very few people existed in this area back then. The first Chief of all Nations had twin sons. Both wanted to be the village leader. It was up to the father to decide which one would do the best job for the people because he was old and knew he would soon be heading to the Spirit lands. Now because they were twins, in order to tell them apart, one wore a raw buckskin and the other wore a dark-stained bear hide. The dark son was born first by a few minutes, and he felt that warranted him the right to be Chief. The dark son also had a selfish, mean streak and belittled and criticized his brother in front of their father. This made the younger brother try even harder in everything he did, and he was stronger because of that. Some felt for that reason he should be Chief.

It came time for the Chief to decide who would take over, so he announced there would be a contest and the winner would be Chief. The oldest brother went out into the deep forest and called up to the Spirits to give him an edge in beating his brother. This attracted the negative Spirits, and they filled and embodied the dark son and he became one with them. The next day the Chief called all the members of the village to witness the competition. They all sat in a circle with the father and sons in the middle. He walked one son to one side of the circle and took the other son to the opposite side. The Chief stood in the middle and looked at the village people and said: "If one of my sons has helped you, please stand by the one that has done the most for you." It wasn't long before most of the people were standing by the youngest son. The older son was furious — he felt tricked, as there was nothing the Spirits could do to help him. The evil in him surfaced, and he stabbed his brother before the village people and ran away, never to return. The younger son survived for one night and woke up with a vision just before his death. The Spirits gave him a message, which is the Prophecy we are talking about. He spoke the words to his father, and they were the last words he spoke before leaving for the Spirit lands."

"So the start of negative Spirits and the start of the Prophecy happened at the same time?" I questioned.

"Yes, it is believed that when a body dies angry and its last breath is a negative one, then the energy that is left to roam the earth is also negative. It is said that that moment was the beginning of the collection of negative Spirits. Over time, the collection has continued; it has grown and grown with every raid, with every death, and the negative energy that is contained within the mountain of the Bear Eaters is overflowing. It is that energy that makes Duran so powerful." We sat in silence as I processed what Pontotok was saying; it all seemed to make sense now.

"So what does the collection of Spirits have to do with the Prophecy?" I was not sure.

"The Prophecy tells of the coming of change, a crossroad of decisions that leads to destruction, change, choices, the unknown. It tells of a force of the walking dead. We know that the bear on the pendant represents Duran." Pontotok said.

"So what makes you think that the negative Spirits have anything to do with the Prophecy?

"Because the collection of Spirits has been going on for generations," Pontotok clarified. "Duran has been collecting for ages, because ... well, some even say he is the dark son." She seemed uneasy saying the words out loud.

"The twin? The dark son that started the collection of negative Spirits? But that means he is hundreds of years old — is that even possible?" I questioned, smirking.

"It does mean that," Pontotok added. I sat, recalling Colbryn's words.

"OK, let me clarify. The first negative Spirit was collected by the dark son when he killed his brother, setting the Prophecy in motion. You think the dark son is Chief Duran who has been collecting negative Spirits in the mountain for generations? He gains strength from the Spirits, which is why he is so strong and why he does not age?"

"Who can say what the truth is, but your on the right track." She bobbed her head up and down, and I felt insignificant again.

"Oh, well, then what purpose does Duran have in gaining all this negative energy? I felt like this was the question of all questions, and the answer to this would be the answer to stopping him. I just needed to find it out.

"We aren't sure. The Prophecy is vague; everything has various meanings, and at this point, it is unclear." Pontotok reached for the air and felt for vibrations.

"Well, let's figure it out! Will you tell me the Prophecy — what were the dying son's last words?" I was determined to figure it all out.

"Well, Put! Do you not think we have tried figuring it out? It's a collection of riddles spoken by a dying man; it's not exactly to the point." Pontotok cleared her throat. "Well, what has been saved and spoken has five parts. It is so fragmented that it seems he was passing to the Spirit world as he was translating the vision, but the first part goes like this ..."

She closed her eyes, took a breath, and released it as a dramatic gasp before she spoke.

"The bird of sorrow abandons half its heart,

with a chance to save the red souls, the choice marks them all."

"As you can see, nothing is spelled out clearly; we think, though, that the reference to the bird must be the dove. 'Abandons half its heart' could mean a lot of things."

"Possibly leaving a great love?" Adoetae suggested, looking at me oddly.

"It could. Who knows? 'With a chance to save the red souls' could be the dove's tribe? 'Choice marks them all' could mean a hundred different things." Pontotok shooed at the air with her open hand.

"So what makes you think that part of the Prophecy belongs to the dove? Bird of sorrow could mean anything. I ask this because you two think I'm the dove, correct?" I asked. They were right — the riddle was confusing. It was a huge guessing game.

"It just fits best. You are either the dove or the eagle. The original gyres, the white gyre and black gyre, of which you have the white ..."

Adoetae interrupted: "Which is why we are sure you are part of the Prophecy."

"Yes, you hold one, each to be passed to the first born daughter. The pendant and the Prophecy are connected — they are both intertwined. The pendants show animals, but we know it is not a war of the animals..." Pontotok was interrupted again.

"Obviously because that would be stupid, they represent people," Adoetae added.

"Am I telling this, or are you?" she scolded him.

"Sorry," he smiled, leaning back into the grass.

"OK, so tell me the rest of it. If each animal on the disk represents a person, and you first said I might be the eagle, then what does that part say, and where does it fit in?" My skin was crawling to hear my fate. The same eerie feeling that had always called to me settled familiarly again in my stomach.

"Well, we just think you could be the eagle but don't know for sure.

Cold blood flows from the one trapped by the sun,

strength comes from those forgotten, one side is done."

Pontotok seemed uneasy telling the Prophecy. I noticed her rocking nervously back and forth and droning up the words from the depths of her memory.

"'Trapped by the sun' — Natani was trapped by the Chief. He is thought to be the dark son. Perhaps it is play on words? 'Strength comes from those forgotten.' You said the men that he takes become strong from the mushrooms, so perhaps they are the forgotten ones?" Adoetae asked. It seemed like a stretch to me, but I went along with it. I was most worried about the part that said 'one side is done' — it sounded ominous.

"Perhaps," Pontotok agreed.

"What do you think 'cold blood' is?" I questioned, hoping someone had a positive guess.

"I don't know. It doesn't sound good." Adoetae looked to Pontotok for more clarification, and I followed.

"Put! I don't know child. There is much to figure out." She rubbed her eyes. I wanted to keep talking, so it worried me that Pontotok was getting tired.

"Cold blood flows from the one trapped by the sun, strength comes from those forgotten, one side is done.'" I chanted it out loud and committed it to memory. At least I would have it to ponder later. "What we need to do is go to the Spirits; it's going to be the only way to figure this out and to understand what all that means. They have to know something that we don't. If you just teach me about the natural powers, I can help you, Pontotok."

Adoetae interrupted me. "Powers? Wait a minute — what have you two been talking about?" Adoetae sat up in protest.

"You have no say in this Adoetae; it's a burden only the eagle or the dove can carry. But you know, child," she turned to me: "You can't carry that burden while you are carrying another life." She pointed to my protruding stomach.

Adoetae protested, "You can't put any more on her. She has been through so much already, and you don't even know for sure which one she is...

the eagle or the dove? I cannot allow it, not alone. Why can't I help with this?" He was angry, and I could almost see the blood pumping through the veins in his neck.

"Natani and I will go to the Spirits and ask them for help. In case something goes wrong and they..."

"They kill the two of you?" Adoetae interrupted once more.

"Then at least you will still be here to fulfill your part of the Prophecy," Pontotok barked.

"Oh, great, I'll be here to fulfill my part of the failed Prophecy ... alone!" Adoetae kicked dirt into the fire.

"You already have a part to play — it's quiet clear. Remember? Is that not enough for you?" Pontotok started to get angry. "I care for you both, but no one said this would be easy." Pontotok looked defeated, and I could tell she was worried.

"Well, I know there are a lot of unknowns. I just know I'm ready to do whatever it takes. If this Prophecy has been building for as long as you two say it has and you're sure that I am part of it, then I accept that and am ready to do whatever it takes. I have no family left. I am not tied to anyone. If I were killed, it wouldn't really matter anyway, so I vote to go alone. Pontotok, you should be here with Adoetae. You have a great talent and are needed by many people. Adoetae, you know how unique and few your tribe is. There is no question that your place is with Cree." I sounded braver than I felt, but hearing the logic in my own words was comforting. I was surprised at how eager and unafraid I was to go alone. The only catch was I had no idea where I was going. I looked at Adoetae; our eyes met, and our concern for each other was obvious.

"You do have family left. How do you think your child would feel if you died, and how do you think we would feel?" I didn't want to argue with Adoetae. He didn't understand, and I knew he would feel this way because his wife had died and Cree was all he had left. But my child was not the same as his child. My child was half-evil, and it would not care if I died. It's not even going to know my name, I thought.

"That's enough for one night," Pontotok said as she got up. I knew this was coming. She always left the conversation when it was at a pivotal place; it was her way of biting off a piece of information and being able to chew it over in her mind without our input interfering with her thoughts.

"Please, we don't have to discuss any more; just tell me the rest of the Prophecy. There are still three you haven't told me." I pleaded, hoping to at least get this much out of her.

"Silent comes the Lion's hesitant heart of stone,

A lesson learned by love — one goes alone.

Silver marks the special one,

Sacrifices great until the river comes undone.

Darkens the evil form, bound by what is born,

Marked to save the red day, from what rides the white storm."

She smiled, but her mouth pinched together and formed a frown that I didn't understand. She then turned from the fire and headed inside. "These old bones need a soft place to fall. Good night."

After she left, Adoetae got up and sat next to me; he approached cautiously, taking my hand. It seemed like he was building up to something. I could tell by his approach that I would most likely not want to hear what he was about to tell me.

"I care for you, maybe more than I should. You bring out my protective nature. Finding you in harm's way only ..." His concern reached my heart, but it was still too freshly damaged to warm it much.

"You can't worry about me. This is something I have to do. You have a place in this, just not now. I heard it: 'Silver marks the special one.'" I couldn't help but pause seeing the Prophecy painted in his very eyes. "That's you, right?"

Adoetae stood, turned, and walked away from me. He took a few steps, stopped, and then turned around as if to say more but only looked back into my eyes a look of wonder and defeat. I saw that same look that I used to love seeing in Colbryn's eyes. It made me look away.

We will both need to make sacrifices, I thought. That night I didn't sleep much. The Prophecy, the Mountain, the evil, it was all playing out in my head. I had a pretty good sense of what would happen. I would either live or die, and either option I could live with, as long as I stopped Duran. Somewhere in the back of my mind I knew that also meant Colbryn's life hung in the balance–I was OK with that.

CHAPTER SEVENTEEN
Bean Eaters

Several days passed. I spent them scribing the Prophecy and toiling over its riddles; it was enough to make anyone a little crazy. Each day I looked for Adoetae to return and to smile like nothing had happened, but he did not visit. I wondered if it was because he was mad at Pontotok or if he was mad at me. I hated not knowing. On the third day after discussing the Prophecy, three men and a woman visited us. The woman's son had been missing for a moon cycle, and they needed to find out what had happened to him. The first thing I thought was that he had been kidnapped by the Bear Eaters. I sat watching. I knew if I saw Colbryn grabbing up a small boy, I would need to be restrained. Good or bad, the Spirits would tell the truth.

As we sat by the evening fire, payment was made, and a possession and the name of the boy were given to Pontotok. I wanted to pay close attention to the words she used in her chants. These days, I was studying her like a hawk, or an eagle ... whatever I was. She addressed the four directions, and soon the image of a young boy appeared. His mother gasped and cried softly, as she watched her young son, bow and arrow in hand, stalking a wounded deer. He had the bow drawn when a sandy-colored shape grabbed him from behind. It didn't take long. The mountain lion had him by the neck, and he was gone. His mother and father wept in each other's arms, and the other two men tried their best to console them. I could feel her pain in the pit of my stomach as if it was my own. To lose a child like that would be horrible. My own thoughts seemed to slap me in the face as I sat days away from handing over my own child to a stranger. Pontotok stood up, chanted her thanks to the Spirits, and asked them to take care of the young Spirit that was in their care. The couple spent the night. I could hear the woman sobbing until sunrise, but then they were gone.

"It is a sad job you do." I said the morning after they left.

"It can be. It also gives closure and justice to both the living and the dead; it is all part of life." I nodded. She was right.

"I know how strong you are, Natani, or you wouldn't be sitting with me now. It probably wouldn't be a job you would have picked for yourself, nor was it what I would have picked, but it has its comforts." She seemed unaltered by the images she has seen over the years. I knew Pontotok was much braver and tougher than I.

"Do you ever wish you had chosen something else?"

"I did not choose this; it chose me, just like you got chosen. But no, I have seen it all: the heartbreak, lost love, death, and greed. If they are good, happy people while they are alive, they will be good happy Spirits. You get out of life what you put into it — same in death. Love is the most powerful force there is, even stronger than evil." The words were comforting.

"Speaking of choices," I paused. "Have you found a good place for the baby?"

"Yes, but I am not going to say anything to the couple yet, just in case you change your mind. I don't want to get their hopes up for nothing." She raised her eyebrows at me, and I wondered what that meant.

"I don't think I'll be changing my mind," I said solemnly, mimicking her gesture. "Time will tell," she answered. I spent my time retracing the words of the Prophecy over and over in hopes I would suddenly be able to figure it all out.

A few days passed, and Adoetae found me in the pasture with the goats. He was in his wild form, which I found strange. He barked at me, and I just laughed. "What? What is it? Why don't you turn back into your normal self so I can talk to you?" Golden Boy gave me a gentle nudge.

He only did this when people came to camp. "What is up with you two?" Then Adoetae grabbed the bottom of my dress and started pulling it hard.

"OK, OK, don't rip my smock. I only have one other. I guess you want me to follow you. I'm coming, I'm coming!" Golden Boy called to the other goats, and they came running. I started following them, but Adoetae pulled me in the opposite direction. The baby was limiting my lung capacity, and it wasn't long before I was out of breath.

"I am going as fast as I can. You try maneuvering with a bolder in your stomach." We were in a clump of trees when he ran off behind a large oak. I stood bent over, panting. "Sorry about all that." I heard him say. I looked in that direction to see him leaning out from around the tree. "What's going on, and why are you behind that tree?" I asked.

"Don't be afraid. I need to talk fast. Men are coming, and I need to get you farther away from here." I could see the urgency in his face.

"Men? What men — you mean Bear Eaters?" I whispered, frantically looking back as the hair on my neck stood on end.

"Yes. So just follow me, alright?" As I was processing everything, he came back, and we were walking again. "So you think they are looking for me?" He gave me a whine that I took to mean yes. "I'm not fast. I use to be but not now, not with this belly. If they find our trail, then I am as good as dead. There's no way I could get away, so you'll just need to leave me, understand?" My voice was harsh and direct, but I wanted him to take me seriously. This wasn't a time for him to be brave; it would be a wasted cause. He snapped at me and nudged me harder.

"Remind me to have you teach me Sib language when we have time." He snapped again.

"You don't need to be so touchy about it." I added. Suddenly, I heard a noise in the distance. Sticks were snapping, and leaves were being crushed underfoot. "Bear Eaters," I whispered, terrified. We crouched down beside a tree; it was hardly big enough to conceal my protruding belly. Adoetae stood at my side. The sound was growing louder by the minute. This would be it — it would be over quickly; they would either kill me right here or take me back to the Mountain. I braced myself. "Adoetae, go! Now!" I kicked him in the side, but he just stood there like a big dumb dog. "Adoetae, don't be an idiot. Go, run, you can't fight them." I was mad. Why wouldn't he run!?

Suddenly, birds were flying off from around me. I closed my eyes and gripped my necklace. The force was great as it barreled toward me like a tornado whipping my hair forward, the smell of wilderness being churned up from the forest floor. I opened my eyes to see Adoetae one last time, but instead of one wild face, I saw several, To my astonishment, it was an entire pack of Sibs. There were ten to fifteen of them, and their large bodies charged right past us like we weren't even there. They were beautiful, and they ran in unison as though they were pulling a sled, only nothing trailed them but settling leaves. Adoetae licked my face, and I began to breathe again. I was so shocked by the experience that I felt weak in the knees and didn't know if I would even be able to stand. Adoetae ran off and left me feeling vulnerable and helpless on the forest floor.

It wasn't long before he was reaching for my hand and transformed back to the heroic man he was. The buckskin he had been wearing around his neck as a collar was now the only thing he wore, wrapped around his waist as a breechcloth. I could see the strength in his arms and chest, and it reminded me of Colbryn — only these arms hadn't killed my family.

"Come on, we need to get some distance between us and them." His voice was stern but reassuring. He stood holding his side.

"What's wrong with you?" I asked concerned.

"You kick hard for a girl." He was still rubbing his side, where the complete outline of my foot marked his ribs.

"Oh, wow, well you need to learn to listen to me; I was serious and terrified for you." I was recalling the anger I had that led me to kick him. I was still mad he hadn't listened to me.

"Terrified for me? Ha! Next time you think Bear Eaters are coming, don't be worried for me. You are the one they want, remember?" He smiled, and I felt foolish. He was right, but it didn't mean I wouldn't still worry for him. Not having a smart comeback, I changed the subject.

"What about Pontotok? Will she be alright?" I worried that she would be unable to defend herself, as she was old and slower even than I was.

"Yes, it's just a small scouting party, five at the most. The pack will cover our tracks and will attack if they have to, but I think they will just stalk from the forest. We just need to keep going and make sure not to leave any traces behind."

"How far are we going?" I wasn't sure how far I would be able to go before I had to rest. I already had a sharp pain forming in my side.

"We will keep going until it is safe." He seemed so serious, and I couldn't help but make light of the situation now that I knew I wasn't going to be killed ... in the immediate future anyway.

"Sorry, I just thought I was seconds from death, and now that I know I'm not, I just feel a little overwhelmed."

"Just calm down you will be OK." He kept looking back to make sure we weren't being followed. It was nice he was being so protective.

"Natani, what are you smiling at? We have a dangerous situation here, and you're smiling." He looked irritated.

"Sorry, I feel I am in very capable paws, I mean hands." I smiled back, and the sharp ridges of his mouth softened. We walked until I was out of breath again. "Is this far enough?" I panted. "No, but we can rest for a bit." He paused, looking at the stress in my face. "When is the baby...?" He pointed towards my stomach shyly.

"Due?" I confirmed.

He nodded without saying anything. "Feels like any time now after that walk." I stretched my back to relieve the pressure. "That's not funny. I've never delivered a baby and would like to keep it that way if I can." I could see the concern on his face.

"Yeah," I huffed. "I wish I had that option." I wanted to ask him about the birth of his son, but I knew the images would be tangled with the images of his dying wife. As we sat, I heard a voice come from the woods. Adoetae stood and froze.

"I will be right back." He ran into the woods and was gone for a short while. I sat completely still regaining any energy I could. The evening was settling in to be a strange one. There was a hint of warmth in the air, which was getting to be very unusual for this time of year. I was glad it wasn't cold yet. Leaving in such a hurry, I was unable to bring a cape, but luckily the extra layer of fat I had put on through the pregnancy would serve me well tonight. Unfortunately, the extra weight was also causing my ankles to swell. The buckskin of my moccasins was stretched tight, and I worried I might have to cut them off.

I wondered if Pontotok was safe. Would Cawttwa or Shosong travel with her? I hated thinking of her out alone and vulnerable. Would she send word when it was safe for us to come back? Different scenarios were playing out in my head when Adoetae came back through the trees. He looked more relaxed, but something told me it was forced.

"They questioned Pontotok to see if she had seen anyone fitting your description. She told them no. That's the good news. The bad news is they are still looking for you. They took off toward the south. Some of the pack are going to follow them."

"So what does that mean for us? Can we go back to Pontotok?"

"Well, I think for tonight we should stay here and head back in the morning. If you will go and find us a place where I can build a fire without it being seen, I will gather wood and maybe scare up a rabbit."

"Sure." I was exhausted and couldn't wait to collapse next to a warm fire. Adoetae silently slipped off into the darkness, so I headed to a close cliff overhang next to a bank of pines. It looked like a safe place to make camp, so I cleared a spot for the firewood and settled down, eager to lean against the rock bank to relieve the pressure on my stomach. I took in slow, calm breaths as I waited for Adoetae to return. No blanket, no food, little water. Ugh! This wasn't going to be pleasant. I was glad to be alone. I needed time to think. Processing all the strange events that were happening seemed overwhelming and unbelievable. I could see Duran's evil eyes gazing into the fog, staring at me, trying to figure out where I had escaped. It would probably be best if I were alone. I wouldn't want the fog reveal to show Adoetae with me. What if the Chief sees that I am pregnant? How hard would he search to destroy his child? It would not help to run, and the Spirits would find me wherever I went. I hated feeling so helpless. These thoughts were making me nauseated, so I got up and walked around the rock cliff, into the darkness, and threw up. I instantly felt a little better. Sitting in the darkness, I felt that warm breeze again blow down across my cheek and through my hair. I had felt it before. It was comforting to me then and now. I wondered from what warm prairie it had come.

"Natani, Natani!" Suddenly, Adoetae's frantic voice called out my name. I got to my feet and stumbled back.

"I was afraid something had happened to you! Are you alright?" He threw his arms around me, and the gesture surprised me. I had only been gone a minute or two, and this sudden burst of anxiety was making me sick again.

"My stomach, I got sick. I think it was just nerves from worrying." His concern made me feel better but still a little bewildered.

"Please sit. I will get this rabbit started, and don't worry, Pontotok will have some answers for us. If I need to take you far away from here, I can do that."

"Far away from here? Maybe you can, but I can't, the Spirits will see me no matter where I go, so what is the point? I just can't travel much farther." I sat rubbing my ankles. Adoetae started the small fire, and I was glad to be able to see his face. Talking into the darkness had made me uneasy because it reminded me of the cave.

"Well, we will do what we have to," was all he replied. The small fire was crackling, and the rabbit was cooking. It smelled delightful. Adoetae took the furs and began scrapping them clean. His hands were very large, and he worked methodically, focusing on every scrape. Sitting silent, I just watched him. Laying them beside the fire to dry, he finally broke from his concentrated trance and smiled at me when he saw that I had been watching him.

"What are you making?" I asked curiously.

"Well, it's something for you."

"Me? There's not enough there to make a fur coat." I replied. He rolled his eyes.

"I noticed that you're busting at the seams there, and that can't be comfortable." He pointed to my moccasins. They were so tight that the beading had popped off, and coarse threads were hanging out.

"Hmm, yeah they are tight, but I really didn't want to cut them off, though. My mother made them. I was hoping the swelling would go down over night." My once beautiful moccasins were looking rather tattered, but they had been with me through a lot.

"Oh, I won't cut them off; it's just a trick I learned along the way. You just snip the threads where the seams are to relieve the pressure, then cap over it with the furs like a decorative strip; it looks like it was made that way, and after the baby is born and all the swelling goes away, you just stitch it back up." He smiled, smirking at me. I couldn't tell for sure from the firelight, but it seemed he was blushing a little.

"Wow, my mom would have loved you." And it was true; he was kind, strong, handsome, and could also sew — it was more than any of the Braves in my village could do, even Talenhill.

"I would have liked to have met your mother. I'm imagining a magnificent woman if she was anything like you." He smiled and scrunched up his nose.

"Yes, she was, and thank you, I think?" I didn't want to discuss my family. I wasn't ready to open up the memories in front of Adoetae, and I sure wasn't ready to start tearing up in front of him. I tried to think of something to change the subject and lighten the mood.

"So how is the young pack doing?" It was my best attempt at conjuring up small talk.

"Oh, they are great. It is always fun watching how awkward they are when they are this age. Their front legs don't seem to be able to keep up with the back. They liked you, you know." He smiled, and I could tell he was very fond of them and was wondering if I was.

"Was it hard when Cree was a baby?" Adoetae was silent, and I quickly wished I hadn't asked that.

"Well, I wasn't around," he admitted solemnly, and I could sense the regret in his voice. "I left. It was a very hard time for me, and I left searching for something."

"Did you find it?"

"No."

"Do you mind if I ask what you were looking for?"

"Mostly for something that would dull the pain, but when I realized that nothing could, I came back. My son and my tribe needed me, and I had a responsibility to them. I realized it was selfish of me to leave. Being there for the pack does help because I can put my energy into something beneficial." He sat snapping a small branch. I could tell this was a difficult subject to talk about.

"I'm sure she was beautiful, your wife."

"She was."

I paused in thought. It must have been nice to be able to pick a partner, someone of your own choosing.

"Well, my husband is real good-looking as well." I tried not to smirk. I wasn't sure how he would take my comment. His eyes turned from shallow and distant to deep and amused.

"Ha, ha, you're a funny one, Natani, and a bad judge of looks I might add. I will take it as a compliment that you are not just beside yourself over me." He smiled and handed me a well-done piece of the rabbit. I was glad that I was able to lighten the mood a little.

"Thanks, you know, sometime when I'm no longer being hunted by forces of evil, battling Spirits, and I have a proper place to cook, I will have to make you my favorite dish of smoked salmon with morels." I bit into the rabbit with a crunch. Adoetae smiled.

"Aw, Pontotok must have told you I go crazy for salmon and morels." He patted his washboard stomach and pretended to fall back off his log. I couldn't help but laugh at the performance through a mouth of tough, crunchy meat.

"Ew, this is tough," he said crunching. "Well, it will make us appreciate the salmon dinner we will have later even more." We both laughed, and it felt good. I was glad I had Adoetae with me.

"Well, it's cold, and it won't be safe to keep a large fire going through the night, not as exposed as we are. If you are comfortable with it, we might need to lie close and just make the best of it." He sat with his hands draped out over his knees. I chuckled a little.

"Well, men have done and said worse to get close to me." It was true. How could I not be comfortable with Adoetae by now? He laughed.

"Well, if it makes you more comfortable, I can sleep Siberian, but I do tend to snore more that way. So what do you prefer, like this or furry?"

"Well, I think both ways are nice, but as long as you keep your hands to yourself, the way you are is just fine with me." He smiled back at me, and I curled up next to him. It was comforting and a little strange at the same time. I had only lay like this with one other man, Colbryn, the night I fell in the well. It was nice lying here with Adoetae. It seemed like we were moons away from anyone. I lay looking out toward the tiny fire. I knew it would soon burn out, and I'd be left with only the warmth of his chest on my back. I allowed myself to feel safe, to feel wanted, a secret I kept to myself.

I still didn't know what my future was going to bring, and I felt that I needed to set boundaries with Adoetae. After everything he had done and been for me, I did not want to get him involved any more than he was already. The eerie voice that has called to me since I was a child was still beckoning me, and for that I needed to be able to go when I needed to. I wouldn't want to break his heart.

Morning came. I was damp from the dew, my back was killing me, and the baby was jumping. I stretched and tried to fix the cramps when I noticed I was by myself. I reached down to my ankles and noticed the new fur wrappings. The extra room made all the difference in comfort. I struggled to my feet and walked out of the rocks to see Adoetae walking towards me.

"Is everything alright?" I asked, glad to see him.

"Yes, everything is fine. I brought some dried fruit and nuts for you." Dried fruits? I wondered where he could have gotten these.

"You went to your village?"

"Yes, it's not far."

"Oh." His village was close yet we slept out here on the ground? I suddenly felt a little hurt that he had not taken me there. Was he ashamed of me because I was pregnant? Was there someone he was interested in that he didn't want me to see? More surprisingly, why was I thinking these thoughts? Why was I hurt? Adoetae was free to do whatever he wanted, and he didn't owe me anything. I turned away from him afraid he would see the hurt on my face.

"Did you sleep alright?" he asked. I shook my head.

"And you?" I asked, still looking down. He came over to me and lifted my chin.

"Something is going on in your head. I can feel it. What is it?"

"Nothing, we need to get started. I have a lot to ask Pontotok." He let it drop, and we started walking.

"Natani, why won't you talk to me?"

"I have a lot on my mind," I said walking as fast as I could.

"I don't believe you. This silence is driving me crazy!"

"I did not realize your village was so close." I tried not to sound obvious when I blurted it out, but I knew he got the picture.

"So that is what it is! You are wondering why I didn't take you to my village?" I didn't look at him.

"I understand a woman in my condition without a husband. I don't blame you." I started waddling off.

"Stop right there!" He grabbed my arm. "It is nothing like that. When you first got here, I wanted to keep you in my village, but Pontotok said it would put the entire tribe in danger. If they came looking for you, someone might say something they shouldn't without knowing what was at stake. So please, don't think I wouldn't love for you to stay here to ... to be mine and to raise your baby as my own. I would do that. I didn't think I would feel this way about anyone ever again, but I do."

I looked into his eyes, and I could tell he was worried how I would react to this information. I could see how sincere he was, and it touched my heart. But my wants had changed. I no longer wanted the Brave, the te-pee, and the family I had once dreamed of, at least not in the near future. I had been damaged by Duran and changed by Colbryn. I was different, and until I got my old self back, I was unable to love anyone. I will admit that this was more than I wanted to hear from Adoetae, but I had no one to blame but myself.

"Adoetae, I appreciate your great kindness. You have been a strength when I have been at my weakest, and for that I owe you a lot. It's just that I am not the girl I used to be, and a lot has happened, as you know. I just can't give you that. I'm not going to raise the baby. Pontotok has a good couple who will take it. All I can focus on right now is helping you and Pontotok. There is too much rage in me to love. Don't get attached to me. It just makes things that much harder for both of us." I could feel the happy vision that Adoetae had pictured in his head dissolve right there in front of me. His eyes dulled, and it was like I had just snuffed out his internal flame. I felt horrible. There was nothing I could do. I could feel the emo-tions in my stomach and the welling of tears behind my eyes like a wave crashing down. I hated that I had become so emotional, that pregnancy was playing tricks with me. I turned, started walking again, and tried to conceal the few tears that managed to escape my every attempt to hold back. I couldn't face him anymore.

"It's too late for that, you know. It was too late that first day I saw you." I heard him walking behind me, so I just kept going as fast as I could. I wanted to run away from the problem, but I couldn't get far. I soon be-came winded and stopped when he was next to me. I turned and wrapped my arms around him and cried into his strong chest.

"Please don't cry, Natani. I would hate to think I caused one tear to fall from your beautiful eyes." He brushed my hair from the side of my face.

"Things are so complicated. I don't know what I am doing half the time," I admitted, looking up at him. It was true. Each day since I stepped foot off Chikitan Canyon seemed to be a story from someone else's life, and I was just stuck in it.

"I know. It's going to be OK." His words were like a drug smoothing over all the rough edges of my mind. For the time being, at least we were at peace.

Chapter Eighteen
Waiting

We got back to Pontotok's that afternoon. She was anxious to see us and scurried out the door with a cup in her hand before she could even see us coming through the forest.

"Oh, thank the Spirits!" she shouted when she saw us. "Here, drink this child, and go lay down. You look exhausted!" I was. I nodded and took a big sip. It reminded me of Eba's tea. The smell was instantly comforting as I walked into the hut. The pile of buckskins had never looked so good. I practically collapsed with a thud. The door was closed, but I could still hear Adoetae and Pontotok speaking outside the wall.

"What happened?" she asked in a rough voice.

"I know you told me not to, but I did." He paused. "I told her how I felt. I had to; it's been driving me crazy. I've felt this way since day one. I just didn't want her to feel like she was going through all of this alone — that I would be there for her and the baby. I thought she'd..." — he paused taking a slow breath — "...well, she didn't, she can't. There, you happy?" Even through the wall, I could feel Adoetae's sadness, and it scraped at my heart like a shale knife.

"You poor fool, you are not the only one who feels that way about her. He came; he was here. I could see it in his eyes, too."

"Who? Colbryn? Here? Are you sure it was him? They all look the same, you know."

"It was him — looked like he'd been skinned alive then put back together. What a mess; she can't be with either of you!"

"You know, I never thought I would feel this way again, and to know that I can't do anything about it — it kills me. Yet she still has feelings for that murderer!" The tea had kicked in. I could hear their voices, but nothing really registered other than the fact that Adoetae was mad and that was the last thought I remember having.

I woke up just as the sun was going down. Pontotok was sitting inside beside the fire. She looked up and smiled.

"I have bread, honey, cheese, and milk. Come eat." We sat in silence for a minute listening to the night coming alive outside the window.

"So how many came?" I couldn't waste anymore time ignoring the question I knew Pontotok was waiting for me to ask.

"Only five. They just looked around and asked some questions." She seemed oddly calm.

"What questions?

"Basically if I had seen a woman or heard of someone with your description passing this way. I said no. I thought it worked, but then they said they might pass back through." She started drawing circles in the dust with a crooked branch. I couldn't tell if she was worried.

"Why would they trace back over the path they had just come?" I asked

"If you are not found, Duran has requested that I come and do a smoke reveal of you." I could tell now she was worried. This could have a bad outcome.

"He can do that? But he doesn't have anything of mine to do the reading with." I had no belongings when I was there, so I was sure nothing was left behind.

"He must have something of yours. Who knows, it could even be something you made. I was afraid he might try something like this. I wasn't surprised when they told me the plan."

"Oh, no, the bowls."

"What?"

"Nothing, so if you do the smoke reveal on me, he is going to see me. He is going to see where I am and that I am pregnant. I will be as good as dead." I felt a chill crawl up my back.

"Settle your soul, child. First of all, it will take many days for the raiding party to exhaust all searching and head back, maybe even a moon or two, so we have some time. Second, the Spirits don't like answering questions for negative reasons, and I can try to send a sign before the reveal to throw it off."

"What if Duran tries to keep you there?" I had never heard of anyone being allowed to just leave the mountain once they had been there. Pontotok was old and weak. She could never escape.

"Old! Put! I'm not that old, and no he won't keep me there. I would do too much damage, too much, and he knows it!" she spouted out, sure of herself.

"Sorry, I didn't mean 'old' like you were old, just that ... never mind." There wasn't any lying to Pontotok. She could feel my energy, and that was something I couldn't hide.

"So is there a plan? What is going to happen, and when do you go to the mountain?"

"Too many questions child. Slow down. I'm old, remember?" She smirked at me and took a large bite of bread, not caring where the crumbs fell. Shosong stood on her lap pecking at each flake.

"So I'm assuming that means Colbryn was one of the five men that was here?" I knew the answer.

"Two large scars running down his face?" she asked. I looked down and then back at her and nodded. It was a strange feeling knowing that Colbryn had been here.

"So what should we do if they come back? Is there a plan? Do I just wait here worrying until you get back?" The thought of Pontotok leaving and me being alone was scary.

"Cawttwa will warn us, and then we will send you off to Adoetae's village. It's a long walk, but it is safer if you go there. Adoetae can take you as soon as we see that they are heading back. You will be long gone before they arrive. If all goes well, I will send word once I get back from the mountain and the coast is clear."

I wasn't sure what to feel. I was terrified for Pontotok, unsure about my trip to Adoetae's village, uneasy about the baby coming, angry Colbryn had come looking for me, and sad I had disappointed Adoetae.

"What is it, Natani?"

"I am so mixed up. I don't know how I feel about anyone or anything anymore." I started to cry again, which irritated me even more. She got up and hugged me.

"Why that's the baby, dear! It makes you feel like you're coming and going at the same time. It will all pass, you'll see. You poor thing — so much to deal with and a baby, too! Do you want to talk about Adoetae?" That just brought on another round of sobs. "Oh, Put! Yes, I understand — back to bed with you. Tomorrow it will rain, and we can just be lazy and stay inside," Pontotok said as she helped me back into the buckskins.

She was right; the next day was rainy, but I didn't feel much better.

"So you think these feelings will all go away once the baby comes? Because I'll never be any good to any one like this," I smiled.

"You will be just fine; it takes a few moons for things to straighten out, but you'll be just fine." Her confidence led me to believe she had been through this before.

"Did you ever have children?" I asked.

"Nope, I never was able to. I raised many though, just never my own. I was never no good to any man, so eventually I just preferred it on my own." Her words were bittersweet; it seemed like an issue that had caused a lot of sadness in her life, but I could tell she was stronger because if it.

"Is that why you don't have a tribe?"

"Sort of — I have a tribe, but I just prefer it on my own. Let's just keep it at that."

The morning started off slow and uneventful just like the lazy rainfall outside. It started early before dawn just like Pontotok had predicted, its soft droplets the only sound. I was well into sewing the beads back onto my moccasins when we heard a knock at the door that turned my blood ice cold.

"It's alright," Pontotok confirmed.

One of Pontotok's acquaintances had come wanting to trade her a large beaver for some medicinal herbs. There were not many beavers where my tribe camped, so I was curious what she was going to do with it. She plopped the large waxy carcass on her work table and smiled with excitement. Curious what she had planned for it, I put down my sewing.

"Hmm, what are you going to do with that? I hope you didn't have to trade much for it?" I was grimacing at the smell, which wasn't setting well with my stomach.

"Aw, well, this is a delicacy. Haven't you ever had beaver sausage before? This one's already been drained and had the hair scalded off, a very good trade." She seemed surprised that I wasn't excited about the beaver.

"No, I can't recall ever eating beaver anything, but beavers aren't common where I'm from."

"You're in for a treat then, child; we can eat on this for days." She slapped the beaver in the head making its teeth click, which made her laugh. I couldn't help but smile at her enthusiasm. I knew Pontotok's ability to eat the same meal for days couldn't be matched, so I hoped she still had goat cheese in the churn. I went back to sewing up my moccasin, but she just stood hovering over the head and staring at me like she was waiting for something.

"Yes? What is it?" I asked, feeling her eyes poking at the side of my face.

"You gonna help?"

"Do I need to?" I asked, hesitantly hoping I had a choice.

"Well, my hands are old. I need some small strong hands to help."

"Help do what?" I asked.

"We need to pop these eyeballs out. Nothing worse than cooked beaver with the eyeballs and teeth left in. But I can get the teeth."

"I need to cut the eyeballs out, really?" I had butchered many animals in my life, so it wasn't anything that made me squeamish. But for some reason, the smell and look of this beaver in combination with its glassy, blue fogged eyes was a little much for my pregnant stomach to take. I got up to help her anyway.

"Just pull it out; get behind it, and cut it from behind. Try not to cut the ball or else you will be oozing stuff all over the place." She handed me a knife.

I didn't want to appear weak to Pontotok, so I pretended this was no big deal. In reality, I was ready to vomit. I struggled with the eye for several minutes. Its tendons were cold and hard, and there wasn't much room to poke my fingers in. Why couldn't Adoetae have been here to do this, I thought?

"Um, it's hard. I can't seem to get a good angle on it. Is there some other way?" I swallowed hard and handed her the knife.

"Keep working it. I told you it was tough. But you're strong, so I know you'll get it." She went back to building a fire and didn't offer any advice.

"Humphf," I tried again, but the cold slimy eyes were not cooperating.

"Maybe try imagining it's someone you don't like." Pontotok slapped the beaver in the head again with enough force to jam my hand under the eye, slice the tendon, and send the eye sailing through the air. "Well, Put! That must be the trick, I guess! Now, go throw that nasty thing out the door. I'm sure one of the goats will like it."

I took the eye and chucked it out the door as hard as I could. It landed in a tree, wrapped itself around a branch, and bobbed in the rain. Glad to be rid of it, I closed the door.

"While you work on the second one, I'm going to go get a fresh gut of water to fill the pot." She threw a shawl over herself and ducked out the door. I was left with nothing but the one-eyed beaver smiling back at me. I was determined to get the next eye out before Pontotok came back, so I could get back to my sewing.

"Alright, give it up willingly." I went in hoping the first one somehow loosened the second. I poked in, squashed it to the side, and pried the knife down.

A nose full of scorched beaver reached my nose. "Ohhhh, you stink!" I held my breath and dug in, a cold spatter hit my face. "Ah, you have to be kidding me!" The eye had popped, and black ooze was now congealing on my face. "Ew, ew, ew!" I dug in and cut the tendon. Getting the eye outside was a must. I scooped it up and headed for the door, but the slime made the door hard to open. The rain was now coming down steadily. I could tell by the sound of it hitting the hut that it had started to freeze. A blast of cold pushed me back when I opened the door. I fought back, chucked the eye out the door, and was glad to be done with my part of the process.

"Hey!" Pontotok shouted. I heard it hit something with a thud.

"Sorry!" I apologized, helping her through the door with the heavy water gut.

"I leave, and you manage to … well, Put, child! Didn't I say not to cut that part? What a mess!"

"Yes, and please never ask me to do that again." I wiped the slime from my face to the sound of low chuckles.

"You did good. I'm proud of you. Don't worry, he didn't feel anything." Her chuckles were low, but uncontrolled, and I couldn't help but see the humor in the situation.

I was glad to get back to my sewing, but from my corner, I enjoyed observing Pontotok's rhythmic process of preparing the meat. She spent the rest of the afternoon boiling and chopping, cooking with sage, and an array of herbs. She was content in her own thoughts. Oddly, after awhile, the aromas of her labor changed from putrid to somewhat appetizing, but I still had a clear view of the eyeball hanging outside the window.

"So when do I get to try that?" I asked, humoring her.

"In a few days. It sits then it smokes then its ready." She spoke without even turning around focusing completely on her cooking. It didn't bother me, the morning's events were still too fresh in my mind for me to be too hungry.

I stared out the small window, thankful I was warm and dry, the sounds of the cook fire popping at my side. The hormonal state I seemed to constantly be in these days was heightened by the somber rain. I sat delving into deep emotions that I would have normally been able to dismiss. The time we had spent together had proved Pontotok dear to my heart. Though rough, her kind soul was immeasurably endearing, and I began to think of her as beloved as any mother, though I knew her coarseness would never allow me to tell her. I thought about Adoetae and Colbryn and wondered where they were. I knew my heart was lonely because I was thinking of them. I hated that I still had feelings for Colbryn. The things he did where unforgivable, so the fact I still yearned for him, sickened me to admit. Would I ever be free of the feelings? Adoetae, on the other hand, was as true and loyal as any friend, and yet I did not share the same feelings. And I didn't know why. Days had gone by since Adoetae had been to see us. I wondered what his absence meant. Had he realized that I was right and that he should not have gotten involved with me? Regardless, I still longed to see him.

Perhaps it was Adoetaes absence or maybe the fact that I was inactive, but the days seemed to come and go slowly. Because of this, I had little to ease my mind. Each day seemed to have only one purpose, and that was to just wait.

CHAPTER NINETEEN

Darkness Falls

Almost with every fingers width of the sun I became more and more uncomfortable. It was hard to sit and hard to stand, and I hated lying around all the time. The rain had stopped, and I decided to venture to my favorite place. I enjoyed spending my days wrapped up under a blanket down by the stream. There was a large oak tree to lean against, and it was within view of the wigwam, so the goats would come and graze beside me. By now the baby was constantly moving, but I tried to think as little as possible about it. Instead, my mind was replaying the events of a reoccurring dream that I had been having. I had dreamt it twice now, and each time it was the same. I was with Adoetae, and we were walking along a riverbank. He was holding my hand, and I felt wonderful being with him. In the dream, I turn from him and look up the river to see a canoe floating towards us. Colbryn is standing inside. I think, why is he standing? He will fall in the river if he doesn't sit down. He calls my name, but I don't answer, so he paddles to shore. He gets out but lets the canoe float on down the river. As I watch it go, Adoetae is suddenly gone, and the pack is running past me. I'm standing there on the riverbank all alone with Colbryn, and then I wake. I wondered what the events of the dream meant, if anything. Could there be a hidden sign, a warning? I couldn't trust my thoughts these days. I seemed to be living in an altered state and figured I would be like this until the baby was born. It would be nice getting back to my normal self.

The sun was a finger's width to the horizon, and the pink-and-blue striped sky resembled hands stretching across, ready to clinch. I knew that sky was the same that stared down on the mountain. Perhaps Colbryn was staring out into the same expanse. Goose bumps rose on my arms just thinking about him. I ran my fingers over my shoulder and down the raised scars that traced the contours of my torso. Would he really take me back to the mountain? Knowing what he had done to my family, would he really be able to go through with the orders to return me to the Chief? He owed me more than that. Surely if I was caught, he would let me go. How many times would he be willing to betray me?

I got up and headed back to the wigwam. I could smell the beaver sausage as it smoked slowly; it smelled sweet and comforting despite the images of the eyeballs. Cawttwa was perched in the corner of the room and hunkered down like a black shadow among his collection of trinkets and odd items. Shosong flitted about the room stealing crumbs from the table.

"I got a good heat going — should dry up nice and well, nice and well," Pontotok spoke, leaning over her pot as I came into the wigwam.

"It smells pretty good," I humored her. She had been working on it for three days now, so it was the least I could do.

"Pretty good? Put!" She shooed her hand at me. "I almost hope you don't have a taste for it, more for me then."

I smiled and took what she had prepared with much appreciation.

We were silent as we each sat eating the sausage. I had to admit it was really good. She had smoked it into dried links, and it was delightful. Pontotok chuckled through her entire meal and enjoyed each bite even more than I. These simple pleasures of sharing a good meal were what I missed most about my family and the way things use to be. After eating, I lay posturing from side to side to stay comfortable. It was pointless. Pontotok seemed preoccupied, so we did not talk. I watched as the moon rose across our small window. There would not be much sleeping tonight, but that was nothing new for me.

By the time the sun rose, the work table was dotted with sachets and supplies all bound in traveling packs. It appeared that Pontotok had stayed up most of the night preparing us for anything and everything that we might encounter. She was sleeping mounded up in her bed, so I quietly slipped outside to let her rest.

There was a stark chill in the morning air, one that warned of the unknown. Despite this, the sun was rising, and I could feel the warmth reaching my skin. A few of the goats met me at our tree and stamped the ground in a playful greeting. I knew I needed to save up as much energy as I possibly could, so I laid in the grass, closed my eyes, breathed in the fresh air, and asked Mother Earth to assist me in strength. A familiar sound broke my concentration as Cawttwa landed a few feet from me and cawed his piercing early-morning hello.

"Good morning, Cawttwa," I smiled at him. Ever since he gave me the silver bracelet, I've held a special place in my heart for him. He squawked at me again, and I tossed a reed at him, but it hit a goat instead as it went bleating off.

"You shouldn't do that; they will stop giving milk," came a familiar voice. I propped myself up to see Adoetae smiling back at me.

"Oh, it's so good to see you!" I struggled to pull myself up to sit. "How have you been?" I asked, trying to calm my overwhelming excitement just a bit.

"I would have walked right by if it wasn't for this strange mound sticking up." He pointed to my belly. "So how are you feeling?" He sat down next to the stream and splashed his face.

"Like a full moon. If I get any bigger, I think I'll explode. What about you? How have you been? I wondered when you would come back and visit."

"Good, it's been real good. It's harvest time, so I brought you two some squash, maize, and beans. Should keep Pontotok busy for a while. He smiled at me with his haunting eyes. I went to the wigwam first to drop them off, but no one was there."

"Pontotok wasn't inside?"

"Nope, I just followed Cawttwa's racket and found you here."

"Hmm, she was there when I left. Maybe she is in the woods getting more supplies. Did you see all the preparing she did?"

"Yeah, I saw it," he smiled. "So are you worried about making the trip to my village?" I followed his eyes down to my crescent belly.

"Yeah, so Pontotok told you we would be coming to your tribe when the time comes. I am worried. I struggle to just get to this tree every day. I can't imagine doing much more."

"Well, you'll have me to lean on. Everything is ready for you when you get there. I made sure of it," he smiled and looked away. I could tell he was trying to disconnect himself from his own endearing words. "I wanted to apologize to you for the last time I was here. I said more than I should have. I realize that you don't feel the same way, and I can accept that. I would still like to be friends."

His words fell bittersweet inside of me. I wished that he were closer so I could wrap my arm around him.

"Thank you for your friendship, Adoetae. That means a lot. Things have just been really confusing for me. I've felt wedged between a rock and a hard place, and it seems the walls just keep closing in. It's caused me to be on the defense. You've gotten the brunt of it, and I'm sorry. You are very important to me, so if I seem a little distant, well, I . . ." He took my face in his hands and kissed me. The sensation was not as strong as it was with Colbryn, but it was very nice and I didn't pull away, not until he stopped and looked into my eyes. His gaze was too intense to hold, and I dropped my head, my hair falling like a sweeping divide and concealing my blushing cheeks.

"Friendship is a good place to start," he whispered, smiling. "I better get back. I told Cree I wouldn't be gone long." He jumped up and left, and

I was alone once more. I was glad we were on good terms again, but the mixed meaning behind the kiss lead me to wonder to what degree he was holding our friendship to. I felt a warm breeze blow through my hair, but not even a leaf or reed stirred beside me. It was the third or fourth time the strange gust of wind had caught my attention. I gathered up the food that Adoetae had brought and then decided to go find Pontotok and see if she had felt anything.

I loaded my arms and waddled back towards the wigwam. As I crossed the clearing, I noticed Pontotok standing with her head against a beautiful painted pony.

"Where did you get that?" I asked. She turned to me with an eager look.

"No time to lose, child. Cawttwa has brought us the warning. You must get to Adoetae's village before Colbryn and the men start down the pass. I have everything ready for you."

"Now? I have to go right now. This soon? But we haven't even talked about the plan. How long will I need to be there? How will you get in contact with me?" The frantic nature of her voice worried me. I felt very ill informed.

"Talk? No time for talk. I've told the pony where to take you; you will go straight to Adoetae's village. He will know the way.

"Oh, no, Adoetae was just here a little bit ago; he brought us this food, and he is headed back home. If only I would have known, we could have traveled..."

"Well, Put!" She wrung her hands and cut me off. "That's OK, just let the pony take you. I fear they will reach the pass today. There is no time to wait. You should be going now to ensure arrival before they have a chance to see you."

The pony got down on his belly, and Pontotok came out the door carrying a pack. She helped me straddle the pony's back and strap down my provisions. I had only ridden a horse one other time, so the act of balancing on one was something I was going to have to quickly master.

"There is food, water, medicine, flint, sinew, and a mess of other items should you need them. Now don't you worry one bit about me; you just get to Adoetae's village and everything will be fine. It will probably be dusk by the time you get there but try not to stop or waste time because you will already have a slow go of it."

"What about the poor pony? I'm practically bigger than he is. He is going to need to rest." The pony struggled to his feet.

"He's stronger than you think — I will see you soon child." And with that, Pontotok smacked it on the rump, and the pony started walking. I could hear the goats baying behind me. I took one last look at Pontotok. We were both crying. Golden Boy took five steps towards us and stamped the ground. I didn't want to leave them.

I rode all day; the pony was unbelievably slow, and my back was hurting almost as much as my rear. We passed a rock outcropping that seemed like the one Adoetae and I had made camp at, but I couldn't be for sure. I was at the mercy of the pony. Finally by evening, I could stand it no longer.

"Please put me down. I can't feel my legs." The pony stopped and dropped to his stomach. I could tell he was exhausted because he did not stand back up. I tried to stand, but that was impossible, so I rolled off the pony's back and sat massaging my calves until I regained the feeling in my legs. Once I could get to my feet, I decided I would walk and relieve the poor creature, so we walked until it started to get dark. It was slow traveling, and I worried that we would run out of sun before we reached the village.

Darkness fell, but there was no village in sight. I settled into a secluded spot and built a small fire. This would have to be my camp until morning. I opened my pack and dug out an array of odd things to eat. The sight of it made me laugh. I missed Pontotok already. I finished my dinner and gave the pony some water before settling against his soft belly to sleep.

Chapter Twenty

Pontotoʒ's Travel

A gut-busting pain balled up in my stomach as I watched her go. Natani was like a daughter to me and seeing her riding off alone in the state she was in, was against everything my gut told me to do. I knew she would be safe in Adoetae's village but watching her go made the hair on my neck stand up. The uneasy feeling that swept over me stayed knotted in my stomach all day. I busied my bones by hiding any sign of her and packing a few things I would need for the journey. Shosong twittered around me nervously, and Golden Boy paced back and forth impatiently.

"Will you two stop that? I am having enough trouble concentrating as it is! Your busy bother isn't helping." They both glanced at me and went right back to what they were doing. Cawttwa soon announced the arrival of my unwanted guests, so I went outside to wait for them. One lone man walked out from the forest and took long strides to approach me. I recognized the scars immediately. It was once again the pieced-together face of Natani's Colbryn.

"Well Put! Tell the others to come out, I won't bite" I said as I spit on the ground in disgust.

"Chief Duran needs you to…"

"Yes, yes I know why you are here, I am ready to go." He looked at me surprised. "Well, aren't you here to get me? I do not like to waste time. Call the other two so we can be off. The sooner we get going, the sooner I get back to my goats." His eyebrows raised, and he called out. Soon a man on horseback came into sight followed by two ponies. I turned to him in surprise.

"We are going to ride?"

"I figured you knew everything. Was the vision unclear?" He smiled back. Another man came from the opposite direction.

"Find what you were snooping for?" I accused as he approached us. He glared back at me and then spoke to Colbryn.

"One pony came and went from that direction."

"I've been known to have a man come around. It's keeping them I don't like. Is that all right with you?"

I knew Colbryn would sense my irritation. "Let's get going. The sooner we do, the sooner you can get back. Yes?" I could see why Natani was so taken by him; his smile was warming. Something about him made me like him immediately even though I saw the damage he had caused and would continue to cause.

After climbing on my pony, I gave Golden Boy and my home one last look. One thing I could not leave behind no matter how hard I tried was the uneasy feeling that Natani was alone. We traveled most of that day in silence. I felt the sun getting low on my back so I hunkered deeper into my cape.

I could not help but imagine Natani settling in Adoetae's village. He had been unable to hide his excitement when we discussed the possibility that she might need to go there. It made me feel good to know that she would be so well taken care of. She should be arriving about now. A smile came to my lips when I thought of her having her baby there with Adoetae watching over her.

"May I ask what has you so focused?" Colbryn said in a curious tone.

"I ... I have a goat that will give birth soon after I get back. They are like my family in a way. I get attached."

He smiled. "Do you not have any family other than your goats?"

"No, not that I know of. I was taken from my village when I was too young to remember. When it became apparent that I was different, it scared all the men away."

"I am sorry we are so short-sighted. I would think it would be very interesting living with someone that has your talents."

"Aww, Put! The rose has left these checks long ago if your trying to blush me out, but good try, good try." I said, and we both laughed.

"What about you? Do you have someone waiting for you when you get back?" I was curious to hear his answer. He looked away.

"I did." He was brief in response. I wondered if he was referring to Natani.

"Did? I am sorry, I don't mean to pry, but what happened?" I could see the pain written on his face, but I dug anyway.

"She now lives with another. We should stop and give you a rest." He added and quickly changed the subject. "Take the horses to the stream." He ordered the others as he helped me down.

"So is it true you can speak to the Spirits?"

"Yes and no. They show what has come to pass, but they do not talk to me like we are talking now."

"Then how did you know we were coming to get you?" He smiled innocently back.

"There are many eyes all around us, even you know that."

"I do, but they don't communicate with me."

"They do more than you realize, Colbryn. Clouds form when warm meets cold, and it's harder to see when the haze follows us." He gave me a curious look.

"Is that supposed to be riddle? You think I am caught somewhere between good and evil?"

"Riddle? Put. I'm too old for games. It's not for me to say where you are caught."

He paused, and the silence set in until the men returned with the horses.

"This will be a good place to stop." He ordered the men to gather wood, and soon a small fire was blazing. We all sat around the flame, and I could tell Colbryn had more things to talk to me about but was waiting for the other men to go away. They offered me dried meat, and I shared my goat cheese. I wondered if I would be treated differently once I arrived at the mountain. The other two men ate and fell asleep quickly. I stayed awake. I knew Colbryn wanted to talk, and I didn't mind the opportunity to torment him a little more.

Colbryn and I sat staring at the flames.

"So what exactly is it your Chief wants of me?"

"He needs you to find someone. Can you do that?" He asked softly and stared attentively at my eyes. I knew he wanted to know the answer.

"I show only what the Spirits want us to see, no more."

"And if this person is dead?"

"If they wish us to see that, they will." I answered. He then turned to me and studied my face.

"And if they live, will you show him that also?" His hand was inching its way to the knife he wore on his belt. My eyes darted to his hand and then back to his face.

"You need not protect this person from me. I will do all in my power to help you." He started to speak then thought better of it. His hand moved away from the knife and turned back to the fire.

"Do you wish to clear the air and tell me about it?" I asked giving him the chance to tell me about his feelings for Natani. "I'm getting the feeling you don't want this person found. They must be very important for you to kill me for." I said as casually as I could.

"I want to know if they're alive, but I do not want the Chief to know. I would kill to keep their safety a secret. I have killed for far less." He answered.

"I bet you have."

"If you won't tell me why it is important to you, maybe you will tell me why this person is so important to your Chief?"

"This person escaped — no one escapes him. They made him look like a fool, and now he is infuriated. The tribe has been growing now by the day, the Chief is enraged. "

"Is it in preparation to find this missing person?" I asked

"I'm not sure, it does not make sense to me." He smirked almost in humor. "I want to find them too but for different reasons." His face gave little away, but I could tell more was going on in this man then he wanted me to know.

"This person sounds like a great warrior. It must have been a great loss to your Chief." I questioned without alluding to anything.

Colbryn choked up smirking and chuckling a little under his breath. "Yes, more of a warrior than I had known — it was a great loss." He turned to me. "They are better off lost." I broke from the grasp of his stare and leaned back to close my eyes. At least we agreed on this point.

At first light, we were back on the ponies heading for the rising sun. The day was warming and leaving frost in the shadows and steam rising from our capes. I heard a crow in the distance and began to think of home I hoped that someone was keeping an eye on things. I spent the time trying to read the wind, but the energy was still and that worried me.

Three uneventful days passed with little or no conversation among us. I was about to ask how much further we were going when I heard the whistle of an arrow behind me. A groan came from one of the men. Someone had been hit. Before I could turn around to see where it had come from, Colbryn had pulled me off my pony. "Put, child, why are you dragging me? I can get along myself you know!"

"Stay here." He ordered then snuck off into the brush to my right. I watched the man that had been shot pull out the arrow like it was some uncomfortable bee or wasp sting, and then he disappeared. Grunts and cries were all I could take in from the heavy bush where I hid. One last piercing scream, and then all was silent. I started to get up when Colbryn shouted.

"Not yet, Pontotok." I peaked above the bushes, and from where I stood, all attackers were dead. Scraping of knife on meat piqued my curiosity, so I slowly rose high enough to see the men cutting thumbs off our attackers. The hair rose on my neck, and my stomach lurched. The thumb was what set us apart from the beasts; it was needed in our afterlife to prepare a spot for our loved ones. The taking of scalps was one thing that did not affect the afterlife, but this was a cruelty beyond that. Shortly, I heard Colbryn's voice telling me to come out. Gathering all the strength I had, I tried to wipe that image from my mind. I stood, then stumbled, and fell into the underbrush. Colbryn came over holding out a hand to help me up, but I could not take it.

"I can do it. I am not so old I can't get out of a bush." The expression on his face was of mild humor — not the look of someone that had desecrated his foe. Rage was still boiling up inside of me, but I had been prepared for this. I knew of the brutality. My life depended on me keeping a cool head on this journey.

"What was that all about?" I asked as I brushed the twigs and leaves off me.

"We are not well liked," he answered with a grin. Chuckles from the other men added to the almost casual atmosphere. The man that had received the arrow wore the hole proudly. His own blood still oozed from it freely. Colbryn helped me back on my horse, and we continued on our journey. The men kept bragging and boosting of their kill, and it was hard for me to keep my mouth shut.

As the day wore on, the landscape changed drastically. Black jagged rocks turned into boulders that turned into sharp cliffs that protruded from the landscape. All of which possessed a smooth glossy shine that I had never seen before. A chill crept over me that had nothing to do with the temperature or time of day. My companions started talking in hushed tones as if afraid someone or something might hear them. The last few rays of the setting sun outlined what appeared to be the head of a man; its size took my breath away. "The mountain," I whispered. Looking closer, I saw the silhouette was locked in a scream. We rode the path, and I kept a blank face. I would need the Spirits to help me with this. The horses started to become skittish, pawing and wining in protest. Colbryn's voice made me jump.

"Well, we get down here." He helped me down but kept a hand around my arm.

"Think I will fly away?" He looked down at me with a slight smile.

"The look on your face was saying just that."

"Yes, well, I suppose you are right that is just what I would do if I could."

"It is very dark for awhile. I did not want you to get lost. This way, please."

The darkness that greeted us was consuming I had never experienced such a void of light before. I began to understand what he was talking about. It was hard to judge distance in such darkness but finally I saw a glow start growing with every step we took. We entered a huge room lit with burning fires on pillars made of rock. The smell of damp earth mixed with stagnant air made me yearn for the outside. In the middle of two stone fire pillars sat the Chief. I had heard numerous stories about him but none compared to the sight of the real man. I could only imagine what Natani had felt the first time she entered this space — to realize she was to marry this man. His menacing look was made more pronounced by the four beautiful women standing on either side of him. One of them in particular gazed upon him with great admiration. It struck me as odd.

"Are you the Spirit talker?" His voice was demanding.

"I am Pontotok, and the Spirits reveal things to me. But no I do not talk to them like we are talking if that is what you are asking."

The Chief gritted his teeth, "I know you must be tired from your long journey. Sit and rest yourself for a little for I have need of your service." Before he had the words out of his mouth, two women led me to a large animal skin beside the main fire. Food and drink were brought to me. I didn't understand all the fuss over me, but I indulged in it anyway. I ate gazed back with the same bewilderment that all the strange faces had as they watched my every move. I could not decide which bothered me more — his gaze or theirs? Finally I found Colbryn leaning against the cave wall; he smiled slightly. I assumed it was to reassure me. I did not get to rest long.

"Spirit woman, are you ready to do my bidding?" I was not, but the same two women started to help me to my feet. So much for the rest.

"What is it you wish to see?" I asked innocently.

"A woman left here, and I wish to know what happened to her." Fear spread through me, not for myself but for Natani. What if the Spirits revealed where she was? She could be in labor at this very moment. The Spirits knew my heart, but would they be indifferent to my plight? I had no way of knowing until it was too late. Stalling, I spoke: "I cannot perform the ceremony without something that belonged to the woman."

The woman next to him bent down and picked up a blanket. "This was used in her room," she whispered to him.

"That will not work. It needs to be something that only she owned." I could feel the relief fill me with hope. Perhaps there would be nothing to do the reading with. The woman bent down and picked up something else from the ground.

"This was hers; she made it." With a toss, a fragment of bisque clay landed in front of me. My heart sank. I slowly picked it up, returned to the animal skin, and sat. Words from a language as old as time became my chant. I spoke low and spastic in hopes no one would understand what I was saying. I asked the Spirits to look into my heart and keep Natani safe from her enemies. Taking the powder from my bag, I threw it into the fire and held my breath as it left my fingers.

Natani appeared. She was climbing a stone wall in the rain, and lightning flashed all around her as she struggled to get to the top. I could tell she was scared, yet the determination that I had grown to know about her was prominent on her face. The cave was deathly silent as all eyes watched her hesitate then jump into the cold river below, her body fading into the darkness. As quickly as the image had appeared, it was gone. Falling like a curtain of sand and ash.

"What trickery is this? You have shown me nothing!" He was on his feet. Rage covered his face and deepened the crevices of his wrinkles that pinched tight between his eyes.

"There is nothing else for the Spirits to show you. Clearly, this person jumped into the river and drowned." I tried to hide the relief I felt. His voice came out in a growl.

"You have not shown me that she is dead! I did not see her rotting body on the shore or anything that would show me she no longer exists!" His anger was reaching its limits, and I was wishing I could just walk out and find my way home. I spoke as calmly as I could.

"Well, Put! I am but a simple woman who raises goats. My powers are limited. I can only show you what the Spirits show me. Please do not anger them!"

"You think I fear the Spirits!" His loud voice echoed around the cave and caused the women to cover their ears. I could feel the energy blow across my face. He pulled out a long blade from its sheath and walked slowly to me. "You will try again." He said almost in a whisper that made every hair on the back of my neck stand up.

I looked him in the eyes for a moment and then started chanting. Walking to the other side of the fire, I asked the Spirits for their understanding and not to take offence. I could feel a jolt come through me. They where not happy. I then threw the powder into the fire and closed my eyes. A strange sucking sound made me open them. To my amazement, the flames that were once leaping across the logs started disappearing. We all watched as one by one the bright flames went out and submerged us all in darkness. Growling vibrated the air around us, and I was thankful for the distance and the dark. My knees weak, I sat feeling the stone in front of me. All was cold; it was as if the fire had never been there. Every sound was amplified, women were crying, and men cursed as they bumped into each other. Teeth began to chatter. Without the fire's warmth, the cave became deathly cold. A speck of light slowly grew from a woman who had left and come back. The Chief grabbed her lantern and tried to light the fires, but it was as if they were soaked in water. The order was given for fresh wood to be brought in. "And bring back more lanterns," he barked to the closest man standing by him. Time seemed to freeze. I knew he could not see me, but I could see him, his face the only thing glowing from the dark. When more lanterns came, he disappeared into the abyss. Colbryn was the only comforting face I could find. Handing me a blanket, he sat down to warm himself by the new fire.

"I thought that went well," he said grinning at the flames.

"Humph, Put!" I said after thanking him for the blanket.

"You're still breathing, which is more than I expected. He must need you later."

"That's comforting." I said with a yawn.

"You should get some rest. If all goes well with the Chief, and you don't make him mad, we will leave at first light." He walked away. It can't come soon enough, I thought to myself.

As promised, Colbryn woke me early. As we walked closer to the cave opening, the sound of rain put dread in my heart. "We can go, or you can enjoy another day here. I will let you decide." He said lightheartedly.

"What about the other men? Don't they have a say?" I asked.

"It's just the two of us. I had a hard enough time getting two ponies for us to use. I told him we didn't need a repeat of last night, and that did the trick."

"So he thinks I did that?" I said in shock.

"Either way, you are free to go. I just need to know when."

"Not many things that can slow me down, and rain is not one of them."

"Then, let's get started." Soon he was back with the ponies and all we needed for the trip. Even the ponies seemed ready to get away from this place. I did not breathe easy until the mountain loomed only in the distance. The rain stopped once the sun was high in the sky. A chill in the air kept us at a steady pace, stopping only to water the ponies.

"So what happens if we are attacked on the road?" I asked, trying to make conversation.

"I'm supposed to leave you and head back," he smiled. "Let's just hope that does not happen. Do you mind if I ask you about last night?" he inquired.

"If you think you must, then I will answer as best as I can."

"I agree with the Chief about not knowing what happened to Natani after she jumped. But the other, the darkness, what was that?" he asked.

I chuckled.

"You push something hard enough it leaves."

"There you go again. Do you always talk like that?"

"Like what?"

"In riddles, without giving anything away."

"I speak straight and true. Perhaps it is you who sees many meanings? That's a good thing. There is always more than one face to a day."

"Humph," he grunted. "So what kind of power can take away every bit of heat and flame from all the fires in the room? How did you do that?"

"You give me far too much credit if you think I did that." I looked at him to see if he believed me. "*I* did not do that."

He thought for a while and then spoke. "You said before about the eyes watching us. Did you mean the Spirits watching us, or is there something else?" I was afraid of where this was going, so I tried to be as vague as possible.

"The Spirits that show the images you saw concern themselves very little with what we do. They only replay what has happened and do not distinguish between right and wrong. That is for another type of Spirit all together — and one that I do not contact. Be assured, there will be a price to pay for the wronging of the living and the dead." He was silent for a long time and then asked.

"But the Spirits that you summoned last night could show if Natani lives — if the question was put to them that way, right? If you had asked where Natani is now instead of what happened to her when she left the cave, they might have shown a very different picture." He was getting to close, so I had to watch every word.

"I did ask just that, and you saw what happened. It is not always as clear as everyone hopes it to be. You take what is given, or else the door shuts." So I lied a little, but I was willing to do what I had to do to keep Natani safe. "As far as the fires going out, I have never had that happen before. It shocked me, too. The Spirits are strong and don't like to be messed with." He rode deep in thought, and I didn't mind the silence.

We went on until dusk; both of us were exhausted from the strain of the night before but were determined to ride until nightfall. After a fire was lit and we ate a meager meal, I did not need to pretend to be too tired to talk because I was. Sharp cold winds made for an uncomfortable night, but we were both ready for an early start the next morning. We stopped a few times for him to listen in case we were being followed, but we weren't. His silence now made me uncomfortable. I wondered what he had been mulling over in his head all night.

When we stopped at dusk, the energy in the air hinted there would be more questions to come. I felt the dirt. Its vibrations created a low hum. Most of the forest creatures had found beds for the winter, and their hearts were beating within the earth. A gentle breeze whispered through bare branches and sang to the twinkling stars above. As I sat and listened to the wind and crackling of the fire, I picked up on a strange expression on Colbryn's face.

"Did you know her well?" I asked knowing much of the answer. I wanted to understand just what this complicated man was to Natani. His scarred, striking face slowly turned to me with a look that was torn.

"How did you know I was thinking of her?" he responded.

"You get a look sometimes, and then you usually follow it with a question about her," I answered. He turned back to the fire in hesitation without responding.

"Well, Put! It matters not what you keep from me I can see what you don't say." I grappled at the air as though I was sucking the information from the wind. He sighed.

"It was like she was fused to me from the moment I saw her. I could suddenly see everything I ever wanted. My life had changed. I longed to have some normalcy again, some connection to a real life. I thought I had found that in her. The touch of her skin sent fire through my cold blood."

He jumped to his feet and like the wind that starts slowly before it becomes a gale, I braced myself for what was to come.

"I had a plan. If she had only waited for me! I just needed to get stronger. I had a plan!" he shouted again to the trees. "Why couldn't she have waited just a few more days?! I don't know what to do with myself now that she is gone." He paced faster like he might be able to catch up to something. Suddenly he turned to me: "Tell me what am I to do with myself. I am no longer alive without her." Desperation echoed in every word and all over his face. He picked up a stone and hurled it into the forest. When it found its mark, it made a sound like thunder.

Slowly his breathing calmed down, and he took his seat again. He whispered softly as if talking to the fire: "I could have saved us ... her." He did not speak for a while. I could feel the torment he was going through. But dared not speak; I only watched. Staring into the glowing embers, he said softly.

"I live only to find her. It is possible that she survived that jump because the Spirits did not show her body. So I still have hope. I see and feel her sometimes. Once I woke, and she was with me as real as you are here. This connection I have with her is not like anything I have ever seen between two people. I cannot explain it. I don't see, hear, smell, taste, or feel like I use to." He hung his head and let out a long breath. "I am the walking dead. Please, if you can help me, I just need to know if she is alive." His sad, pleading eyes began to soften my heart. I wanted to help him.

The fire snapped between us as an ember landed on my hand. "Ow!"

I felt like I had awakened from a trance or spell. Something was at work here other than a lovesick man. The temptation I felt to tell him about

Natani was suddenly gone. Something inside of me told me to keep silent. It was a strange feeling. The air moved in a way that warned of something.

"I wish I could, but I cannot comfort you, Colbryn. Some things are beyond my vision to see." He looked hard at me, which sent a chill down my back, and then he spoke in a harsh tone I had not heard yet from him.

"Or is it you are not willing to try? If I thought you knew..." He stopped short and stared back into the fire. I watched his anger wash over him.

"Well, Put! I offer a hand, and it's been slapped. I remember now why I keep to goats." It was time to change the subject. "I shall be happy to see my goats again. I hope they are doing well. Is it much farther?" I did not think he heard me because it took him a long time to answer.

"If we ride hard tomorrow, we should be getting close." Locked in his own thoughts, he sat gazing into the fire while I tried to get comfortable enough to sleep. That feeling of fear crept over me again. He was capable of killing me, of that I was sure, and there would only be so much warning I could take from the wind.

The morning chill made every bone in my body pop and ache. Getting old was something I had a hard time getting used to. Colbryn was already tending to the ponies. How long had he been up? It was hard to say. We shared what little food I had left. I noticed him take something out of a pouch he wore around his waist and eat it. I thought about asking him why he did not share, but I did not want to cross him so early in the day.

We did not speak as the day wore on, but I didn't mind. My thoughts where on Natani and what had transpired since I had left. My daydreaming was suddenly interrupted. Colbryn took the bow from around his shoulder and notched an arrow with the speed that made my head spin. Before I could react, the arrow whistled through the air and found its mark in the tall grass. The rabbit was skinned and gutted before I could get down from my mount and walk over to see what he had.

"Find us some wood, and I'll cook this rabbit for us." His tone told me nothing of his mood. So much for pressing on hard, I thought. The sun felt comforting as we rested with full bellies. I longed to get moving again but didn't want to appear overly eager either. I leaned back against a tree, looked around, and realized I suddenly knew where we were.

"Humph! I'll be. I know this place. I have grazed my goats here." I had a sudden case of nerves and excitement as though something had snuck up on me.

"You have been very kind to me, Colbryn; I feel sorrow for your situation. You deserve more from life than what has been handed you. Do not worry about me. I know my way home from here. Keep on your quest if you must, but I don't hold much hope that you will find what you are looking for. His smile was brief, and I could feel his eyes penetrating me.

"Thank you, Pontotok, but I want to see you home. I am in no hurry to get back.

A sinking feeling washed over me. What if Natani had come back and was there? "That is kind, but I am not afraid of what wild thing I might find between here and there." He started to speak but was interrupted by a very familiar sound. Colbryn whisked his arm through the air and had an arrow pointed before I could even react.

"No! Don't you dare." I shouted in protest.

Looking back over my shoulder, I saw Golden Boy followed by the other goats coming through the woods.

"They have come to greet me. I won't need an escort now." We were soon surrounded by them. Golden Boy was impressive with his massive horns. He eyed Colbryn unnervingly, and I hoped nothing bad would come of this.

"May only good Spirits be with you," I said to him. "And with you," he added. We hesitantly parted ways, and the feeling of dread finally left me. I would be home by dusk.

CHAPTER TWENTY ONE

Lost

The stars had never seemed so clear and bright. In the distance, an owl called to another. I worried about Pontotok. Would she be alright? I wondered if Colbryn would take care of her and if he would sense that she had been with me? Would he kill her if he found out she was lying to him? I hated not knowing what was going on.

When morning came, I loaded up the pack. I was too sore to ride or even climb onto the pony, so I walked instead and followed behind him.

"You know where you're going, right? I kind of thought we would have arrived at the village by now." The pony did not respond, and I hadn't expected it to, but I was quickly beginning to doubt his directional abilities. After morning turned into high noon, I stopped and sat down. I had not been feeling good all morning but figured it was the salty dinner that was not setting well with me. I rubbed my stomach and then my legs. By now, even the fur alterations that Adoetae had made for me where stretched taut. I brushed the dirt from the beautiful rabbit fur and made a startling discovery: A thin stream of moisture was running down my thigh. This can't be good, I thought.

I started walking in earnest now. I knew little about giving birth — just that I had seen women die of it. Surely, I'm not going into labor. I can't be. "Not here, not alone!" The pony jerked ahead, startled by my outburst. I just need reassurance. I thought, "It's going to be okay. It's going to be okay, just keep going. You're almost there." My words did little to ease the frantic feeling that had swept over me.

Each step seemed harder than the last. I followed the pony, sometimes poking it to go faster. It felt like we were walking around in circles. The terrain seemed familiar, but where was the village? Where was Adoetae? I tried to steady my breathing, inhaling deeply and slowly letting it out, but I was panting from walking too fast. Only short gasps of air were coming out. I was sweating from head to toe, and tears of determination and panic were rolling down my hot cheeks.

The sun was getting low in the sky, but I was thankful I still had sunlight. I came to a fast-moving stream and collapsed at its bank. Bending down to get a drink, I felt a sharp pain run through my entire body.

"Ahhhh! Adoetae!" was all I could cry out. The pain stopped, and I was able to get to my feet again. Once standing, I noticed the most welcoming sight I had ever seen. Thin purple strands of smoke were rising up into the orange sky. I thanked the Spirits; this had to be Adoetae's village. Relieved, I waded across the stream and left the pony behind. I had only one thing to worry about right now, and for once, that was myself.

I had just crossed the water when I was hit by another pain that forced me to bend taking me to my knees.

"Ahhhh!" I clinched the dirt so hard my hands hurt. "Get up, just get up!" I told myself. I clamored to my feet and headed toward the smoke. The setting sun was leaving dark blue shadows on the east side of every hill, and with each blue shadow I made it through, it seemed like a hundred more still stood in my way. Eventually, the sun was gone, and only blue shadows remained by the time I was able to crawl between the first two tepees. A woman practically fell over me carrying several water skins as I reached for her in desperation. Another pain hit and sent me into a coil in the cold dirt.

"Here, dear, let's get you inside." A feeling of relief came over me as she spoke. I hadn't noticed until now that the wind had picked up and turned cold and steady, and I could hear thunderheads in the distance. "It is a good night to be born!" She smiled at me, and I appreciated her enthusiasm and confidence.

Was it a good night to be born, I wondered? Hopefully, it wasn't also a good night to die because that was what I felt like I was doing.

Once I was inside her tepee, a man slightly older than myself stared back at me with a strange grimace on his face.

"Tetome, looks like you need to spend the night with your brother again," she spoke softly to the man I assumed was her husband. He just shrugged and gathered up some blankets and was gone before another pain ripped through my body.

"I am Comesue, the healer here, so you have come to the right place. What is your name?"

"Natani" was all I was able to get out before a loud clap of thunder snuffed out my voice.

"Lie down, and let me see how far along you are." She acted like she knew what she was doing, so I would have done anything she asked of me. I could hear her concern for me in her voice as she spoke low. "Natani, looks like we are going to have a long night. Try to get comfortable. I need to get my water skin outside, and I will be right back." She left the tepee.

I didn't know what to say to Comesue. This did not seem like Adoetae's village. She came back, put more wood on the fire, and crushed dried leaves into a stone bowl that she placed close to the flames. She took the steaming water from the fire and poured it over the leaves. A relaxing, fresh aroma filled the tepee, but it didn't stop the pain.

"Do you have a man here by the name of Adoetae?" I asked.

"No, no one in the Red Hawk tribe goes by that name. Is that your husband?" she asked. The question stunned me, and I didn't know what to say, so I faked another pain and gritted my teeth. Where am I? I wondered. Wind whipped the tent, and rain pelted its sides from one direction then another. But I paid little attention to it. I had my own torment to deal with.

"Is this your first baby?" she asked.

"Yes." I tried not to screech.

"Well, I am sure it won't be your last." She smiled.

"Do you have children of your own?" I asked her.

"No, we haven't been blessed yet, but I keep hoping." I could tell by her age she must have been hoping for a long time.

How perfect, I thought. She seemed like a good and happy woman. She would make a great mother. She would never know about the evil bloodline, and therefore she would never judge or resent the baby. That was what I wanted for the child. It had to be fate that brought me here; the Spirits had directed me to Comesue. I was grateful for her. She was a stranger to me and yet treated me as a daughter, a child she never had, but one that I could give her.

"Ahhhh!" I clinched the blankets with all the energy I had left. The tepee shook from the force of the rain; it seemed like the world was in as much upheaval as I was.

"Push, Natani! Push hard!"

I pushed with all my might. I could feel the veins in my face bursting and the sweat protruding from my pores. My muscles were straining. There was no controlling the pain. My insides were literally being ripped out of me. "Ahhhhh!" I could hear my screams. They shouted back in protest to the thunder barking down at me. The pain finally hit an apex, and there was relief. I lay exhausted somewhere between sleep and death. The pain echoed through me with every movement, so I lay motionless against the soiled blankets.

"Natani, she is beautiful!" I could hear the envy in Comesue's voice. "What is her name?"

I hadn't thought about that. Even now I didn't want to think about it.

Giving her a name seemed to make it too real. The question caught me off guard a little. What should I say? I didn't even deserve to give her a name.

"I don't have a name yet," was all I could say.

"Plenty of time for that later. You rest now, dear."

Sweat was still running from my forehead and burning into my eyes as it pooled in my lashes. I knew the worst of the pain was over, but I still had to leave. Comesue was wiping the baby with gentle strokes. I could hear sweet sounds coming from her, but I didn't want to hear it. I didn't even want to see her. It would only make things harder.

Comesue turned back around with the tiny bundle and knelt down beside me, but I closed my eyes. I couldn't face her. The small baby that I had birthed — would she look like Duran? Would she have horns and evil green eyes just like him? I didn't move. I didn't look. I couldn't. She would grow to hate me — I knew that — but the best thing I could do for her was to let her go. She deserved a family that could love her without the judging, resentful eyes that I would see her through. I hoped Comesue would take her and let me sleep, but she didn't. She left the baby lying warm against my chest.

"I will leave you two to sleep," she touched the baby on the head with a gentle caress and then got up and headed to the other side of the tepee.

I lay there with my eyes closed, afraid to open them, afraid to see her. Moments passed to the sounds of the popping fire and the innocent breaths below my chin, and I finally peered out and saw the face of my baby girl. The first glance sent chills rippling through my soul. In that moment, I realized that what terrified me more than her looking like the Chief was the fact that she looked like me.

I took a slow, deep breath and tried to memorize the moment. I burned the image of her face into my mind and my soul. I held her tight as she slept. She was not as I had expected. She did not resemble Duran and did not have horns like I was afraid of. She was beautiful, but I knew with time I would see something that resembled the Chief and it would make me resent her. I knew she deserved better than that. She deserved a safe, loving life. In these moments, I allowed myself to question what I was about to do. If I kept her and the Chief found me, he would take her to the mountain and put her with all the other lost babies. I couldn't have that happen. Nor would I be able to join up with Pontotok and fulfill whatever my part of the Prophecy was. It was best for her here. I had made my decision. I enjoyed these moments we spent together. The rain poured fiercely outside, but for us, it was a peaceful understanding between mother and child as we both slept exhausted by our separate journeys.

I woke before the first light. Looking at the tiny sleeping face I had just given birth to, I still felt little of what I thought a mother should feel for her child. Comesue was sleeping soundly on the other side of the tepee; this is as good a place as any, I thought. I looked again at my daughter. Taking off the pendent from around my neck, I stamped it with my blood onto a piece of leather. The image transposed clearly across its surface. I then slid the pendant around her tiny head and tucked the leather piece in my pack. How sad, I thought, that I would never know her.

"Someone else will have to provide the rest for you, little one." I kissed her forehead and snuck out into the early-morning air. I was sore and aching and still exhausted from the night, but I knew the less I knew about these people and the less they knew about me, the better. I had very few regrets in my life, and I worked hard at keeping it that way, but leaving my baby was harder than I thought it would be. She will be safer with Comesue, I kept telling myself. If I had kept her, she would have been in constant danger just like the rest of the people in my life. I looked back toward the village one last time and then turned and tried to forget the child that I was leaving behind. Completely depleted of energy, I crossed back over the path I had crawled though only the day before.

I waded over the stream again, and the icy water numbed my lower body providing instant relief. I found the pony where I had left him, and once again he lowered himself so I could straddle his back. Exhausted and still in pain, I leaned forward against his warm back and let him take me away from this place. Sometime in the afternoon, I awoke to the sound of him drinking from a stream. We crossed it and kept climbing into a mountainous area filled with pines. I had no idea where we were, and nothing looked familiar. But it didn't seem to alarm me because I was falling in and out of a dazed state. I was so tired I could barely keep my eyes open ... and cold, why was I so cold? Slowly sitting up, I realized the crimson saturated leggings and the thin streams of blood that webbed down the pony's side. Was this normal? I knew I felt weak, but wasn't that normal after giving birth?

The sight alarmed me — it was a lot of blood, but I knew the only thing I could do was to keep going. The air got colder, so I put my arms around the pony's neck to feel his warmth. I could feel him moving, so I closed my eyes as images and faces came and went in my head. Everything began to blur. Adoetae, Eba, and my father all called to me from far away. I tried to concentrate on what they were saying, but I was just so tired, I wanted to be left alone to sleep.

Noises were all around us in the pines, but the melodic sounds of the pony's steps were comforting. I opened my eyes, but it was hazy and grey. I didn't want to squander away the energy it took to focus, so I closed my eyes and lay back on the warmth of the pony's back as he rocked me back to sleep.

The face of my mother appeared. She had come to scold me and shook her finger in anger. I kept telling her I was sorry, but she just would not listen to me. She was replaced by my brother running in the tall grass. I tried to catch him, but my legs were so heavy I couldn't make them move. Then I saw what he was running from. A large bear was coming after us, its ears pinned back, its teeth frothy as it chopped its jaws at the air. I could see a raw hatred in its eyes, and as it came toward me, I could do nothing to stop it.

"No!" I screamed as the bear ran past me, and its eyes locked on Natan. "Nooooo!" I yelled, jerked myself up, lost balance, and fell from the pony onto the ground's damp leaves. With a thud, I landed on my back knocking the air out of my lungs. I lay rolling and trying to catch my breath. I knew I was breathing because I could taste the pungent earth on my tongue. Between the spastic jerks of my body struggling to breathe, I looked to see where I was. It was an overcast evening, and the clouds seemed so low that I could reach up and swirl them around with my hand. I heard the running gurgles of a nearby stream. Was this a different stream, or was it the same stream? I couldn't tell.

I knew the feeling of blood on my hands, and I was covered in it. This is not normal, my mind warned me. My head spun, so I put my cold sticky fingers to my temples to try to focus. Soft white flakes fell casually through the grey air to the forest floor around me. I lay back against the ground and tried to collect myself. My breathing became regular as I watched the snow drift through scarce branches. It was like I was falling through frozen stars.

If you stay here, you will die, my inner voice spoke to me. It was my own voice, but it was calm and strong.

"I know, but I'm so tired. Can't I just close my eyes and rest for a bit?" I was conversing with my mind. Couldn't I convince myself that resting was the best thing to do? Nothing answered back, so I closed my eyes. I felt so far from anything familiar.

CHAPTER TWENTY TWO
Spirit Search

I quickened my steps as my goats followed. I did not look back. Reaching my hut, I greeted Shosong and Cawttwa.

"Sheshebackinall, go see, go see" I asked them to see if I had been followed. They got back about the time I finished milking the goats and were silent. All was well at last, and the dread was over.

Adoetae's voice surprised me and made me jump with the day's anxiety still fresh. "Hey, good to have you back. I was getting tired of the milking chore. Where did you two go? You better not have taken her to speak to the Spirits in her condition." I spun around.

"What!" My heart stopped. "Is she not with you?" He gave me a confused look.

"With me, no why would she be with me? I have not seen her."

"Put! Put! Put! This is bad!" I stood pacing in bewilderment.

"What Pontotok? What is going on?"

"She is supposed to be with you. I sent her off on a pony to your village six days ago! Six! I was taken to the mountain, Duran summoned me for a smoke reveal. She was on her way to you."

Adoetae's anxiety now matched my own. "I must find her? Which direction did she go?"

"She was headed toward your village, but if she did not end up there, then who knows where she is!"

"I will head that way!"

"Wait! Before you go running all over, let's see what is going on first. She could be safe in another village somewhere." The last glow of the day was ending, which added to my new wave of panic. Would Natani be alone another night? I lit a fire, gathered an item of hers, and asked the Spirits to reveal her to me once more. The image came into view as the sight confirmed our worst possible fear. We both gasped and I could feel my blood reversing within my skin. She was lying on the ground with flakes of snow drifting slowly around her pale face — a sharp contrast to the dark red blood covering her body. We both let out a cry.

"THIS CANNOT BE!" Adoetae cried, his eyes swimming in tears. "I must find her." Cloaked in bewilderment and confusion, he jumped up.

"Please, Adoetae, I have a faster way. Come, I need your help. We hurried into the hut, and I sat on my cot.

"We don't have time for you to rest. We must find her!"

"Yes, I know. You must listen very carefully because much depends upon your doing exactly what I say! I will be leaving my body behind, and you must guard it. Do you understand?"

"Yes ... No! What? Guard your body from what?"

"Once my Spirit has left this body, other Spirits will want to take it over, and I will not be able to get back into it."

"This is crazy, Pontotok. Is there no other way?"

"I wish there were, but I have got to find her in a hurry." He looked around the room as if to find some other way hanging on the walls.

"Adoetae, we are running out of time. Can you do it?"

"Yes, I will try."

"You must do better then try."

"Just tell me what I need to do."

I tossed him the toad pouch that hung from my neck. "Repeat this, and remember it! Spirits of the afterlife, this is not your body. Be gone. Then shake the pouch over my body." He repeated it and shook his head.

"Please, help her." Adoetae's eyes burned with desperation and turned a silver hue that seemed void of any color.

"Yes, yes, now hand me that pouch in the basket at the corner." I placed the dried yucca leaves below my tongue and stretched out. I was instantly on my way.

"How long does this take?" Adoetae paced, wishing he had something to take his mind off the image of Natani's lifeless body. At about his fifth turn around the room, he heard a voice he had not heard in many years. He turned in horror to find the faint form of his father reaching to him.

"Adoetae, it is such happiness to see you. I have longed to be with you again. Come, my son, and help me up so we can smoke the pipe and talk of many things."

"Father?"

"Well, who else do you think I am?" he grunted.

"You traveled to the Spirit Land seven years ago." When Pontotok said Spirits would enter her body, he had no idea they would take the form of people he once knew and loved.

"Oh, father, I have missed you, too, but this is not your body so you must go back."

"Send me not away for I long to live among my people once more. I can help you. We can have good times again!"

Adoetae's hands went up into his hair as he struggled with the torment within. "I am so sorry, my Father, but ... *Spirit of the afterlife, this is not your body. Be gone.*" As soon as he had said the words, the image of his father was gone. The feeling of betrayal swept over him. Turning away, he dropped to his knees and cried: "Please, forgive me, father. I had no choice!"

"Adoetae?"

The voice made him freeze in a sobering instant. Had he imagined it? Rising up, he didn't even dare turn around.

"No" he whispered quietly, his shoulders relaxing as he sunk into submission. "This can't be." He covered his heart as the voice pierced deeper than a spear.

"Adoetae?" The seductive voice came again beckoning him.

"Shelna?" Lying on the cot was his beautiful wife.

"Oh, no, no, this cannot be. This cannot be happening." He grabbed her face as tears of doubt and longing welled within his.

"Adoetae, come to me. Wrap your arms around me and kiss me. Tell me that you still love me. I so long to hear your voice again." Mesmerized by the appearance of her, he could hardly move. Long, graceful arms reached into the air and ran up his back. How many times had he longed to hold her one more time, caress her long black hair, and tell her how much he loved her. How much he had needed and missed her.

"Our son looks so much like you. He is growing so fast. He took his first steps just the other day. You would be so proud of him."

"Oh, I am, and I am so proud of you. Help me up. I want to see Cree so badly." Her words were slow, soft, and mesmerizing in every way.

Adoetae moved closer and then stopped. He needed to think. Could he have his wife back just like this? It would be wonderful, a second chance with the woman he loved. This was torture. He knew he needed to send her back. He sank down to his knees and wept.

"Don't cry, my love. We can be together as we once were. I love you still. There is nothing that will separate us again. Come to me." Tears streaming down his face, he reached his arms out to her in an embrace and then held her face again.

"I have missed you more than the Spirits will ever know. I loved you with my whole Spirit and will always love you, but our love can no longer be in this world. This is not real. *Spirits of the afterlife, this is not your body. Be gone.*" The words choked from his mouth, and he watched as she faded from his hands. Once she was gone, Adoetae got up, staggered to the door, and punched the oak support beam.

"Augh!" he cried out in anger. "I don't know how much more of this I can stand!"

"Aahhhwww." A groan came from the cot.

Adoetae was afraid to turn around. If it was his wife again, he knew he would not have the strength to send her away again.

"Adoetae, are you alright? Put! You are bleeding? What did you do to your hand?"

"Pontotok, I don't think I have ever been so happy to see anyone in my life. Did you find her, and where can I go to get her?"

"Get me some water, Adoetae. There is much to tell you."

CHAPTER TWENTY THREE
Natani's Silence

"Chickitan Canyon," I mumbled into the cold evening air. The warmth of my breath let go of my lips with every word. Memories played against the backs of my eyelids, and my two best friends, Tecka and Ottowa, were running and laughing in the sunshine. My mother was cooking, and my father was teaching my brother the bow. Life was perfect, but that was no longer my life. It had been stolen from me.

I lay motionless. My mind could function, but my body no longer could. This was what dying was. I felt something come over me. Like a jolt of lightening, it sucked the air from my lips as I drew back my breath. I inhaled a familiar dampness, the recognizable smell of trapped stagnant air. I was back in the cave, and cold, damp blackness surrounded me. I moved my fingers beside me, and instead of the snow-flecked leaves, I now felt the slimy rock surface. Had I died? I heard the deep groans of the Dwells beneath me, but worse of all, I heard his cruel laughter echoing through the chambers. Duran? I opened my eyes, but when I did, I was looking down at myself lying on the dead leaves in the forest. I looked so peaceful, but I wasn't with my body.

"Natani!" A familiar voice caught my attention. It was Pontotok. My heart ignited with joy to see her. Our Spirits swirled together like smoke curling and dancing when there is no wind.

"Natani, you must stay with your body. Help is coming!" she kept saying to me. "Please, I need you. Adoetae needs you. Go back, go back now. Help is coming!" She seemed upset, but I didn't want to go back to my body. It was dead. She was fading, leaving me grasping at her through the air, but with every movement of my arm, her image dissipated.

"But I want to be with you! Please, Pontotok, it's so dark and cold. Take me with you, Pontotok!"

BOOK TWO OF THE LEGEND

CASEY VOIGHT & BARBARA WENDLETON

COLUMBIA, MISSOURI 65202
hauntpublishing@aol.com

PROLOGUE

It was the most violent storm the tribe of the Red Hawk had ever seen. Even old Brown Tooth, the eldest of the tribe, could remember only one imbalance as fierce as this one. The thunder seemed to come from farther up in the heavens than just the clouds.

"There is a face to this storm," said Brown Tooth in his slow, deep voice. The monotone drones of his voice box ratted with the start of every word. "It watches us, it sees without eyes, it is growing in strength, and I sense its power will bring a voice."

The winds whipped, stirring up small dust devils, which danced between the hide huts. The sun had just about reached its final embark and was simmering below the two Compton Mountains as though the mounds had trapped its red Spirit. Above it, capping the night and forcing out the day, thunderheads marched in steady and black. The children ran excitedly through the village. A nervous energy cloaked them as the change could easily be felt.

"Ahhh, the rains are coming," said Brown Tooth. "The Spirits are fighting this one, and they shall bless us with more than just silver spears."

The group of old men known as the Grey Hairs grunted in response. They had many years behind them, and age had marked them with the shackles of time. Too old to hunt or be of much use, they would gather in their Gojo around evening fires and repeat the stories of old. Their wisdom seeped continuously like the tobacco smoke from their wrinkled lips. Each was nestled beneath the rock overhang, peering out upon the valley, and anticipating the coming rain.

There was an oddness to this evening despite the coming storm. There was a smell of organic matter as though someone had just tilled the basin line. Thunderheads continued to tumble above the Red Hawk camp, as the old tribe sat, puffing smoke into the dry air, as it danced in rings about the Gojo. The village sat in a sober anticipation. Any moment the heavens would release the rain. The children huddled around the fire counting distant rumbles and jumping as the bellows echoed through the Duca Canyon.

"I've heard the heartbeat of a warrior. This story is close, and life is surfacing," bellowed Brown Tooth. The other elders peered out below their aged brows, and their slow movements petrified against the walls of the Gojo. Brown Tooth knew something was about to happen. Whether he had a premonition of it, or it was just a hundred years of being wise, he knew. The rumbling ceased as though to tell all to go to sleep. The families huddled down within their tepees as the old tribe sat circled around the glowing fire listening to the rain move across the prairie. The cool fall breeze blew in once more and brought with it a stillness, and for a moment, nothing stirred. Then, as though the canyon drew back its breath, the wave of rain raced across the canyon, the noise like a growing applause. Through the sound came a small cry. No one knew the significance of this night, but Brown Tooth knew and let out a deep laugh. Relief could be heard and felt throughout the camp as all fell into a restful sleep.

All but one.

CHAPTER ONE

Found Objects

When we have gone past the point of helping ourselves and succumb to the notion that all hope is gone. When giving up is the only thing left to do. There is a time, a brief time, between living and death that the fading voice of our soul whispers out, 'Let go.' We are hit with a comforting feeling that all is at peace — that we can head to the Spirit Land with no worries — but my soul did not say these things to me.

I was staring up at the white ghost-like flakes of snow, their dancing bodies falling to die against mine. I knew I had lost a lot of blood — too much. I could feel it seeping into the Earth below me, back to the place where all things come. My heart had slowed to a sporadic quiver. This would be where I would die.

My fingers flinched at my side. Could I cross my arms and die in a noble position? Could I manage to turn and face the ghostly silhouette of the moon to follow it into the Spirit Land? Could I reach the buckskin that had the pendant mark pressed into it? It was the only connection I had to my baby. I thought all these things, but the only thing I could do was blink my hazy eyes.

When would my Spirit tell me to go? When would I feel the peace?

"Can I go?" I whispered out into the night.

No, my soul spoke back.

I closed my eyes. I could feel the strange familiar breeze dip down from the treetops and brush my face as it blew my hair away from my cheek. Even Pontotok's voice could no longer reach me.

All was silent.

Contact

www.caseyvoight.com

caseyvoight.wordpress.com

Facebook: /caseyvoight

Twitter: /caseyvoight